Dirty Plans

LILY & LONDON

THE ONE NIGHT STAND CLUB
BOOK ONE

CARISSA KNIGHT

To Colin—my real-life London,

In the labyrinth of life, our paths crossed and intertwined in the most unexpected, yet destined way. Your love has been a guiding light, illuminating a path I didn't know I was searching for. You've shown me that sometimes, life's most profound truths are hidden in the heart's silent whispers.

This journey, akin to Lily and London's, is a testament to the power of authentic connection, the courage to embrace change, and the beauty of finding true love in the most serendipitous places.

Thank you for being my steadfast friend, my unexpected love, and my constant inspiration.

For infinities,
xo Carissa

THIS BOOK WAS NEVER MEANT TO BE.

I've been an urban fantasy author for over a decade and never intended to write romance. Believe me, the irony isn't lost on me.

Yet, somewhere in the back of my mind, the inklings of something new emerged. I just didn't understand what it was.

This story (or more accurately, the series concept) has whispered to me for over *six years*. And for as many times as I tried to ignore its call, it never backed down. It continued to insist: I needed to write this. *You* needed to read this.

So, *for you,* Dirty Plans exists.

And The One Night Stand Club comes to life ...

Prologue

LONDON (TEN YEARS OLD)

My heart hammers in my ears as I slip out of my bedroom window. My feet hit the ground, and before I know it, I'm running across the dewy grass.

Lily's house isn't far but it still feels like every step means I could get caught.

But I have to do it.

My chest aches because in a few hours, my family will be moving and I'll never see her again.

My best friend in the whole wide world. I can't even think about it.

I've seen her every day since the first day of kindergarten and that's been almost exactly half of my life now.

When I reach her window, I tap quietly and struggle to keep my breathing under control.

What if she doesn't wake up?

The thought makes my insides feel sick. We're leaving at first light—*my mom's words*—because we have a long drive ahead of us.

I can't *not* see her before we go.

After a few seconds, the curtains pull back and her sleepy face comes into view. Her hair is in a messy ponytail, with strands sticking out everywhere.

She's so cute it hurts.

The window slides open.

"London? What are you doing?" she asks, her voice low and eyes wild.

She's in the unicorn pajamas I made my mom buy for her tenth birthday and it does weird things to my belly.

I reach a hand out, trying to keep it from shaking. "Come on. I want to show you something."

"But what about sleep? You're leaving in the morning—" Lily protests.

"*Please*, Lily?" I'm not afraid to beg at this point.

She sighs, then nods. "Okay. Let me grab my slippers."

She vanishes into her bedroom and a minute later, her fuzzy foot comes into view as she sticks her leg out the window. I reach out, giving her something to hold onto as she crawls through.

"If my parents find out I snuck out, they'll have a heart attack," she mumbles, followed by a big yawn.

"They won't find out. Besides, we'll just be in the backyard," I whisper, leading her to the treehouse next to her garage. "Wait here."

I drop her hand and climb the ladder so I can dig out the blankets I hid up there earlier in the week. Thankfully, no one goes in the treehouse anymore, so the blankets are right where I left them.

"Look out," I say, standing over the door and dropping them to the ground.

Lily is gathering them up by the time I get back down to her.

"What are we doing?" she asks, clutching the blankets close.

"Isn't it obvious?"

She shakes her head.

"We're going to stay up all night." I grin.

"I've never done that before. I don't know if I can," she admits, biting the side of her lip.

"Me neither. But I wanna try. I want it to be with you," I say, shoving my hands into the pockets of my jeans. I'm already dressed for our move. One less thing that will take any more time away from Lily.

She smiles sweetly. "Okay."

We move to the middle of her big backyard. Far enough from the tree, so we have an open view of the night sky.

She helps me lay the big blanket on the grass, then we sit down on it, covering ourselves up with the smaller blankets.

"I would have brought pillows but Mom would have noticed if they were missing," I say, leaning back.

"It's okay. It'll make it easier to stay awake," she says, lying down, too.

Her words make me smile as we settle in.

We lay there for a little while, just watching the stars and taking in the nighttime sounds.

"It's so peaceful this time of the night," she finally whispers, breaking the silence.

"That's because the latest we've ever stayed up is eleven. And even then, it was the Fourth of July, so it was noisy all night," I say, resting my head in my hands.

"That's true. What time is it now?"

"Three, I think. I had to make sure Mom and Dad were in bed before I came over. They were up late packing."

"Oh." She doesn't say anything else, but I can hear in her voice that she's sad. I made her sad by bringing up the move again.

Great move, London. Real, good.

I clear my throat and roll over, propping myself up on my elbow.

"My dad said once there was a radio broadcast about the Martian invasion. It was before the internet and people started freaking out over it," I whisper, watching her expression shift.

"Really?" Lily says, rolling over to face me. Her eyes are lit up now. I love they way they do that.

I nod. "Yeah. It was just a story. They didn't know that, though. It's funny now, but I guess people were really scared. They thought the Martians were actually attacking."

"That's crazy," Lily breathes, then a devilish grin appears on her face. "I wish we would have heard it."

"You would have loved it."

Her expression turns quizzical. "How do you know?"

"Because I know you, silly." I roll my eyes. "Why do you think I brought it up?"

Another sad smile rises and she lays back down. "Thank you."

"For what?"

"This. I'm going to miss you so much." Her voice cracks and when I turn to look at her, tears are welling up in her eyes.

"Lily, don't cry. Please. I didn't want to make you cry."

She wipes the tears away with the back of her hand. "You didn't."

"It sure seems like I did." I frown.

She shakes her head, refusing to look in my direction. Instead, she stares up at the stars until her breathing goes back to normal.

I sigh, wishing none of this was happening. That my parents weren't moving my brothers and me to Colorado. That we were just staying here—right next door to my best friend. And this was any other normal night.

I hate them for doing this to me.

I'll never forgive them. *Never.*

For the longest time, I lay there, mad at my parents and the world.

Then I notice Lily's eyes have fallen shut and she's asleep.

So much for staying up all night.

Well, for *her* at least.

But there's no way I'll miss a single second.

Rolling onto my side again, I watch her for the longest time, trying to memorize everything about her.

I wish I could tell her how I feel but I don't even know what this is. I just know she's a part of me and not even moving away will change that.

Suddenly, a strange urge comes over me and no matter what I do, I can't seem to talk myself out of it.

I hold my breath, scared I'll wake her up, but my hand moves toward her. Every inch closer makes me feel more alive—and kinda scared out of my mind. But I know I can't leave without doing it.

Slowly, I take her hand in mine, feeling the warmth of her palm as it rests in my own.

I exhale.

This is what home feels like. *She's* my home.

I'll be back, Lily. I promise.

CHAPTER 1

Lily

I f it wasn't for these dirty bitches, I don't know how I'd make it through the week. I'd probably end up one of those lonely, drunk ladies who has way too many cats and an impressive collection of yarn.

"Hey, Lil, can you flip the open sign off for me?" Tasia asks as she stumbles into the reading alcove of her adult bookstore with two dark brown folding chairs tucked under her arms. They almost look like extensions of her body since the color is nearly a perfect match to her beautiful, dark skin.

Beside me, Anna calmly sets her phone in her lap, then pushes her large-framed glasses up her face. Without missing a beat, she raises her right hand and flips the bird toward the front of the building. "Got it."

Tasia's expression deadpans. "Hilarious, Chang. Ever think of going into comedy?"

"I aim to please," Anna retorts with the kind of straight face only she can manage. Maybe it's her Korean roots showing. Or a prerequisite for being a female computer programmer. Pretty sure those ladies major in *'Smart Ass.'*

Trying to hide my smirk, I push off the small purple loveseat and stand up. "On it."

Tasia's dark eyes sparkle as she beams her giant smile at me and sets the first chair out. Then she turns to Anna and says, "See, that's why *she's* my BFF."

"Kiss ass," Anna says, pretending to sneeze as she picks her phone back up.

I laugh under my breath and weave through the bookshelves toward the front of the store.

So far, only three of us are on time—me, Tasia, and Anna. We're waiting on Vivian, who's notoriously late, but for some reason, it would be weird if she wasn't.

The *Dirty B's* have been meeting every Thursday night in the back of Tasia's bookstore for the past three years. In that time, the four of us have built something I hadn't realized I was missing in my life.

Friendship.

Camaraderie.

Hell, a fun group of women who like to sit around, drink wine, and talk about dirty books in a bookstore with more than enough reading material.

Best of all, they don't care about what kinds of books I read, the ones I won't touch, or ... *how I look.*

That last piece has been a blessing.

It's not always easy finding friends who can look past the slightly odd shape of my nose and the scar that tears its way from my upper lip to my left nostril.

Hell, not even my husband can seem to do that.

So, yeah, it's been nice to be around people who see me for *me* and not my birth deformity.

Truth be told, it's been eighteen years since the last time I felt like I was really seen for who I am. That was back when my best childhood friend, London, was still around.

There are times when I still can't believe his parents forced him to move to Colorado. But that's the way life goes, right?

People move on.

I walk over to the front door and flip the switch on the open sign. It goes dark just as the door lets out a shrill ding, announcing a newcomer.

Vivian waltzes in with a brown paper bag in her arms and a smile on her face. Her bleach blond hair is up in a messy high ponytail and she's clad in bright pink yoga pants, paired with a black crop top that shows off her ample cleavage and midriff.

I'd be jealous of her annoyingly perky body if I didn't know the woman it was actually attached to. I'll keep my average weight and height, thank you very much.

"Hey, Flower," she says with a quick wave of her free hand. Vivian is the only one who thinks calling me *Flower* makes more sense than *Lily*.

"Hey, Viv. We're just about to get started," I say, jabbing my left index finger toward the back of the store. "Was it your week to bring the wine?"

"Yup." She nods and glances into the bag like she's surprised it's still in there.

"Nice."

Vivian might always be late, but her taste in wine is impeccable. Plus, as one of Duluth's most sought-after interior designers, she has the budget to afford the good stuff.

"Sorry I'm late. I was sucking Jordan off before he left for Tahoe and the man has stamina. But I had to leave him with an impression, if you know what I mean." She winks at me and wipes at the corner of her mouth with the tip of her middle finger like she's cleaning up whatever he left behind.

My face heats and I suck in a quick breath.

With Vivian, you never know if she's serious or just saying something for shock value. However, the way her hair is slightly disheveled leaves me envisioning her boyfriend's hands groping at it as he thrusts...

Fuck me.

I press a knuckle to my right eye socket.

She chuckles and continues through the store without elaborating further—*thank god.*

It's been two months since Seth and I had sex and it's starting to do weird things to my brain.

Shaking it off, I walk back to the alcove to find Vivian in my seat. Anna locks eyes with me and slowly raises hers to the ceiling like she's praying to the gods to save her.

Instead of fighting it, I grab the vacant fold-out chair and pull it closer to the coffee table between us.

"I have glasses, ladies," Tasia announces as she enters from the backroom with four wine glasses poking through her splayed fingers.

Other than talking about dirty books and the book boyfriends we'd love to bang, drinking wine and chilling with these ladies is a highlight for all of us. There's no judgment and no shame. Only fits of giggles and the occasional drunk butt dial.

Tasia gives Vivian a once-over, then shifts her gaze to me.

I can tell she's wanting permission to kick Vivian out of my spot, but as my best friend, she also knows how much I hate that kind of confrontation.

I shake my head and shrug.

It's really not a big deal.

Tasia huffs a sigh and sets the glasses down on the table. "I really need to get a couple of recliners in here. My ass is getting too old to sit on straight-up aluminum for hours on end with you bitches."

"You know, I could totally help you with the—" Vivian begins.

Tasia cuts her off with a swipe of her hand. "I'm not looking for an interior designer."

Vivian's face falls.

Anna, on the other hand, chuckles but doesn't drop her phone. The woman is glued to her tech.

Tasia takes the seat next to me and points to the glasses. "Viv, you're the last one here. You can pour."

I catch her side eye and smirk as she leans back.

She might not make her move seats but she'll get back another way.

That's my girl.

Grinning, I shift the chair a little closer to the table when the doorbell dings again.

Everyone stops what they're doing to exchange confused glances.

"You shut the sign off, right?" Tasia asks, standing back up.

I nod. "Absolutely."

"But you didn't lock the front door when Viv came in?" She looks like she's hovering between hiding back here and going to the front.

I butt the palm of my hand to my forehead. "No, I got kinda distracted. Sorry, Tash. My bad."

"Oooh, dropping down the BFF scale," Anna chides, continuing to scroll.

I shoot her a look of annoyance but she doesn't even glance up to catch it. Instead, she chuckles softly under her breath.

"It's my fault. She was busy doing mental gymnastics about me and Jordan," Vivian interjects. Again, she winks when she catches my horrified gaze.

"Is this pick on Lily night? Did I miss the memo?" I counter.

"Hello?" A woman's voice calls out into the bookstore.

Tasia shoots everyone a look of consternation. "*Behave.*"

Then, she's moving toward the sound of the voice. She doesn't make it far before a short, curvy redhead full of freckles comes into view. The woman has deep-set dimples like me, but they look so much better on her.

"Is this the ... Dirty B's book club meetup?" she asks softly, as she wrings her hands together.

Tasia glances back at us and scratches her forehead. "Um, yeah. That's—that's us." She circles her pointer finger around the rest of us.

The woman visibly relaxes. "Oh, good. I thought this was the right place, but you know, the directions weren't very clear."

Anna drops her phone and arches a black eyebrow above her frames. "You found directions?"

As resident tech nut, Anna created an app for the four of us to communicate during the week about the books we're reading. But as far as I'm aware, there's no website or anything that would house directions. Each of us has been specifically recruited by Tasia at one point or another.

The woman nods but doesn't elaborate, so we all just stare at her as we try to process.

Vivian clears her throat and stands up. "Well, hi. I'm Vivian." She thrusts her hand out across the spans of the coffee table.

"Carlie," the newbie says, her smile broadening. She steps into the room with her arm outstretched.

Before she can make contact with Vivian, her knee bumps the coffee table, and the four glasses of wine clatter together.

Without dropping her phone, Anna presses a foot to the other side of the table, stabilizing it before it becomes a disaster.

Carlie pulls back. "Shit. Sorry." She shakes her head and her cheeks turn a bright shade of pink.

"No big deal. Hardly a spill," Tasia say with a shrug of her shoulder. She gives Anna a pointed stare, then turns toward the break room. "I'll go grab a towel and another glass."

With her hands by her sides, Carlie appears frozen to her spot.

I shake out my surprise and stand. "Hi, I'm Lily." I opt for a wave. Seems safest at this point.

Her grin is back, melting some of the ice in the room. "Hi."

I twist slightly and raise my hand toward the loveseat. "You met Viv, and the lady running to the back is Tasia. This is Anna."

Anna tips her chin but doesn't say anything. I've known her long enough to know that she has a perverse need to watch people squirm.

Carlie nods, her smile plastered on her face like she's too scared to drop it.

"So…" I begin, turning back to her. "You found us online?"

Her gaze drops onto the table. "Well, not exactly."

Anna snickers and crosses her arms over her torso. Her phone is still clenched in her right hand.

Carlie clears her throat. "I—I'm not super social. Bet you couldn't tell, right?"

I smile and hold out a fist. "Introverts for the win."

She fist-bumps me and continues, "I was searching for book groups in the area and I was coming up empty."

Anna's eyebrow twitches. "There are tons of book groups in Duluth."

"Yeah, no—I meant *romance-related* book groups," Carlie clarifies.

"You mean *smut*-related," Vivian corrects, a wicked grin appearing on her face. She wiggles her eyebrows for effect.

Carlie smiles and nods.

"Did any of you bitches lock the door yet?" Tasia asks as she enters the room with a towel and another wine glass. When no one answers, she rolls her eyes. "Vivian, can you take care of it?"

Another attempt at retaliation.

Smooth, Tash. *Smooth.*

"Why me?" Vivian complains.

"It's either that or clean up." She tosses the towel in her face.

Vivian groans and drops the towel to the table. Without even verbalizing her decision, she gets up and walks through the bookstore.

"Do you really trust her alone up there?" Anna asks, blinking slowly. "Remember what happened last time?"

Carlie's eyes widen. "What—what happened last time?"

Tasia blows out a breath. "Let's just say ... Viv has *sticky hands*, if you know what I mean. Shit, I better keep an eye on her. Chang, take care of that." She points at the spill and dashes off to the front of the store.

"Quick, take your seat back before I have to spend the entire night envisioning stabbing Vivian through the boob," Anna hisses at me, her voice low and urgent as she wipes up the wine.

I point to the back room. "But I should probably grab another folding chair for Tasia."

Anna's expression is devoid of any interest. In fact, it almost looks like she's trying to glare a hole through my head.

"Oh, it's okay. I can just sit on the—" Carlie begins, pointing toward the floor. She makes an attempt at dropping down and nearly takes out the floor lamp beside her.

Anna pops up. "I'll get the chair. Lily, sit your ass down next to me. Carlie, grab a chair." She hurries off to the back room before I can protest.

I shake my head and hold my hand out to help Carlie stand back up. "I promise, we're not normally this chaotic."

"I wish I could say I'm not normally this clumsy but that would be a lie." Carlie huffs a laugh.

"Well, if it's any consolation, you'll fit right in."

"Thanks," she breathes, her shoulders sagging a bit. "I'll admit, I was pretty nervous about coming tonight."

I smile at her as Vivian and Tasia come into view. "Shit, I better sit down or I'll be getting eye daggers from Anna all night."

"Go," Carlies says, shooing me toward the loveseat.

I sit down just as Anna enters the room with the folding chair. She dumps it in Carlie's hand and practically dives head-first into the spot beside me.

"Hey, I was sitting there," Vivian whines when she sees me.

"Actually, it was Lily's spot first. You stole it but no one was man enough to kick you out," Anna declares, picking up her phone and feigning boredom again.

I jab her in the side with my elbow.

"Just suck it up, Viv. You can tough it out with me and Carlie," Tasia says, taking a seat. "Come on, Anna, hook me up." She wiggles the tips of her fingers toward the glasses on the table.

Anna bends forward slowly and starts working as book club bartender. She tops up all five glasses and divvies them out.

"I'd like to propose a toast," I say, raising my glass in salute.

Everyone stops in mid-sip to stare at me.

I clear my throat and continue, "To old friends and *new ones.*"

"Who are you calling old?" Vivian scoffs playfully.

"Cheers," I say, ignoring her as I hold my glass higher.

"Cheers!" The rest chorus.

I take a sip, letting the notes hit my tongue. Blackberry, cherry, and a hint of something else—*something really sweet*—lingers on my tastebuds.

"Okay, so who actually read *'Fuck Me Sideways?'*" Tasia begins. "Carlie, I know you're new so we don't expect—"

"The one by Anita Bang?" Carlie interjects.

Tasia nods.

"Great book. God, wasn't Banner the *perfect* grumpy to Tess's sunshine?" Carlie croons, clasping her hands together and holding them under her chin.

Tasia shoots us a look of surprise. "You—you read it?"

Carlie nods. "It was raunchy and I love it. Plus, I'm friends with Anita."

Anna coughs on her wine. "You're *friends* with Anita Bang?"

She nods.

"I can't even say her name without squirming in my seat," Vivian says, then bites down on her lower lip.

Carlie double-takes at Vivian. "I mean, her real name is Christie, but yeah. She's great."

"Okay, you're gonna have to dish. How is it you're friends with Anita?" Tasia asks, clutching her glass to her chest.

Carlie swallows hard and shifts her gaze around the room.

"You don't have to tell us," I say, trying to give her a way out. It's pretty clear this question is making her uncomfortable.

"No, it's—" Carlie begins, her lips twisting to the side. "It's okay. I knew this was going to get asked at some point."

"Ooooh, goss. Spill it," Vivian practically cries out in glee, leaning in closer to her.

Carlie smiles uncomfortably and says, "I write ... *romance.*"

"*Really?* Are you published?" Tasia asks.

Of course, she would. It's literally her job.

Again Carlie nods.

"Anything we've heard of?" Anna asks, clearly as curious as the rest of us.

"Probably," Carlie hedges with a grin bordering on grimace.

"Oh my god, the suspense is killing us." Vivian taps her toes on the ground and squeals like a little girl.

Tasia takes a sip of wine. "So, I'm assuming you have a pen name, as well?"

Carlie points at Tasia. "Very astute."

"We won't tell anyone," I say, mesmerized by the fact that we have an *honest-to-god author* in our midst.

Silence fills the room for a few beats as Carlie chews on the side of her cheek.

"Guys, she wants her privacy. We need to respect that," I interject, reading her hesitation.

Carlie flashes me a relieved smile. "It's not that I don't want to tell you guys. It's just—I mean, we just met and ..."

Tasia waves a hand between them. "Totally get it."

"I would totally bone Banner," Anna spits out.

We all turn to face her. While a comment like that from Vivian is to be expected, hearing it from Anna is something totally different.

"Seriously? I thought you liked the nerdy smart ones who end up being a total kinkster?" Vivian gapes at her.

Redirection accomplished.

Anna shrugs.

"I totally agree. When Banner had to go into the bathroom to relieve his desires because he couldn't handle the forced proximity with Tess ...” Tasia fans herself.

“Oooh, and then she walked in on it!” I fire back.

“So, are you saying that turned you on?” Vivian gasps in mock seriousness.

“I mean, well,” I mumble, flustered. My face heats up and I reach for my glass.

Vivian leans in, her eyes trained on me. “I thought you were, and I quote, *only turned on by the sweet, romantic ones.*”

I bite my lower lip. “I mean, there’s something to be said about the way he was so different with her.”

“Say it, *he was hot,*” Vivian presses.

I press my lips tight. After a few seconds of deliberation, I spit out, “Fine, the way he was *depicted* was hot.”

Vivian lets out a howl of approval. “Yes. I knew it. I knew we’d break you one day.”

I look up at the ceiling. “Oh, for godsake.”

“Things still strained between you and Seth?” Tasia asks, her eyes full of concern. She’s the only one who knows how things have been going and I’m not overly in the mood to change that.

I shift in my seat and stare down at my empty glass.

“Things are strained? Do tell,” Vivian says, twisting to face me.

She’s a magnet for drama and crazy shit. So when things are going good in her own life, she’s looking for it anywhere else.

“You need to divorce him and move on,” Anna says

without a hint of empathy. When my jaw drops open, she just shrugs. "You deserve better."

"Look, things are *fine*. He's just gone a lot and things have been—"

"She hasn't had sex in over *two months*," Tasia fires back. "Sorry, Lil. You need some tough love here. It's not normal."

I blow out a slow breath and wait for the onslaught.

"You know *he* hasn't gone two months," Vivian blurts out, then covers her mouth.

My eyes shoot to her.

"Oh, Lily, I'm sorry." She backpedals.

"Let's drop it, okay," I say, wishing the next bottle of wine was already open.

I know things are strained with me and Seth. I'm not stupid. But we've been married for almost ten years. I've come too far to turn back now.

Besides, my sister Angie would have a field day.

"Oh, guys, I almost forgot. Our new bookmarks came in," Tasia interjects, changing the subject. "Anyone feel like going next door to grab them?"

"Why are they next door?" Carlie asks, confusion clear across her freckled face.

"Tasia owns Dirty Books *and* Dirty Deeds," Anna offers by way of explanation.

"We get more deliveries at Deeds, so I just send all the mail there," Tasia says with a shrug. "Plus it's fun to see the vein in Quinn's forehead bulge when he thinks he's being overworked."

Everyone except Carlie laughs at that thought. Quinn

is the sweetest gay guy you'll ever meet but he does get hilariously agitated over too much work.

"You own the adult toy shop, too?" Carlie replies, her eyes distant as she processes.

"Yep," Tasia says, letting the P pop.

"I'm impressed. I assumed it was some dirty old man." Carlie chuckles after a moment. "I guess that was a bit presumptuous."

"What can I say? I'm a rebel. Stereotypes are the bane of my existence," Tasia quips. "Now, who's gonna go hound Quinn for the mail so you can relay back to me whether his eye twitches or his scowl concretizes?"

"Why do you bother asking? You know little Miss Goody is going to go," Anna drawls, picking up a new bottle of wine and grabbing the opener.

All eyes turn on me.

After an awkward stare-down, I slap my thighs and stand up. "I guess I'll go."

At least when I come back, there will be more wine. And Anna better save my damn spot.

CHAPTER 2

London

I stare at the email, but for as long as I take in the splotches of black on white, I can't make heads or tails of it.

It doesn't make a damn bit of sense.

I've been back in the Twin Ports for six months, peanuts compared to most of my employees, but even I know that Club Nocté has a reputation for being the area's best-kept secret.

It's a big *fuck-you* to the people who, in my mind, deserve it.

Plus, there's an air of mystery to the club that you don't get with most businesses.

It's refreshing.

I've worked nightclubs since I was eighteen but this one—it's different. It has two modes of operation and because of its rules, it draws in an interesting clientele that needs an outlet for their ... *frustrations.*

But this email...

I'm supposed to figure out how to host an event that could fuck it all up. If word gets out, the rules of the club could break down, and outsiders will try to force their way in. People with deep pockets and greasy hands.

All the *wrong* people.

I might be the manager, but I'm not equipped to handle this kind of bullshit and neither is the rest of the staff. Things have been going fine. At least, I thought they were.

However, the order came down from *'on high'* and it's not my place to question it. The boss gets what the boss wants.

Besides, his crazy ideas have gotten Nocté this far.

There's gotta be a master plan buried in the details somewhere. I'm just not privy to it.

"Hey, Saint," Cal says, rapping his knuckles on the frame of my office door.

My eyes shift from the computer monitor to him.

Nocté isn't due to open for another few hours, but like clockwork, Cal is one of the first ones here. As head of security, he likes to spend a few minutes kicking the shit with me before making his rounds.

Gotta say, right now, I could use the distraction.

"S'up, Cal?" I mutter, as I push away from my desk and lean back in my chair.

"You looked awfully engrossed. Watchin' porn?" He grins, sliding into the room like a golden panther. He takes up his typical spot on the opposite side of my desk.

People often underestimate him because he's short and has an easy-going air about him. Probably because of that damn dirty blond hair and goofy grin. They don't expect him to go stone-cold badass at the first sign of trouble.

That's why I hired him.

"Nah, nothing that exciting," I fire back.

"So, cyber-stalking your mystery girl, then?" Cal's dark eyes glint with that lethal humor of his.

"Very funny." I make a face and flip him the bird.

"Seriously, dude. You've been here half a year and you haven't even looked her up? Aren't you curious?" He leans back, clasping his hands behind his head.

"I'm sure she's long gone," I counter. But the response falls flat, even to me.

Besides, of course, I've damn well looked her up.

He narrows his gaze, but his left eyebrow twitches suspiciously into an arch. I could have let that go, but then the asshole has the audacity to smirk.

"Fuck off," I mutter, eyeing the email again. Maybe it was the lesser of two evils after all. "Did you need something?"

Cal snickers. "Since when do I need a reason to harass you?"

My expression deadpans and a low growl rumbles from the back of my throat.

That makes him full-on guffaw.

Prick.

"Seriously, man. I've never seen a guy wound so tight at the mention of an old friend," Cal continues. "Are you sure you don't have feelings for her?"

"We were ten, man. And she was my *best* friend." I

lower my eyebrows. "Of course, I have feelings for her. Just—*not like that.*"

"Sure, sure," he says, nodding.

I roll my eyes. "You gotta point in there somewhere?"

"Saint, you're pining for a girl you haven't seen in damn near twenty years. The least you could do is put your feelings to bed by tracking her down, asking her out to coffee, and realizing she never went through puberty like the rest of us. Or that she's an ogre or some damned thing. Christ," he mutters.

"First of all, I'm not pining—"

Again he raises an eyebrow.

"Hey, Saint, we're outta stir sticks," Myles says, knocking on the doorframe the way Cal had. She tips her chin to him in acknowledgment. "Oh, hey, Cal."

"Hey, Myles," Cal says, looking over his shoulder.

I turn my gaze to the best damn bartender this side of Lake Superior—who on occasion is also one deluded mofo. Her pixie-style haircut is a mixture of black and purple this week. It was red and gold last week. Dressed in the goth garb she frequently wears, she looks like a pissed-off fairy.

"This is my problem how?" I fire back, leaning forward so I can plant my elbows on my desk and steeple my fingers beneath my chin.

She arches a well-sculpted black eyebrow and crosses her arms. "Did you approve my entire bar order last week?"

"Is there a well-stocked bar out there?" I quip,

knowing damn well she's been putting everything away for the past hour.

Besides, she and I both know that between the two of us, if the stir sticks got forgotten, it wasn't on my end.

Her eyes narrow and her mouth purses. "Well, *shit.*"

I shake my head and turn back to the pointed stare Cal's throwing in my direction. He's not done with his stupid conversation.

"You know what?" I say, standing up quickly. "Why don't I come help you look?"

Cal's eyes narrow at me, so I make sure to grin big as I walk on by.

"You know, you really don't have to do this—" Myles sputters, taking a step into the hallway.

I can tell by the tone of her voice, she's well aware that she's the reason there are no stir sticks. It doesn't stop me from following her to the bar anyway.

"*Hey*, Saint," Rebecca says, entering the club with her coat dangling over her right arm. She bats her eyes like she's one of the twitter-pated cartoon animals from Bambi.

She's dressed in skin-tight black pants and a low-cut black top that leaves nothing to the imagination. Her dirty blond hair is up in a long pony which makes her neck look far too long.

There was a time when seeing her dressed like that would have made my pulse race and my dick hard. But now, I just want to get far, far away from her.

On the upside, she should rake in drink orders dressed like that.

I shoot her a pained smile and continue following after Myles.

"She's not real quick on the uptake, is she?" Myles whispers, leaning in close so only I can hear her.

I shake my head. "You have *no* idea."

In fact, I'm pretty sure Rebecca is the reason blond women are stereotyped. It took me nearly three weeks of dating her to realize it, though. Once the magical spell of her perky tits wore off, there really wasn't much left that I could connect with.

Myles laughs. "Still don't know what you saw in her. She's just so ...*perky*," she says, plucking the word right out of my previous thought.

"I am gonna laugh like hell if you end up with a blond bitch." I chuckle, nudging her on the shoulder.

"Not in a million years. My girl is gonna be dark, broody, and fuckin' hot in bed," Myles counters, wiggling her eyebrows suggestively.

"Glad you're keeping an open mind, then." I snicker.

"So, what were you and Cal talking about that had you running to my bar. You know the stir sticks aren't fuckin' here," Myles says, grabbing a bar rag and tossing it over her shoulder.

I glance over mine to make sure no one has managed to sneak up. "Yeah, I know. And it was nothing. Cal just likes pushing my buttons."

"Uh, huh." She crosses her arms over her torso and leans against the back counter.

"Swear down," I say, holding up my hands. "I was more worried about the email I got from the boss."

"Shit, what now?" She makes a face.

"Noah wants us to put on this fancy dinner event for Nocté's *Upper Tier.*" I run my hands through my hair.

Myles looks confused. "I don't get it. That's not so bad."

I pin her with a knowing stare.

"Oh," she breathes. "*Oh.* You meant the *other* club."

"Yeah," I spit out. "And if it goes well, he wants us to continue them. But if word gets out—"

"It will mess with the *club*," Myles finishes.

I nod. "That's what I'm afraid of."

"Well, shit. You need to hire someone with finesse for this sort of thing," she replies. "Know any event coordinators?"

"Oh, yeah, for sure. I hang out with that crowd on the weekend," I huff, rolling my eyes.

"Well, I'm not handling the planning," Myles blurts, raising her hands.

"What are we planning?" Rebecca asks, leaning forward on the bar. She crosses her arms and her breasts practically jump ship.

"Not a goddamn thing," I say, turning on my heel.

She chases after me. "But Saint, if you need help, I could totally make it *magical.*"

I groan.

Everything with her is fucking *magical.* You'd think she walked through life in a goddamned fairytale. Hell, I bet she still watches all the Disney Princess movies every weekend.

"Seriously, I'm good. But thanks for the offer," I respond, my tone clipped.

She pulls up short and pouts.

I swear to god, if the woman starts crying ...

"Saint, I still need those stir sticks," Myles calls out.

"Well, then go."

"I can't. I have to check the barrels and we have a trainee coming in," she says.

"Fuck me," I ground out. "Then *I'll* go. Wouldn't want to put anyone else out."

At least it gives me an escape route.

I move past Rebecca, not even acknowledging her bullshit.

"Thanks, Saint," Myles says, batting her crazy eyelashes at me and blowing a kiss. "You're the best."

I walk out the door with my middle finger held high.

The bitch just laughs.

CHAPTER 3

Lily

There was a time when walking into Dirty Deeds would have made my pulse race and my mouth go dry. I'm not the kind of girl who frequents adult toy shops.

Or, at least, I didn't *think* I was.

Then I met Tasia and all that went out the window.

Though, it helps to know the people who run the place. If there was one person in the whole world I wouldn't be ashamed to buy sex toys from, it's Dirty Deed's manager, Quinn.

He's a take no prisoners kinda guy and gay as the day is long.

I adore him to pieces.

"Hey there, lover girl," Quinn beams when I walk through the door. He's shaved the sides of his head since the last time I saw him and on top is a bleached white pile of messy curls.

I can't help the smile that breaks across my features.

Instead of answering him back, I run around the counter and give him a big hug.

"Got the raw end of the stick, did ya?" he purrs, laying his innuendo on thick.

I poke him in the chest when I step back. "From what I hear, that's you."

"Touché," he says, grinning like a madman. "So, you're here to pick up the boss's dirty mail, I presume."

I nod. "You presume correctly."

He starts digging around behind the counter, nodding to himself. "When I realized it was Thursday, I figured Tash would send one of you in to do her bidding. But my money was on Vivian."

"Oh, it was touch and go there for a minute. There was hair pulling, wine was spilled, but in the end, I won." I beam at him.

He places a box on the counter and swats the air. "Oh, stop. You'll make me blush."

"A hard feat, I hear," I fire back.

He chuckles. "Oh, honey. You have no idea."

A woman walks in, glancing in our direction long enough to make eye contact. A shadow of a smile floats over her features, but she continues on a path to whatever she's looking for.

"You can tell an awful lot about people by the way they walk in here," Quinn says conspiratorially as he pushes the box of bookmarks toward me and leans forward on the counter.

Instinctively, I move in closer and raise an eyebrow. "Oh really? Do tell."

He tips his chin. "See that guy in the back? The one who's checking out the bondage?"

Slowly, I twist around and glance in the direction of the back wall. Sure enough, there's a tall man in the section. He's dressed in a cowboy hat and flannel shirt and is fondling a ball gag.

I turn around with wide eyes and nod.

"Now, you'd think by the way he's massaging the merchandise that he's a go-getter who knows what he wants," Quinn whispers. "Maybe he likes a little pony play."

"He's not?" I ask, unable to help myself. Granted, I have no idea what he means by pony play, but I let that slide, fairly certain it's better that way.

"Not if the first few seconds in the store have a say. He slunk into the room and ducked behind the shelf as quick as he could. Never looked in my direction or made any kind of eye contact. He was either hiding from the potential onlookers from the street or was too embarrassed to look me in the eye," he says. "My guess is the latter."

"So?"

"Well, it says he's got hangups and isn't owning his sexual prowess just yet. But he's working on it. I'm already conjuring up recommendations for when he manages to muster the courage to waltz his ass up here," Quinn quips with a wink. "Now, the other guy—the one by the party supplies, he was a man on a mission. He walked in here right before you did, strutting like he owns the place—which he doesn't, *obvs*. Strong eye contact. Even tipped his chin and said, *'Hey, how's it goin'?'* He either has a bachelor party to plan or he's about to be the gag-gift giver of the century. Either way, he's a man who's secure with who he is and has *zero* fucks to give. I bet he's an absolute *beast* in bed." Quinn places his chin in his hand and sighs loudly. "Which means he's *probably straight.*"

I rotate to get a look at the guy, but his back is turned to us. All I can make out is a dark head of messy brown hair and a great build. Clearly, the man works out because he has shoulders for days. Plus, he's got the kind of ass that fills his faded denim *really* nicely. Too nice, in fact, for the tingle that hits this married woman's nether regions.

I clear my throat and shift my gaze.

"What about that one?" I ask quietly, eyeing the woman who walked in a moment ago. She's now standing with her hands on her hips in front of the wall of vibrators.

"Oh, honey, she's done with *his shit* and ready to take matters into her own hands." Quinn chuckles. "Literally."

"Who's shit?" I ask, turning back to him.

"Does it matter?" He shoots me a WTF look. "She is fed up with a capital *F*. Any minute, she's going to ask for my *oh-so-worldly advice* on which one of those silicone beauties will turn her vision technicolor and I'll give it to her. Oh, that reminds me. You have *got* to check out this new Swedish brand we just got in." He twists around and pulls up a couple of black boxes.

Without a second thought, he opens the first box, plucks the silicone toy out, and waves it proudly between us. Then, he passes it to me.

It's a bright blue number that looks more like the letter V than a vibrator.

V for Vibrator. I guess it works.

"Meet Hugo. I'm officially in love and no longer need a man to complete me," he swoons, fanning himself. "It has a prostate massager and eight *hands-free* settings. Seriously, I've never come so hard in my life."

"Oh, dear god." My face flushes and I pass the monstrosity back. "Well, that's lovely for you. I don't have a prostate, so ..."

His face brightens and he wiggles his eyebrows. "Which is why I am pleased to bring you this next piece. Say hello to *Enigma*," he says, removing a dark pink vibrator from the other box. This one is shaped more like a question mark to match the questions in my mind.

What's with the abstract shapes?

He hands it to me and I turn it over in my hand, confused about how you'd even use the damn thing.

As if reading my mind, he begins his sales pitch. "Fully waterproof, this bad boy is sure to be your best friend from here on out. Now, this piece fits inside to stimulate the G-spot." He taps the curved part of the question mark. "And this amazing little spot here is the super-sonic clit stimulator. Like, seriously, from what I hear, it's supposed to exorcise your demons and give you a glimpse into heaven itself."

Behind me, someone chuckles. My first instinct is to freeze. Because, dear Lord Almighty ...

Quinn arches around me and gives whoever it is a good once-over. I'm too terrified to look.

"Don't let me stop you," a man's deep voice says from behind me. "Please, carry on. I'm very interested to hear about how this super-sonic feature works. Heaven certainly has an appeal."

With the vibrator still in my hand, I chance a glance over my shoulder and come face to face with the dark-haired, perfect assed man from the party section.

Of course.

Tucked under his left arm is a box of lewd stir sticks. His eyes sparkle with amusement as a dazzling smirk appears.

"I, this isn't—" I begin, fumbling with the vibrator. I nearly drop it but manage to grab it by the G-spot curve. "I mean, he was just showing me ... But this isn't ..."

To my horror, I bump into his box of stir sticks, sending them flying. Somehow, he manages to reach out and grab them before they hit the ground. I'm dazzled by the way his biceps flex and the tattoos on his forearm dance.

"Whew, good reflexes there," I blurt out, still mesmerized by his arms.

The guy's smoldering dark blue eyes survey me, still with a hint of humor, and somehow, the weight of worlds. There's a gravity there and it's like he strips me down and sees into my soul as a strange energy passes between us.

He looks like he's about to say something, but stops short.

Of course, mind-in-the-gutter-girl that I am, already turned on by the toy I clearly need for myself, all I can think about is what Quinn said earlier—and I'm inclined to agree.

Beast is definitely the word that springs to mind for this guy.

It's suddenly too hot in here.

"You know, I should *go*." I twist back to Quinn and thrust the Enigma at him. When I catch his eye, I mouth, *I want one.*

He winks at me and mouths back, *After.*

Oh, you bet I'll be here after book club. I have a date with the Enigma tonight.

I pat the counter and move quickly to get out of the way.

"Lily, don't forget the bookmarks," Quinn calls out, thrusting them after me.

I butt the palm of my hand to my forehead. "Oh, right."

Just as I pick up the box and clutch them to my chest, the man grabs my elbow. He twists me to face him, now looking far more serious. "Lily? It *is* you ... I thought—but I wasn't sure ..."

Confusion clouds my mind as I blink at him, now towering over me. He looks vaguely familiar, but with the way he's staring at me, it's like he's seen a ghost.

"Do I know you?" I ask, dropping my gaze to where his hand is clutching my arm. It's like an electric current has turned on all the nerve endings where his palm makes contact.

He doesn't release me like I expected him to. Instead, he sets the box in his other arm down on the counter and tugs me to him for a full-blown embrace.

"Holy shit," he mutters. "I can't believe this. I was just—I never thought I'd see you again."

I stiffen at the sudden contact with the wall of muscle and shoot Quinn a confused glance.

Cops? he mouths.

Suddenly, I'm standing upright again as the man holds me in front of him, grabbing onto both of my forearms.

Again, he pierces me with his dizzying gaze. "Lily, it's me, *London.*"

I blink hard, unable to force my mouth to form words.

London?

As in ... *my London?*

As in, my former nerdy best friend? The one who lived next door, who would stay up all night, talking through walkie-talkies about aliens and the meaning of the universe?

That London?

Oh my god, I've lost the ability to speak.

Quinn glances from London, to me, and back again. "Uh, Lily ... Do you want to fill me in? Are Duluth's finest gonna need a call? *Or—?*"

"No—" I spit out, holding out my hand. I turn back to London St. James. I haven't seen him since we were ten and he was waving from the back seat of his parent's minivan as they drove away.

Holy shit, he filled out well.

"London?" I breathe, barely able to get the word past my lips.

His grin melts my heart. "In the flesh."

"H—*how?*" I manage to sputter.

"I, uh—" he runs his hand along the back of his neck. His eyes suddenly widen and he eyes the box on the counter. "You know, those aren't for me."

"Oh, I get it. That's not mine," I say, pointing at the pink magic still clutched in Quinn's hand. "I mean, not now. I mean, maybe someday, but that's Quinn's. Apparently, they're very good at—"

Quinn's eyebrow rises and I clamp my mouth shut.

Stop talking right now, Lily.

My god. You almost told London about the vibrator's usefulness.

Quinn looks far too smug and my cheeks heat as I turn back to London. "You know, I really need to get back." I jab a thumb toward the door.

Disappointment floods London's features. "Oh, I'm sorry. I didn't realize I was keeping you."

"I mean, I'm just next door. Book club," I say, trying to backpedal and sound more reasonable. Or adultish. That's a word, right?

Now it's London's turn to raise an eyebrow. "At the dirty bookstore?"

I narrow my eyes, realizing it wasn't the smartest thing to bring up. "I mean, yeah."

"Our girl here *loves* her dirty books," Quinn offers, butting in.

"*Quinn*," I hiss.

When I look back to London, he almost looks impressed. I take a deep breath and clutch the box of bookmarks to me like a lifejacket.

I need to go. *Now.*

"Well, we should catch up sometime," London says, reaching out again and pressing his hand to my elbow. "Coffee, maybe?"

"Coffee," I repeat, but the word hasn't settled into my brain. It's still floating around the universe as I try to make sense of the alternate reality I've fallen into.

London is here. He's back ... and he's *hot*. And, oh my god ...

"She'd ... *love to*," Quinn interjects, rolling his hand. "Right, sweetie?"

I nod, still not sure what planet I'm on. "Right. Coffee. Coffee is good."

"*Ooookay.* Give the nice man your number, so I can ring up his purchase, and get away from this awkward-fest," Quinn retorts, tossing me a pen and sticky note. "And that's definitely saying something, considering where we all are."

In an absolute daze, I write down my number and hand the paper to him. Before I can set the pen down, he takes it from me and grabs my hand. He presses the pen tip to my palm and writes down seven digits.

"This way, you don't lose it," London says, clicking

the pen and handing it back to Quinn. "I doubt that's changed much."

When we were kids, my head was always in the clouds. I was forever losing things.

But he's wrong.

I've definitely gotten better at keeping track of details. In fact, some of my clients consider me a master of it.

I blink hard, not telling him any of that.

Instead, I shoot him what I can only consider is a bewildered, crazy smile as I back out of the shop.

When I get outside, my heart finally starts beating again.

London is here.

He's back.

And I just gave him my number.

CHAPTER 4

London

I watch her leave, and her expression is as dazed as I feel.

She looks so fucking good.

Definitely not an ogre. And puberty had definitely hit her *just right.*

Thanks for that, Cal.

My brain can't even fathom what just happened.

After the talk with Cal, what are the chances I'd run into her?

"So, you and Lily, huh?" the store clerk says, ripping me from my thoughts.

I blink back at him, then clear my throat. "Um, what?"

He scans only one of the plastic bags of stir-sticks and shoves the rest of the box at me. "You and Lily. You were a thing?"

"No," I mutter, but my strangled laugh doesn't really emphasize the point I was trying to make. I clear my throat and repeat myself, trying to sound more sure. *"No."*

The guy quirks his pierced eyebrow. "Seriously? Because I definitely caught a vibe—"

"There's no vibe," I spit out. *There was definitely a vibe.* "She and I were best friends."

"Oooh," he says, leaning in closer and fluttering his eyelashes. "Is this my lucky day? Are you batting for the other team?"

I chuckle softly, damn flattered.

"Nah. Sorry, man," I say, patting him on the shoulder. I might not be gay, but I'm no prude either. Besides, thanks to Nocté, I know plenty of gay guys who are not only awesome people, I've come to think of them as good friends.

His face falls. "Yeah, I thought so."

I open my mouth to tell him I could set him up if he wanted, but he cuts me off, sounding completely confused. "Friends? *Really?* Are you sure?"

I nod. I don't know why I even feel the need to explain anything to his guy, but I find myself clarifying anyway. "We were *ten*, man."

His eyes widen and he crinkles his nose. "Really?"

"Really." I grab my box and start to leave. I'll put out my feelers to some of the guys to see if I can point a couple single ones toward Dirty Deeds. He doesn't need to know I was involved.

I get as far as the door when he calls out, "Thursdays."

I turn back to him. "Huh?"

"In case she doesn't call you or blows off your attempts to call her, because, let's face it, that's *totally* a Lily move," he says, rolling his eyes and giving me a sheepish grin. When I don't respond, he continues, "She's in Dirty Books every Thursday night for book club. They almost always walk out of there by eight. A little tipsy, mind you, but mostly in a good mood." He winks at me.

"Oh, thanks," I respond, shooting him an appreciative glance before I walk out the door.

"You didn't hear it from me," he calls after me, holding his hands up. "And if you try to throw me under the bus, I will deny it until my dying breath."

I can't help but grin. "Understood."

He tips his head, then wanders out from behind the counter and heads over to the woman standing in front of the vibrators. "Honey, allow me to blow your mind. I have just what you're looking for."

I huff a laugh and push the door open. A rush of chilly lake air greets me as I walk down the block to my vehicle. It might be May but the ice hasn't even fully melted off Lake Superior yet. The chill it brings is enough to make even the most hearty of midwesterners shiver. I have to admit, I forgot how long it takes to warm up here.

When I reach my Escalade, I pause before getting in. My gaze drifts over the two stores. Dirty Books and Dirty Deeds sit side-by-side, taking up half of the city block.

Part of me wants to walk over to the bookstore and wait for Lily right now. But that would be nuts. Besides, it's barely six-thirty and Myles will flip her shit if I don't come back with the stir-sticks before the doors open.

When I got the idea to piss off Myles with these dirty replacements, I had no idea it would turn my world upside down. I just thought I'd travel to the west hillside of Duluth, to the closest novelty shop I was aware of, and get a good laugh.

But now...

I shudder from the realization.

Things feel ... *different.* And I have no clue what any of it means.

I open the door to my vehicle and hop in, tossing the box of stir-sticks on the passenger seat. Within minutes, I'm on the bridge heading back to Superior and totally lost in thought.

I need to get back to my computer so I can do some digging. It's been months since I looked Lily up online. It was a mostly dead-end then, with only a few mentions in the newspaper. No pictures.

Now, I'm kinda grateful for that because if I had seen her, there's no telling what I would have done.

Instead, all I got were snippets—she graduated from UMD with a Bachelor's in business.

There was also a mention of a wedding—*but that was over a decade ago.*

A lot can change in a decade.

Please, don't be married still.

The thought makes me grip the steering wheel.

Our relationship isn't like that. *We're not like that.*

I have to admit, though ... Of the many ways I envisioned running into her again, I can't believe we reconnected in a *sex shop*, of all places.

Despite myself, my fucking body reacts like a teenager when I think about her standing there with her tiny hands wrapped around that vibrator.

I adjust in the seat, ignoring my stupid cock. It clearly hasn't gotten the memo that we're just friends.

Though, if I'm honest, I would have paid good money to see the look on her face when the guy at the counter told her about how it's used.

I blow out a labored breath.

Get it together, London. This is Lily.

Seeing her today was awkward and she seemed shaken—but damn, she was beautiful. Her hair is darker than I remember. It used to be a light shade of blond that really made her brown eyes stand out. The freckles across her nose were also more pronounced in my memory, too. I suppose it was from all the time we spent outside, running the streets of Duluth.

We owned that damn town.

Memories of her running, her long hair flowing behind her, flit into my mind. All the times spent at Enger Tower, Lester Park, or just down at the shore of Lake Superior.

She used to have freckles all up and down her arms, too.

I wonder if they're still there?

My mind veers toward wildly inappropriate thoughts by the time I get back to Nocté. I'm actually thankful for the distraction from my own mind.

When I walk into the building, Myles shoots me a confused look. "Where are my stir-sticks, man?"

"Fuck," I mutter, turning back around. Didn't even grab the damn box.

"You had one job," she calls out after me.

"Yeah, yeah," I mutter. I'd forgotten completely about the stir-sticks and my plan for them.

I stomp out to the Escalade, yanking open the passenger door, and grabbing the box. There's barely enough in here to last the night, which will really be the thing that gets her knickers in a twist. As much fun as that would be to watch, I have better things to do now.

"Shit." I walk to the back and open the hatch, then I drop the box of dick sticks and grab the bigger box of plain stir-sticks I picked up at Costco.

I'll mess with Myles another night.

"Whatcha up to?" Cal's voice booms from somewhere behind me.

Despite myself, I nearly jump out of my skin. I spin around and shake the box of stir-sticks by way of explanation.

"You're an awfully jumpy fucker tonight," Cal says with a hint of a smirk.

I rub my left index finger over my eyelid. "Yeah, well, you have a way of sneaking up on people."

"I wasn't sneaking," he responds, giving me a once-over. "Just doing my rounds before we open."

I nod. "Good. Well, I better head in."

Without adding anything else, I close the back hatch and hit the lock on my key fob. Then, I walk past him and back into the building. I can feel his eyes on me the entire walk back and it puts me on edge. If he knew what just happened, I'd never hear the end of it.

"Here's your damn stir-sticks," I say, shoving the much larger box across the bar.

"'Bout time," she says, grabbing hold of the box and yanking it open.

I sigh loudly and lay on the sarcasm thick as I walk away. "You're welcome, Myles. Don't mention it."

Now, I regret not giving her the other box.

Dick sticks for a dick move. Shoulda stuck to the plan.

I shake my head and walk through the club and toward my office. Time's ticking and the doors are gonna open soon. Once that happens, getting a moment of silence will be impossible.

When I get to my office, I pull up my chair and wiggle the mouse to wake up the computer. Once I log in, I pull back, staring at the email that's still front and center on the screen.

"Shit," I mumble, ignoring it and opening up Chrome.

I type in Lily's maiden name into the search bar:
Lilian Boyd

Holding my breath, I lean in and scroll past the first two because they're about some *Lilian Boyd* in Pennsylvania who scored for her girl's basketball team.

I click on the one I really don't want to read.

LILIAN BOYD AND SETH LARSON

Lilian Boyd and Seth Larson were married on August 18th at the Anchor Point Community Church in Duluth, Minnesota. Lilian is the daughter of Daniel & Tracy Boyd of Duluth. Seth is the son of Miranda and Trent Larson of Hermantown. The Matron of Honor was Anastasia Wilde, a friend of the bride. The Best Man was Ben Strode, a friend of the groom. The bride and groom met at the University of Minnesota. The couple resides in Lester Park.

The first time I read that article, I was appalled by whoever wrote it because it was as bland as humanly possible. A wedding announcement should have char-acter—and symbolize the kind of love the couple shares. Don't get me wrong, I don't think I'd want to read that, either. But that's what it *should be.*

At the time, I was pissed they didn't even post a picture to go with the boring ass announcement. Now, I have to admit, I'm glad I don't have to stare at her husband's face or see how excited she was on her special day.

I should have been there.

Sighing, I do what I didn't have the strength to do last time.

"Fuck, I hate social media," I mutter, opening up my ancient Facebook account. I haven't touched the damn thing since I was in high school and even then, it was infrequently. I was too busy joyriding and getting tattoos to dispel the nerdy image I used to have to think about social media.

But if I know Lily, she'll be on there.

First, I type her maiden name and pray she shows up.

Of course, she doesn't.

I close my eyes, fighting internally.

I should leave it here.

If she wants to tell me her life story, she can do it over coffee.

But of course, my fingers type the name anyway:

Lilian Larson

A few seconds later, the search results come up. There, at the top of the list, is the woman who just blushed her way through the door of Dirty Deeds.

Fuck. She's still married.

I stare at that beautiful smile. Her dazzling eyes and deep dimples capture the entire scene.

But underneath her name is a short bio. My heart skips a beat and I lean forward, rereading it because I can't believe my luck.

Right there, in black and white, it says:

Freelance Event Coordinator. Creating an unforgettable event is an art form. I can help you plan and execute it. Reach out. The planning starts over a cup of coffee.

Suddenly, this stupid event the boss wants just might be the best fucking thing that's ever happened to me.

CHAPTER 5

Lily

Holy shit.

A wave of panic crashes over me as I close the door to Dirty Books and flip the lock. I clutch the box of bookmarks to my chest like it's my only anchor to the planet, and slide down the door until I'm resting on my backside. I breathe in and out, trying to will my heart to slow back down.

It doesn't overly help.

I flip my palm over and stare at the numbers written across it. In his handwriting.

London's handwriting.

After all of these years, *sure*, I've imagined what it would be like to see him again. I've wondered how he turned out and if he and I would still be friends as adults.

Hell, if he even still remembered me ...

But one thing I never imagined was how *good* he'd look.

For some reason, that sort of thing never occurred to

me. I suppose because he was my friend and at ten years old, I was more concerned with whether or not he thought aliens created the pyramids.

"Lily, is that you?" Tasia calls out, breaking me from my mini freakout.

"Yeah—" I croak. I clear my throat and attempt to stand, but my legs aren't getting the memo.

"Well, get your ass in here," Tasia hollers. "And lock the damn door this time."

I don't even respond to the jab. Instead, I focus on pushing down all of the emotions that are threatening to take me under, so I can deal with them later.

Right now, I need to act like nothing out of the ordinary happened. If these ladies sense blood in the water, they'll turn into sharks and pry it all out of me. The last thing I need is to spend the next hour hashing out my nonexistent love life when we should be talking about dirty books.

"Hi guys," I say, plastering a big grin on my face when I get back to the alcove.

Everyone turns my way. Well, everyone except Anna, whose nose is in her phone, per usual.

"Who walked in on who naked?" Vivian blurts out.

"What?" I ask, my voice raising an octave higher than it should have.

She narrows her gaze.

Even Tasia shoots me her side-eye of suspicion before pointing at me. "You gonna hand those over?"

I glance down and realize my fingers are digging into the box of bookmarks. "Oh, right."

Tasia holds out a hand and I relinquish the box. Then, I take a deep, calming breath as I move past her and back to my seat. Thankfully, Anna kept Vivian from stealing it.

"What's got your panties all twisted up?" Tasia asks. "Did Quinn talk about his latest vibrator experience or something?"

"No—" I exclaim, then realize I was thinking about London standing behind me while I was holding the big pink monstrosity. "I mean, *yes*—but that's not what ..." I clamp my mouth shut.

Anna looks up from her phone, turns to me, and slowly quirks an eyebrow.

Even the new girl is eyeing me expectantly.

Shit. Shit. Shit.

I feign ignorance by scratching at the spot under my left eye and clearing my throat.

"So, uh ... Let's see those bookmarks, huh?" I say, pointing toward Tasia and hoping the redirection sticks.

Instead, Tash places the box in her lap and covers it with her hands. "What in the absolute fuck is up with you?"

"Nothing," I squeak.

"Oooh, this is gonna be good," Viv says, a giant grin spreading across her face.

"I promise, there's nothing to tell," I respond, pressing my hands to my cheeks to keep them from flaming.

"Maybe she's trying to spice up her marriage and found some sexy lingerie when she went next door. Or maybe she's secretly planning a surprise threesome," Carlie interjects, strumming her fingertips together.

We all turn to face her.

"Sorry, hazards of the job." She shrugs, totally not fussed.

Vivian grins. "Maybe Flower here is into the kinky stuff and just ran into her Dom."

My head whips to her and I gasp, *"What?"*

Why on earth is that the only thing my brain can fire off?

Vivian beams back. "That's it. Isn't it?"

"No." I blink hard, trying to get the image of London being a Dom out of my head.

Thanks, Viv.

"You know, if you're not going to spill it, I could just walk next door and ask Quinn," Tasia says with a ghost of a smirk as she jabs her thumb toward Dirty Deeds.

My stomach drops and my heart skips at least three beats. Cold sweat literally bursts from the skin on my forehead like a faucet was turned on.

When I don't say anything, she makes a move to stand.

"Okay, fine. Christ, just sit down," I mutter, holding out my hands.

She resumes her seat and crosses her hands over the box.

I sigh. There's no way I'm going to get around this. If I don't talk, Tasia will one-hundred percent go ask Quinn.

"Quinn would just blow it out of proportion," I mutter my next thought out loud.

"You were blowing Quinn? I thought he was gay," Vivian says.

When I turn to her, she looks positively scandalized.

"What? *No.*" I make a face at the thought and my word choice as I shake my head.

"He's not gay?" She looks as confused as I feel.

I pinch the bridge of my nose and take a deep breath.

"Vivian, how you make it through the day is one of life's greatest mysteries," Anna mutters, returning her gaze to her phone.

"Just lucky, I guess," Vivian chirps with a shrug.

"More like dumb luck," Anna claps back.

"Getting back to whatever Quinn would have blown out of proportion ..." Tasia interjects with the roll of her hand. She holds my gaze with the kind of intensity that could make even Vivian squirm.

I inhale a deep breath, fighting the urge to up and run.

"Do you remember ..." I hedge as I try to pick the right angle for this discussion.

"Should we channel Michael Jackson and sing the rest of that song? Or were you gonna finish that thought?" Anna asks, barely even giving me a sideways glance. However, I catch the smirk on her lips.

"Shit, I don't know how to say this without all of you freaking out," I huff.

"I won't freak out," Carlie says with a sweet smile.

"That's because you're adorable and don't really know us yet," I retort, smiling softly.

"Come on already. The suspense is *killing* me," Vivian complains.

I roll my eyes to the ceiling and blurt out, "Do you guys remember me talking about my childhood best friend?"

"Wasn't his name England or something?" Vivian asks, pulling up her long legs into a crosslegged position on the folding chair. I cringe at the motion because I'd never be able to unpretzel myself if I pulled a move like that.

"This is a *he?*" Carlie interjects, her expression the epitome of interest and surprise.

"It's not like that. He's a friend," I counter, albeit too quickly.

"What about *London?*" Tasia asks.

"Oh, right... London," Vivian says, nodding to herself as if she's the one who remembered.

I nod at Tash. "Yeah. London."

"Did you just run into him on the street?" Tasia asks, her eyes wide.

"Worse." I cringe, knowing where these ladies are going to take things now.

Vivian's eyes widen. "Oh, my god. *Oh, my god.* You ran into him at Deeds?"

Without voicing it, I just nod.

"That musta been hella awkward," Anna snickers beside me.

"Oh, you have no idea," I breathe.

Vivian claps like a school kid who was just told they're going to get ice cream. "This is going to be *soooo* good. What happened? Don't skimp on any details."

Anna sets her phone down in her lap and turns to me. "Yeah, I'd like to know, too."

I make a face. "I sorta … I kinda …"

I glance around the room. Everyone's attention is rapt, as if they're all too afraid to breathe and miss it.

"So, Quinn was showing me the new *line*," I start, then chew on the side of my lip.

"*Vibrator* line," Tasia interjects, filling in the gaps.

I nod. "Yeah, that."

Vivian places her hands on her knees and bounces in her seat.

"Did he walk in on Quinn's colorful description?" Tasia guesses.

"Oh yeah, that he did. Then I practically bitch slapped London with it when I turned around." My cheeks flame.

"He got dong slapped?" Viv's mouth gapes open.

"Not exactly. It was an abstract-looking thing, but he definitely knew what it was. He wanted to hear the rest of Quinn's sales pitch," I say, covering my face with my hands. "I'm so freaking mortified."

"Why would you be embarrassed? You were there, sure, but so was he. What was *he* getting?" Vivian interjects, ever the pragmatic one.

"Girl's gotta point," Anna says, clearly impressed.

"Stir sticks that were shaped like penises," I whisper.

"That's it?" Tasia says, clearly not thrilled by the purchase. "Are you sure?"

I nod. "Yeah, and I nearly knocked them across the store's floor with the pink vibrator of doom."

My cheeks are on fire and I know I must be resembling a lobster right now.

"Did he remember you?" Carlie asks, her eyes sparkling with the kind of enthusiasm only a writer could have given this situation.

"Oh, yeah." I nod. "I didn't even recognize him at first."

She grins slowly. "But *he recognized you.*"

"That's hot," Vivian purrs, nodding approval at Carlie.

My eyebrows lower as I shoot her a look of annoyance. "In what realm is any of this hot? And besides, *married.*" I hold up my left hand and flash her my ring finger. "Remember?"

"Psh, formality," Vivian counters, with a swipe of her hand.

"That is *not* a formality. What's wrong with you?" I fire back, mortified.

Vivian shrugs.

"What's he like?" Tasia asks, her voice low and face serious.

I inhale and exhale, trying not to swoon. Married women don't swoon. "He's *London.* Just older."

"Yeah, I think we're gonna need a little more to go on there," Anna says.

I glance in her direction. This is the longest I've seen her off her phone and I'm not sure how I feel about that fact.

"I don't honestly know. We only talked for a few minutes before I had to get back here," I offer with a slight raise of my shoulder.

"More like ran away," Anna responds under her breath.

I elbow her but she just laughs.

"That's it? He didn't even ask you to meet up or anything?" Vivian asks, sounding disappointed. As if the idea of bumping into a long-lost friend in an adult toy store isn't exciting enough for her.

"Well, I mean, yeah," I sputter, glancing at his number written on my palm. "He wants to meet up for coffee sometime."

"That's great," Carlie responds, her eyes sparkling.

"Sure. But I don't think I'll go," I say, shaking my head and closing my fist.

"Why in the hell not?" Tasia fires back.

"Because," I huff, as if the word by itself should be all the evidence I need.

"You *have* to go," Vivian says, uncrossing her legs and leaning forward.

"I agree," Tasia throws her two cents in.

"Ditto." Anna nods.

Again, I run a hand over my face. "I can't go. I mean, what would Seth think of me going out with a guy he's never met?"

A huge grin spreads across Vivian's face. "He *was* hot. Wasn't he?"

"What are you talking about?" I deflect.

"You've got your panties in a bunch and you wouldn't be getting all flustered and creating all of this *'what would Seth think'* drama in your mind if he wasn't," she says with a smirk.

Anna harrumphs. "Twice in one night. Didn't think you had it in you to surprise me, Viv."

She beams back.

"Look, fine. Yes, he was hot. But he's my best friend," I say, feigning nonchalance.

"*Was* your best friend," Tasia quips with a pointed look.

"Right, right." I nod like a bobblehead.

This whole thing is freaking me out. I need some time to think.

"Besides, you meet male clients all the time," Anna points out. "Seth isn't going to give a rat's ass."

Vivian nods and pretends to shoot Anna with her index finger.

"I'm totally not comfortable with how much we're in agreement tonight," Anna says, picking up her phone. "The world has fallen off its axis."

A smile floats to my lips.

"Girl's got a point," Tasia says, a lopsided grin slowly creeping onto her face. "You meet clients all the time. Why would it matter if you had coffee with an old friend?"

I blink hard. "I mean, I guess it doesn't."

Tasia nods. "Good. Then it's settled. You're gonna meet him for coffee. Now, how about we check out these bookmarks."

CHAPTER 6

London

F*our.*
Four calls. Four separate voicemails.
Two excruciatingly long weeks.
And *zero* reciprocation from Lily.
Totally ghosted.
Had the guy at Dirty Deeds not warned me, I probably would have just let it go and taken her lack of reciprocity as the hint to fuck off.

Well, okay, letting it go would have been more difficult than that, but I would have done it anyway because that's what guys do, right?

Move on and pretend it doesn't phase us?

Instead, I'm standing beside my Escalade, in the chill May wind of the Twin Ports, so I don't miss her when she exits the bookstore. It's just gone past eight o'clock and I'm hoping I can convince her to go to dinner with me before Myles sends someone to hunt me down and haul my ass back to Nocté.

For whatever reason, I have this perverse need to see her—to get to know her as she is now. I just hope her husband can live with that. Hell, I hope *she* can.

"Hey there, lover boy." I shift my gaze from the storefront of Dirty Books to the sound of the voice. The store clerk from Dirty Deeds is marching in my direction. "Waiting for our girl, huh?"

I nod. "Yeah. Thanks for the tip."

"Left ya on read, huh?" he says with a slight shake of his head.

"Uh-huh." I nod.

"Knew it. Lily might be a bit of a flight risk, but she has her heart in the right place. I'm sure she's just trying to weigh things against her pro-con list," he offers.

The thought makes me smile. Even as a child, Lily was always the one who needed to find order in chaos. She always wanted proof that life has meaning or that we're not alone in the universe.

I push off my vehicle and reach my hand out when the store clerk is close enough. "I'm London, by the way."

"Quinn," he says, giving it a shake. Then, he takes up the spot beside me and leans his back against my truck. "Still no sign of them, huh?"

"Not yet. But I'm patient," I offer with a smirk.

"I can see that," Quinn says. When I turn to look at him, he wiggles his eyebrows.

I narrow my gaze but let that one go. Instead, I take a step back and lean against my door, crossing my feet at the ankles and arms over my torso.

"So, shouldn't you be in the store? Are you going to get into trouble being out here with me?" I ask. It's not that I dislike his company, I just don't want him getting fired over it.

"Store's empty." He shrugs. "And since the only way in is through that there door, I'm pretty sure I'll know when duty calls."

"Fair enough." I shift my gaze back to the bookstore and grin.

"What's your game plan?" Quinn asks after a few minutes of comfortable silence.

I snicker softly and turn to face him. "What do you mean?"

He huffs like I've insulted his intelligence. "I *mean*, when Lily walks out of there, what are you going to do?"

I stare at him for a beat, taking in the seriousness of his light brown eyes. "I mean, I guess I just thought I'd see what she's doing after. Maybe we would grab a bite to eat. You know?"

His eyebrows rise until they vanish into his curly white hair. "Like a *date?*"

"No, not like a date. Like two friends grabbing some dinner," I fire back.

He crosses his arms over his chest and shakes his head. "She'll freak."

A sensation not dissimilar to panic claws at my insides. "You think?"

"Hell yeah," he breathes. "First of all, she'll feel pressured because you're calling her out in front of the Dirty

B's and they're gonna want a show. Vivian alone will make a scene. Second, she won't want to let you, or anyone else, down so she's gonna be torn on what to do. Third—"

I hold up a hand. "I get it. She'll freak. So, what do I do?"

"Before I agree to help, I need to know your motivations. I can't work my magic if I don't know what your end goal is." His lips press tight and he watches me the way my grandma would when she thought I was about to lie.

I sigh, glancing from him, to the door of the bookshop, and back again. "I don't know. I haven't seen her in so long. I just want to get to know her again, I guess."

"You know she's married, right?"

I nod. "Yeah."

"So, this isn't a sexy Alpha male making a move on her while her husband's away kind of thing?"

The shit this guy comes out with.

I shake my head, trying not to laugh. "No."

"Shame," he murmurs, his shoulder falling limp. "She needs a little Alpha male in her life."

A strange part of me can't help but feel ridiculously happy about that statement.

"Are you saying she's not happy in her marriage?" I ask, trying to step lightly. I don't want her unhappy, but that would be good information to know.

"Honey, she hasn't been happy for a very long time." Quinn swipes his hand through the air between us.

"Why not?" I turn to face him now, wanting to hear more.

Quinn follows suit and turns to face me. "Between you and me, Seth—*her husband*—is gone a lot. He cares more for his job than anything else."

"What does he do?"

"He's some big-shot travel blogger. Travels, like, nonstop." Quinn rolls his eyes.

"You don't like him?" I ask, probably overstepping, but it slips out.

"Seth's fine. I mean, as far as human beings go, he isn't terrible. I just think Lily's lonely and deserves better than she's admitting to herself."

"Why doesn't Lily travel with him?"

"I think she did in the beginning. But it's hard to run a successful event coordination business when you're never in town to coordinate the events." He shoots me a pointed stare. "Lily is an independent woman who still wants to make her own mark. The last thing she wants to be is just arm candy for some travel influencer, however adorable she might be."

I tip my chin. "Makes sense."

Lily never was someone who would sit idly by. She was always full of enthusiasm—chasing one interest, then another.

Quinn watches me for a moment, then offers, "Let me do the inviting. Once they realize you're here, the girls will want to chat you up. Well, more like interrogate you ... All the good stuff. Once the other B's go, I'll invite her to dinner at Fitger's. I'm closing up soon anyway. Then,

I'll invite you, too. She won't feel crazy pressured because I'll be there as a buffer—and the invitee."

I scratch the side of my right eyebrow. "That's actually ... not a terrible idea."

He feigns being heartbroken. "Are you kidding? It's brilliant."

I laugh at his confidence. "You're not wrong. So, will you stay the whole time or—"

"I'll read the room." He smirks at me. "If it seems like the two of you are in the clear, I'll make up an excuse to go."

"You don't have—" I begin.

Just then, the doors to the bookstore open, and out stumble five slightly tipsy women. They're all chatting amongst themselves, without a care in the world.

Of course, Lily holds my attention in the back, as she leans against a shorter woman with red hair and wraps her arms around her.

My heart hammers in my chest and I take a big inhalation to try to tame it.

"Showtime," Quinn says under his breath. He bumps me with his shoulder. "Don't freak her out."

"I'll try not to," I whisper, swallowing hard.

"And remember, you throw me under the bus and I'll return the favor tenfold," he hisses in my ear right before he plasters on a big grin and calls out, "Ladies! Which book boyfriend do I need to fall in love with this week?"

"Quinn—" the group of women croon in unison.

"*Oooh,* who's your friend?" a tall blond asks when her gaze lands on me. She's dressed in skin-tight teal leggings and a top that looks like it was picked out of Rebecca's wardrobe.

Quinn turns back to me and extends his right arm. "Actually, this is Lily's friend, London."

The entire group pauses to give me a solid once over before exchanging a significant glance with one another. The look they share is something I can't quite decipher, so I'm hoping like hell it's not a bad thing.

Lily breaks from the group of women and walks toward us. "London, what are you doing here?" Her voice is breathy and I have to force myself not to glance at her chest when I notice she's breathing heavily.

"Oh, he came in to talk to me," Quinn says, cutting me off. "Had to rave about the sexy stir sticks. Right, London?"

I blink hard, but find myself nodding in agreement. "Yeah."

Despite the fact I still haven't pranked Myles with them yet, I'm hoping Quinn has a reason for the misdirect.

Lily's face flushes and she glances down. "Oh."

I step forward, not wanting to disappoint her. "I was hoping I'd run into you, too, though."

Quinn shoots me a look of annoyance and mouths, *Freak out!*

"Sorry to be the first to bail on what's clearly about to be an awkward situation, but I have an episode of the *Last of Us* that's calling my name. I've been dying inside all week and must have the unresolved questions answered," the Korean woman says, jabbing her thumb over her shoulder. She doesn't wait for recognition from the other women before she saunters away with her face glued to her phone.

"Lily, I think you should introduce us," the tall black woman standing on the other side of Lily declares. Dressed in an off-white designer blouse, paired with navy dress slacks and heels too high for most women, she has an air of importance about her.

For all I know, she could be a senator or something.

Lily presses her fingertips to her forehead. "Oh, sorry. Of course. Everyone, as you know, this is London." Her dark eyes search mine for a beat. There's a curiosity and fire in those brown orbs that I wish I could read. She clears her throat and twists around. "London, this is Carlie, Vivian, Tasia—and the one about to run into a light pole is Anna."

She points to the redhead first, then the blond, the senator woman, and the Korean who's no longer in sight.

I raise a hand, feeling entirely too self-conscious as I wave. "Hi."

"So, London ... Lily tells us you used to be best friends," the blond—Vivian, if I remember right—declares.

I nod. "Yeah, it was a long time ago."

"It was nice to meet you, London. But I need to head back, too." The redhead says. She smiles in my direction, then turns around and gives Lily a hug. It looks like she whispers something in her ear, but I don't catch a word of it.

"Bye, Carlie. Call me later, okay?" Lily says when they separate, her cheeks slightly more pink.

"You bet," she says with a wink. "Bye, everyone."

"Bye, sweets," Quinn calls after her, crooking his index finger and wiggling it in goodbye.

"So, Quinn, are you locking up? Looks like a slow night," the senator woman asks.

"Yeah, I think so, Tash. It's been dead since seven," he says with a shrug. "I guess everyone's all kinked out for the night."

"Guess so." She smiles. "Come on, Viv. Why don't you help me out inside?"

The blond turns back to Tasia as if she just asked her to light her hair on fire.

Tasia's eyes widen and she tips her head toward Dirty Deeds.

"But I wanted to learn more about—" Vivian protests.

Lily springs to action, taking Vivian by her shoulders and pointing her toward the door. "No, I think Tasia's right. She needs your help."

"But I—" she complains.

Before she can continue, Tasia is sweeping Vivian into the building next door.

"Nice to meet you, London," Tasia calls back before the door closes.

Quinn rolls his eyes, then turns to Lily and says, "Hey, Lily, I'm starved. You up for a little Fitger's?"

"Well, I—" Her apprehensive gaze meets mine before she turns back to Quinn. "I probably *should* eat. Anna brought her favorite wine and I think I had four glasses. The stuff was good."

"Okay, cool. Let me go close up shop and I'll drive. Sadly, I haven't had a drop," he mutters, then holds out a hand like a stop sign. "Hang out here with London until I get back."

Without waiting for her response, he turns around and walks back to the store. I gotta hand it to him, he's smooth.

Lily turns to face me, then takes a deep breath. "So..."

"So," I repeat. "We meet again."

She laughs softly, then drops her gaze. "Sorry, I haven't—"

"No need to be sorry. I'm sure you're busy."

She scratches at the spot behind her ear. "I wish I could say that's my reason. I just—"

"Feel awkward?" I offer.

She nods, then lifts her eyes to meet mine. "Yeah, sorta."

"It's okay. It's fuckin' weird. I get it." I shrug.

A broad smile cracks across her features, lighting up her whole face. "It really is. It's not that I'm not happy to see you—I totally am. It's just been so long."

"Right?" *Eighteen years, two months, and eleven days. But who's counting?*

Quinn practically skips his way from the store over to us. "My night has officially been made. Tasia offered to close up for me. Ready?"

"Oh, yeah," Lily says, nodding in agreement. However, I notice her hesitation.

"Tasia works at Dirty Deeds?" I blurt out, surprised that the senator woman would work for a place like that.

Quinn full-on snickers. "No, cupcake. She *owns* it."

My eyebrows rise. Now that sorta makes sense.

"London, what are you doing right now? Did you want to join us?" Quinn asks with a gigantic grin.

"I'm, uh," I hedge. Should I say I'm free? Or should I try to play it cool?

Relief flashes through Lily's features and she reaches out to touch my arm. "Yeah, please come. It would be great to catch up."

Despite wearing a coat, my arm is hyperaware of how her hand clings to it.

"I don't want to intrude," I say, opting for playing it cool, when everything in me is screaming *hell yes, I'll come.*

"Nonsense. The more the merrier," Quinn beams. He's pretty damn proud of himself for his puppeteering mastermind.

I nod. "All right. As long as I'm not intruding, I'd love to join you. Did you both want to just ride with me? My car's right here." I point at the vehicle behind me.

"Catch a ride in an Escalade? Yes, *please*," Quinn says, not giving Lily a chance to pick a different option. He opens the rear passenger side door and is already inside before I can turn back to Lily.

Lily just laughs. "I guess that's a yes, then."

I nod, following her to the passenger side, so I can open her door for her. She smiles at me, then takes her seat.

When I close the door, I take a few deep breaths and I walk around the back of the truck, rather than the front so no one can witness my mini-panic attack.

My heart is thundering in my chest and I'm about to break into a cold sweat, but I got what I wanted. Lily's in my vehicle and we're gonna have dinner.

Quinn isn't just brilliant. He's a *goddamn genius.*

CHAPTER 7

London

"Y ou're kidding me?" Quinn says, cough-laughing into his napkin. "Lily was a ten-year-old *conspiracy theorist?*"

Lily rolls her eyes. "It wasn't *that* bad."

I try really hard to keep a straight face, but I can't seem to manage it.

She was a *borderline* conspiracy theorist. She was convinced that aliens had been here before. We just didn't have proof. Or if we did, we just didn't know it when we were looking at it.

"Oh, that's just too good," Quinn responds through fits of giggles.

Lily picks up her napkin and throws it across the table at me. "Thanks a lot, *you.*"

I catch it in mid-air, grinning like a goddamn Cheshire Cat.

I haven't had this much fun in years. *Hell, maybe ever.*

I can't even complain about having Quinn along for the ride. He's managed to buffer the awkwardness between Lily and me and encourage a more natural conversation when things started to feel weird.

"Yeah, well, he's a Trekkie," Lily fires back, jabbing her index finger in my direction.

I narrow my gaze. "Ignore her. She's clearly had one too many margaritas."

She glances down, noticing her second strawberry margarita is nearly gone. "Shit, where did it go?"

"You *drank it,* hon. You're clearly a tequila whore. If I find you laughing at the ceiling fans, I'm going to pawn you off to the nearest alien," Quinn quips, bumping her left shoulder with his right.

She snorts into her empty margarita.

Quinn insisted he sit on her side. I only found out after she went to the bathroom that it was so she could focus on me better without cranking her neck sideways to get a look at me.

I wish I had a Quinn in my life. All I have are asshole friends. Don't get me wrong, I'd take a bullet for every single one of them. But if they had heard Lily say I was a Trekkie at ten, I'd never live it down. I'd have to change my name and move to a different state.

Lily reaches out, grabs another chip, and dips it in her remaining guacamole. Despite having a Fiesta Burrito the size of her head, she's still devouring the homemade corn chips from Mexico Lindo.

I kinda love that. She's not afraid to eat in front of me—or Quinn.

"Well, shit," Quinn mutters, glancing down at his watch. "Is that *the time?*"

I glance at my own watch, surprised like hell when the time is closing in on eleven.

"Holy," I blurt, surprised I haven't gotten any irate messages from Myles. Either she's pissed, or it's been too busy for her to realize I'm still gone.

Quinn turns to Lily and pats her on the shoulder. "Sorry, sweetie, but I need to get back home. I'm supposed to take Ma to the doctor in the morning."

Lily's eyes widen and she drops the chip she was bringing to her mouth. "Oh, I'm so sorry. I didn't realize—"

She makes a move to get up, but Quinn presses her back down in her seat. "Sit, *stay*. You don't have to leave on my part." He turns to glance in my direction and shoots me a wink.

"Don't you need a ride home?" I ask, wanting to make sure we're not putting him out.

He waves off my concern. "Nope. I live a block and a half away on East First Street."

"Are you sure? I don't mind—" I begin, but stop when I get a death glare from him.

"*Totally* sure," Quinn grounds out, exaggerating the words. He scoots out of the booth, then plants a knee where he'd just been sitting, so he can lean in and press a kiss to the top of Lily's head. "Have fun. Don't do anything I wouldn't do."

I swear Lily's cheeks flush. "That doesn't leave much."

He grins slyly. "I know."

With that, she bends forward, taking another sip of her nonexistent drink.

"Bye, London. It was lovely to meet you. I trust you can get our girl here back home?"

I nod, suddenly extremely nervous about this endeavor. "Yeah, totally."

"Good." He seems pleased as he turns to go.

"It was great to get to know you, man," I call after him.

"Back atcha, Tiger." With that, he walks off toward the door.

Both Lily and I watch him go, but when he's gone, we turn back to each other a little less comfortable than we were a moment ago. I don't want this evening to end, but I don't know how to continue either.

"So," I say, by way of my brilliant conversational skills.

Lily picks up her discarded chip and digs it into the guac. "So."

I clear my throat and point to her nearly empty glass. "Did you want another drink?"

She thinks on it for a moment and shakes her head. "You know, I better not."

"Okay," I respond, my word close to a whisper as I reach out and spin my glass of water. The ring from condensation makes it rotate easily.

Just when I'm sure she's about to pull the plug, she asks, "So, you haven't really talked much about yourself. Did you go to college?"

A wave of relief washes over me and I lean back in the booth. "No, never quite made it that far. I ended up working for a nightclub in Colorado Springs. From there, I hopped around, learning the club scene. I'm a manager of one now."

"Ah, you like your nightlife, huh?" she says with a smug grin.

I narrow my gaze. "I guess. Why?"

"Remember how many nights we'd pretend to go to bed, then sneak out of our houses so we could stare at the stars for hours and hours?" Her brown eyes sparkle as she holds my gaze.

"Yeah, I remember." My heart thumps unevenly at the memories that float to mind. They were some of the best in my life.

"Most nights, we were up until at least ... *ten,*" she giggles.

"More like ten-thirty, for sure." I laugh, scratching at the side of my eyebrow with the back of my thumb.

There were so many nights where I'd stay up, fighting the siren call of sleep just so I could be close to her. She always had a way of making the night feel spellbinding. Like everything *really was magical*—and not in the Rebecca kinda way.

"It just seems fitting that you'd find a job that lets you stay awake into the night," she whispers, dropping her gaze to the table.

I take a deep breath and drop my own gaze.

She's kinda wrong there. It was never about my

innate desire to stay awake. Not then and definitely not now.

In fact, it never occurred to me until this very moment why I really chose this line of work. It's so I can fill the void in the loneliest hours of my day.

I blink the realization away.

"Uh, so Quinn mentioned you're an event coordinator," I say, trying to steer the conversation to my ulterior motive. "How do you like that?"

She chews on the side of her lip, and the movement draws my attention. The scar above her upper lip is barely visible and it makes me wonder if she ever had more surgeries for her cleft lip and palate.

Not that I'd bring it up.

She had always been so scared about the ones looming in her future. Back then, I would have done anything to trade places with her so she didn't have to go through with them.

"It's fine," she finally offers.

I quirk an eyebrow. "Just fine?"

She eyes her empty cup and sighs. "Yeah, just fine."

It's obvious things are *not* fine. But I don't know how much I should pry.

"I bet *you* went to college," I say, redirecting things for now.

She nods. "Yeah, UMD. I studied business. I always knew I wanted to be an entrepreneur. I just didn't expect it to be so ..." her voice trails off.

I don't know if she's thinking about her husband and wishing she was traveling. Or if it's something else.

"Hard?" I offer, hoping it's the right choice.

Again, she sighs. "Yeah. *Really* hard." Her eyes meet mine and there's a glassy quality that wasn't there before.

"Shit, I don't mean to upset you—" I say, suddenly feeling like an ass.

She swallows hard. "No, it's not you. I think it's—it's just the drinks. I should have stopped after two." In a movement so quick, she swipes at her cheek.

I could kick myself. Of course, this is a sore subject. Quinn all but told me that it was a contention in her marriage and that his traveling put a strain on her business.

Lily takes a moment to compose herself. "I just really expected things to be easier. I mean, I went to business school. I *know* what I'm doing. But it turns out, I suck at marketing and finding clients. It's hard to dazzle them with my event planning skills when they won't even give me a chance."

I watch her movements, the way the corners of her mouth tip downward and her shoulders slump. She looks like a defeated woman and it makes me wonder what's caused this in her.

Even when things didn't make sense, she was always the kid who would dig in until she figured it all out. She'd never wave a white flag in defeat. I hate seeing her like this.

"You know, I could really use an event planner," I say tentatively.

This wasn't the way I wanted to ask her—like I'm

doing her a favor—but I'd do just about anything to shift her into a better place.

She eyes me with a hint of curiosity and skepticism. "Are you just saying that?"

I chuckle softly. "Not even a little bit."

Lily watches me for a few beats, her eyes surveying me like she can assess my truthfulness simply by scanning me up and down. Finally, her curiosity must win out, because she says, "What kind of an event?"

I lick my lower lip, trying to decide how much I can tell her. My boss, Noah, will expect me to follow protocol, and that will mean bringing her back to Nocté to sign an NDA.

I clear my throat and hedge, "It's a sort of dinner party."

"A dinner party?" she asks, sitting up straighter. "At a *nightclub?*"

I press my lips together. Yup, walked right into that.

I scratch the back of my neck. "It's complicated."

She looks enthralled now, though, as she crosses her arms on the table and leans forward. But the one rule I promised myself I wouldn't do slips as I drop my eyes to her cleavage, barely visible from the v-neck of her shirt.

Shifting in my seat, I wait for her to ask another question because I don't trust myself not to lay everything bare.

"You don't know, do you? You're totally lying to make me feel better," she huffs, leaning back.

I breathe a sigh of relief to no longer have the view down her shirt. "No, I know more. It's just ... I would need to have you sign an NDA before I can describe it fully. My boss would kick my ass."

She narrows her eyes and damn near pouts. For the briefest of moments, it reminds me of Rebecca—only it looks so much more adorable on her.

"All right, I'm in. When can I sign the NDA?" she proclaims, holding her chin up.

"Tomorrow, if you want. I'm in the office by three —" I say, fighting my surprise and elation.

She runs her left hand in her hair and twirls the ends of it for a moment. A serious expression takes over her face and she nods. "I can make three work. What night-club are we talking about here?"

I fight back the smile threatening to summon the angels in heaven to sing their songs of joy. "Club Nocté."

"Where's that?" she asks, her eyebrows pulling in.

I can almost see her flipping through the Rolodex in her brain, trying to figure out where we're located. I'm not surprised that she came up empty.

"It's in Superior. Give me your phone. I'll put the address into your contacts," I say, outstretching my hand and flicking my fingertips at her.

She looks appalled. "I know how to add contacts into my own phone."

"Are you sure you can type after two margaritas and four glasses of wine?" I shoot her a pointed stare that could rival the ones Cal gives me.

She makes a show of flicking open her phone and pressing on the screen. But after a moment, her eyes narrow and her expression turns serious.

Then she drops her head and extends her hand to me without a word.

I chuckle under my breath and type in the details, including my direct line. I also take a moment to add my personal contact info, including my home address, into her phone.

Just in case.

CHAPTER 8

Lily

"What do you *mean* you can't come with me?" I practically channel Vivian as I whine, ready to throw a full-on temper tantrum.

It's not often I ask for help, so when I do, it means I really need it. Tasia knows that.

I lean forward clutching at the glass counter of Dirty Books as if it might help me get a different answer out of her.

Tasia gives me her best WTF expression and sweeps her arms out. "I'm working, darling. As much as I love you, I still need to pay the bills."

"I *know*," I drawl. "But I can't go alone."

For whatever reason, I don't feel like I can trust myself alone with London. There's a strange kind of energy in the air whenever I'm with him and I don't know what it means. I just know I like it way more than I should.

Besides, I haven't told Seth about him yet. I don't

even know how to bring him up, to be honest. Had Quinn not been the instigator of things last night, there's no way they would have turned out the way they did.

As it is, I can't believe I said yes to helping London with this dinner event. It must have been the margaritas talking because it's *bonkers*.

I should not be working for my former best friend who has a way of making me feel like a confused, horny teenager.

"Do you bring a friend to all of your work meetings?" Tasia asks slowly blinking at me. "If so, I think we may have put our finger on the lack of client signups."

Tasia has bright, metallic purple eyeshadow on today and lipstick that practically matches. Every time she blinks, I'm dazzled by the sparkle in it. It looks awesome with the purple sweater she's sporting and a wave of self-consciousness washes over me. There's no chance I could ever pull something like that off. Yet, somehow, she makes it seem like nothing less than that will do.

I glance down at my plain, blue button-up and black plaid slacks and shudder. I look like a third-grade teacher.

I tap the edge of the counter with all of my fingertips. "No, of course not."

Tasia just arches a shaped eyebrow.

"Maybe I should cancel," I blurt out. Besides the weird vibes, the last thing I need to do is turn up looking like I should be escorting a nine-year-old to the bathroom.

I mean, I want to make a good impression, too.

What was I thinking when I dressed in this outfit?

Tasia narrows her gaze and crosses her arms over her torso. "He's really getting under your skin, isn't he?"

My eyes snap to hers. "What's that supposed to mean?"

"It means," she begins, drawing out the words, "you're not usually this neurotic. A little nutty, sure. But this is a bit much. What's going on in that head of yours?"

So many of the emotions I've been trying to tamp down bubble up.

My eyelids flutter as I try not to cry. Instead, I take a deep breath through my nose and whisper, "I don't know."

But I do know. *Sorta.*

"You were supposed to have coffee with him two weeks ago," she presses.

"I know," I murmur, still looking at the ceiling so I don't let the tears threatening to spill over loose.

"You said you had a great time last night," she continues.

"I know. *I did.*"

"Quinn loves him already." Tasia laughs. "He couldn't stop gushing about how much fun he had last night with the two of you. He's practically adopted London."

I snicker under my breath. "It was a lot of fun."

"So, what is it? What's going on?"

He looks really good and I don't know why that's getting to me. He's funny and gets along with Quinn—who is notoriously hard to please. He has tattoos and they're oddly hot, even though tattoos have never been my thing. I want to know what they all mean. And he makes me feel ... things. Things I have no right to be feeling as a married woman. And, oh yeah, I suck.

I take another deep breath and meet her confused expression. Holding it for a moment, I finally confess, "Being with London feels different than being around other guys—*clients.* We have a history, and I don't know what Seth would think."

"You haven't talked to him about London?" Tasia prompts gently.

I point my index finger at her. "Very astute."

"Well, you're just friends. Right? I don't see why Seth would care." She narrows her eyes. "Unless there's some reason he *should* be worried."

I break out into a cold sweat.

All of the Dirty B's have been very vocal about their feelings about my marriage. While they don't think Seth is Satan or anything, they think we've grown apart.

They're not wrong. It's just—I wasn't ready to give up on things yet. But maybe it's because I didn't have a reason to really question it.

"No—I mean, I don't know. *Maybe?*" I whisper.

The whites around her dark brown irises appear. "Maybe?"

"I don't know what it is about him, Tash. When I'm with him, there's this weird buzz of energy in the room. I'm feeling *things*—things I haven't felt in a really long time. Maybe since the last time I was *with him*. I don't know what any of it means and the last thing I want to do is put myself into a situation I might regret," I say by way of word vomit.

She watches me intensely and I expect her to tell me *I only live once*. Or that I should follow the signs my body's giving me—because, let's face it, Tasia is a rebel when it comes to all things sex and relationships.

Instead, she asks, "Have you asked Anna to go with you?"

My lips shift to the side and I nod. "Yeah, but she's working on a new app for a client and she's on deadline. So ..."

Tasia nods. "So, she can't go."

"Nope."

"Maybe you should try Carlie. She works from home, too," Tasia offers, clearly doing her best to help me out.

However, while I might be new at this whole panic over a guy thing, it did occur to me to ask the Dirty B's who work flexible hours before trying to arm-wrestle Tasia into it.

"She can't come. Something about seeing a nutritionist this afternoon at St. Mary's," I mutter, shaking my head. I can't believe none of my friends can help me when I'm clearly going to implode.

"What about—"

I glance up and glare at her. "If you were going to say Vivian, I swear—"

"What about me?"

Like a ghost ready to haunt me at a moment's notice, Vivian is suddenly behind me.

I practically scream. Incredibly ladylike of me, I know.

"I, uh—" I hedge, trying to figure out what to say and how long she's been standing there. Did she hear the whole conversation?

Dear god, tell me she didn't.

I'll never hear the end of it.

If she did, she doesn't give me any signs.

When I turn back around, Tasia gives me *the look.*

You know, the one that says, *'You're out of options, Lily. Don't be so picky.'*

I heave out a sigh and turn to face Vivian. As much as I hate to admit it, beggars can't be choosers. And right now, I'm definitely ready to grovel on my knees.

I plaster on a big smile and ground out, "I'm looking for someone to come with me to a club in Superior. Are you"—I swallow hard—"*free?*"

Warning bells are going off in my head, screaming, *'Danger, Will Robinson, Danger!'* But it's too late to back out now.

"Flower, I never took you as a mid-day partier," Vivian says, laying her mock-surprise on thick.

At least, *I hope* it's mock-surprise.

Truthfully, with the way she's staring at me, it could be genuine.

I laugh uncomfortably. "No, I have a client I need to meet at three and I just don't want to go alone. I thought maybe you'd like to join me."

Tasia shoots me a sideways glance, but thankfully, doesn't say anything. Then, she turns to a small stack of books beside the cash register, flipping through them one at a time. Evidently, she's openly eavesdropping on the rest of this conversation.

"Which club is it?" Vivian asks, drawing my attention back to her.

I clear my throat. "Um, Club Nocté?"

I don't know why I say it like it's a question. But when you're as far out of the club scene as I am, it's hard to be sure if I'm even saying it right.

God, I feel like a grandma. Maybe I should go with my Bingo stamper and walking cane. That should be enough of a buffer, right?

Vivian claps in front of her chest making her boobs practically bounce out of their holsters. "Oh, I've been wanting to go to Nocté! This is perfect. I kept trying to get Jordan to go, but we were always too busy having sex to make it happen."

I blow out a puff of air and turn back to Tasia, trying hard not to make a face. Deep down, I know that wasn't a dig at me, but it felt like it anyway.

Tasia reaches out and places her left hand over mine.

Of all the Dirty B's, she knows how hard all of this has been on me.

For a moment, I think about telling Vivian to forget it. That I'm a grown woman and I can do hard things. But then I remember the magnetic pull that kept threatening to take me over last night.

Maybe it was all of the alcohol, but after Quinn left, being around London made me feel so nostalgic for those nights staring at the stars with him.

We would talk about all sorts of things—big things, little things. It always felt like we could solve the world's biggest mysteries in those late hours.

I didn't realize how much I missed that kind of connection until last night. When he dropped me off, I almost asked him to join me in my backyard to stargaze.

Thankfully, I sobered up enough to come to my senses.

There's no way I should have asked another man over to stargaze in my backyard when my husband's away on a work trip. I'm sure that goes against our wedding vows somewhere.

If nothing else, it sends the wrong message.

"Well, wanna come with me? I leave in—*oh, geez,*" I double-take at the clock behind Tasia's head. "Is it already two-thirty?"

"Yup," Tasia says without even checking the clock.

"Now," I spin back around to Vivian. "I'm leaving *now.*"

Vivian shrugs. "Sure. I was just helping Tasia design the new alcove, but I think I've got all the specs to get started."

I throw a look over my shoulder at Tasia. She swore she wasn't letting Vivian at the alcove. Her words were, and I quote, *'Over my dead Black ass.'*

Tash just shrugs. "She's doing it for free as long as I give her a testimonial. I figured why not? Now, stop worrying about what I'm doing and focus on what *you* need to do." She gives me a pointed look.

My heart hammers in my chest and I take a deep

breath, trying to calm down. But the more I think about it—going to see London and now having to bring Vivian—the more I freak.

"Come on, Flower. Want me to drive?" Vivian asks, oblivious to my crisis state.

I barely register myself as nodding.

She takes me by the hand and leads me out the door in a haze, chatting away, even though I have no clue what she's saying.

"You'll be fine, Lily. Take a deep breath and relax," Tash calls out before the door closes behind us.

"Relax," I repeat, following Vivian to her pink BMW.

Oh yeah. Easier said than done.

CHAPTER 9

London

"You look fuckin' sick," Cal says as he drops into his usual spot on the other side of my desk. "And I don't mean in the dope kinda way, either."

"I feel sick," I admit, glancing up at him.

Last night went better than I could have imagined. Even with Quinn there, dinner with Lily made me realize how much I've missed in her life.

She's still the same, quirky girl she was as a kid—but she's also got a layer of hurt that wasn't there before. It's hiding just beneath the surface of who she wants everyone to believe she is, but I can feel it like it's a palpable thing.

I can't help but wonder how it got put there and whose ass I need to kick.

"What's up?" he asks, leaning back and crossing his right leg over his left knee.

There's no point in hiding things. Lily's due to arrive any minute now.

I level my gaze and force a sigh from my nose. "She's on her way here."

He snickers. "She?"

I continue to hold my expression.

Cal drops his leg and sits up straighter. "Are we talking about ..."

"Yes. Fucksake, *yes*. Who the hell else would I be talking about?" I fire back.

"Shit," he says, sounding impressed. "Explains why you've got a stick shoved up your ass."

"Great. Wonderful. Glad life's mysteries have all congealed in your brain." I pinch the bridge of my nose, trying to force my nerves to settle.

"Why's she comin' here?" Cal presses.

I lick my lower lip and laugh under my breath. "She's a fucking event planner if you can believe it. And I need one to plan this damn event Noah wants us to do."

His eyebrows fly up, then he shifts forward in his seat, pressing his palms over his knees. "Hang the fuck on. You're telling me you've finally connected with this girl after *two decades of pining* and your first thought is to hire her? You realize how nuts that is, right?"

I lower my eyebrows and hold up my middle finger. "First, I wasn't pining. Second, it wasn't my *first* thought. It just kinda worked out."

"In what universe is that working out?" Cal responds.

I swallow hard and scratch the back of my head. "It seemed like a good idea at the time."

He blows out a puff of air and shakes his head.

"Look, I get the whole '*I wanna spend time with her*' thing that was probably going through your mind here. But you realize that if she comes on board, she'll have to be brought up to speed on—"

"I know," I cut him off, pressing my fingertips to the center of my forehead and spreading them out. It does fuck-all for easing the tension. "Trust me, I haven't been able to think about anything else."

"Do you think she'll back out if she knows?" Cal asks, narrowing his gaze.

I shrug, despite my heart taking a plummet. "Honestly, no clue."

The worst, though, would be if she saw me differently because of it—and not in a good way.

There are so many ways this thing could go tits up, but none of them mattered when it was all just hypothetical. Now that she's agreed to sign the NDA, the reality of it feels like a swift kick to the balls.

Great, now I feel sick again.

Myles knocks on my doorframe and steps into the room. "Saint, there are two ladies at the door asking for you. One of them says she has an appointment. Want me to let them in?"

Two ladies?

I shift my gaze to Cal just in time to see him take a deep breath.

Fuck. If he's nervous, it might just be the start of the goddamn apocalypse.

I nod and stand up, fiddling with the cuffs of my shirt. When they suddenly feel too stuffy down, I end up rolling them up to my elbows. "Yeah, yeah. Let 'em in. I'll be right there."

"On it." She spins on her heel, vanishing down the hallway.

"I sure as hell hope you know what you're doing," Cal offers with a skeptical look.

Doubtful.

I step around my desk and pat him on the shoulder as I pass. "Thanks for the vote of confidence, man."

When I get into the hallway, I close my eyes and take a deep breath to level myself.

Don't fuck this up, London.

Before I can open my eyes, Cal shifts past me. "Don't keep her waiting. You've done enough of that."

"She's married, Cal," I fire back.

"And?" he asks, spinning around and walking the hallway backward.

I throw my arms up in exasperation.

He narrows one eye and grins. "But you're *not* pining."

My eyebrows tug in as I watch him retreat down the hallway. When he's gone, I take another deep breath and make my way into the club, proper.

It looks totally different this time of day. Without the neon lights that paint the space bright colors and a mass of bodies gyrating to music, it looks way too big for the bar on the far end.

Lily is standing against the bar talking with Myles. She's dressed in a beautiful blue shirt, with form-fitting black plaid dress slacks. Definitely more formal than last night after her book club, but it suits her.

Sitting on a stool next to her is the blond from last night—Veronica, I think?

Shit, I suck with names.

I'll just call her *V.* Seems pretty safe.

"Hey, ladies," I say, walking up behind them, and giving Myles a quick nod.

Myles eyes me suspiciously, but thankfully, she knows when to keep her mouth shut.

Unlike Cal.

Lily spins around, her light brown hair fanning out in the motion. For a split second, I'm mesmerized by the way the golden lights of the bar make the blond streaks in her hair sparkle.

"London, *hi.*" Her voice is breathless and it stirs my insides.

"*Oooh,*" V says when she turns around and notices me. I'm not sure what that's all about, but I hope like hell it's not bad.

After holding my gaze for a moment, Lily turns to indicate V. "I hope you don't mind. I brought Vivian with me. She really wanted to see Nocté."

Ah, Vivian. Not Veronica, then.

There's something in the way she moves—kind of fidgety—that makes me think that's only part of the story.

"Sure, no problem. Do you ladies want a quick tour?" I ask, hoping that going through the motions of a tour will iron out the rest of my own nerves. But at this point, who the fuck knows?

Vivian practically jumps off her bar stool. "I'd love a tour."

"Sure." Lily nods, smiling softly.

I tip my head. "Well, you've already seen the bar," I say, swiping my hand toward Myles and her station. I turn around, pointing at the large stage on top of the platform. "That's where the DJ performs his magic every night. Obviously, the rest of this space is the main level of the club."

"I love the semicircular seating," Vivian says, walking over to one of the lounge areas. "The sequence cushions are a nice touch. I bet they look amazing when the lights are going."

"Vivian's an interior designer," Lily offers.

"Ah." I grin. That explains her friend's interest in the furniture.

We walk around the rest of the space, letting Vivian evaluate the design aesthetics. Based on the way she gushes about it, she approves.

"What's up there?" Lily asks, pointing to the black-out windows on the upper level.

"VIP rooms," I respond. It's usually enough to keep people from asking too many questions.

There are eleven large rooms in all that overlook the main club on either side of the building. However, they're definitely more exclusive than just VIPs.

"Ooooh, I want to see," Vivian says, clapping.

I shake my head. "Sorry, against club rules. They're invite-only."

"We can't even *see* them?" Vivian asks, aghast as she presses her fingertips to her clavicle.

I shake my head. "Sorry."

As much as that's gonna sting—I also know it adds to the mystique that Club Nocté represents. She'll get over it—and probably be curious as hell. Which is exactly what we want.

Vivian's face falls but she nods.

"So, Lily," I say, turning to her. "Do you want to join me in my office? We can go over the details for this event."

She inhales sharply as she turns to me. "Yeah. Okay."

"Vivian, feel free to hang out with Myles. She'll take care of you. Drinks are on the house," I offer, pointing toward the bar.

Vivian's blue eyes brighten. "I'll never turn down free drinks."

She sashays off leaving Lily and me standing awkwardly in the middle of the dance floor.

"So, wanna ..." I make a feeble attempt at pointing toward the direction of my office.

"Yeah, yeah," she responds, nodding and extending her hand.

I take the lead, making my way to the inconspicuous door hidden behind an enormous velvet curtain. With the keycard in hand, I swipe it and open the door to the hallway. I hold it open and let her step inside before I close it.

"I'm this way," I say, pointing to the other end. Stepping out in front again, I lead the way to my office, trying to tame the pounding in my chest.

Lily doesn't say anything. She just clasps her hands in front of her body and follows after me.

When we reach my door, it's the only one in the hallway that's wide open. Light cascades into the black-painted hallway from my window and the LED overhead lighting.

"Come on in. Have a seat," I say, standing by the open door and sweeping my hand inside.

She smiles at me and walks by, wafting the scent of her perfume as she does so. It's a subtle mix of lavender and vanilla and despite myself, I commit it to memory.

I give myself a count of three before following into the room.

She takes the seat Cal typically chooses and I walk around to the other side of the desk, relieved to have a buffer between us.

"So, before I can really discuss anything about this event, I need you to sign this NDA," I say, picking up the stack of papers I printed out earlier.

She swallows hard and nods. "Sure."

I extend the papers to her and she accepts them, her gaze immediately falling to the writing as she leans back and gets comfortable.

A grin plays at my lips.

Of course, she's going to read them.

There's not a lot of people who actually take the time to read the NDA in its entirety. Most of the time, when we offer a position, they're more than happy to just sign so they can finally get more information about Nocté.

Rebecca was the last hire I offered the NDA to and she didn't even bat an eyelash to review. She just signed. I'm fairly certain she still has no idea what really goes on up there since I never felt the need to fill her in.

"This says that I'm not even allowed to discuss Nocté with my spouse or friends," she says, flipping the page.

"That's right," I say, nodding.

Her lips press tightly and I wonder what she's thinking. Does she usually tell her spouse everything? And if so, will keeping Nocté under wraps be a problem?

"I can't even allude to what I'm doing here?" She says it like a question, but she keeps reading, clearly not expecting an answer.

My pulse thrums in my ears, making it impossible to think of anything but the blood rushing through my goddamn body. I shift in my seat, letting her read.

When she reaches the end, she looks up. "This is an awful lot of secrecy for a nightclub."

I nod.

She makes a face, one that's hard to read. It's like a cross between determination and consternation.

I lick my lower lip. "If it makes you feel better, it will all make sense after you sign."

"I figured." She taps her bottom lip with her index finger, rereading part of it.

I swallow hard. "And if you decide you don't want to take the job afterward, I'll totally understand. You'll just need to stick to the NDA, even if we part ways."

The last few words leave a bad taste in my mouth.

Again, she looks up sharply, then holds my gaze. "Why wouldn't I want to take the job?"

"Reasons," I mutter, sheepishly.

Honestly, I have no idea how she'll react when she finds out what else we do here. I don't know this new, older version of her. Not really. For all I know, she could be a prude or a religious zealot. She did get married in that church on the east hillside.

She blows out a puff of air.

"Saint," Myles calls out, knocking on the door frame the way she usually does.

I glance up to see her eyes widen as she shifts from foot to foot.

I narrow my gaze. "What do you need, Myles?"

She clears her throat. "We may or may not be out of stir sticks again."

I roll my eyes. "Fucksake."

"And uh," she shifts again from foot to foot, "can I talk to you out here for a sec?"

I shift my gaze to Lily. "You okay for a second?"

She nods. "Yeah, I'm going to just look this over one more time."

"Okay." I get up and walk out into the hallway with Myles. "What the hell else—"

"Get that blond bitch away from my bar. I'm *begging you*," Myles rush-whispers.

I pull up short, barely stopping myself from snickering. "What? Why?"

"She keeps asking questions like, '*Who designed the*

bar?' 'What's the thought process on how the bottles are laid out?' 'Did I pick out the dish rags?' The *dish rags,* Saint. Can you believe it? She won't stop talking … *incessantly.* I might stab her. The day is young," Myles hisses.

I level my gaze with her. "Myles, you deal with talkative drunks every damn day, all night long. How can she possibly be getting to you after a few minutes."

She raises a hand and mimes stabbing someone.

This time, I can't help but chuckle. "All right. I'll see what I can do."

"Thank you," she breathes, her shoulders drooping with relief.

"And I've got another pack of stir sticks in my office. Let me grab them," I say, walking past her and back into the office.

She follows after me and shoots a quick smile at Lily. "Sorry for the interruption."

"No worries," Lily says, holding up the papers in her hand. "I was riveted by my reading material."

Myles huffs a laugh. "Oh yeah, that's some goddamn Shakespeare right there."

I reach into my desk drawer, grab the box from Dirty Deeds and shove them at her. "Here."

"Thanks," she says, grabbing the box and spinning on her heel. When she reaches the door, she mimics stabbing someone again.

"Bye, Myles." I laugh.

She whips her head and stomps off.

Lily sighs and shifts forward in her chair. "All right. I'm ready. Can I borrow a pen?"

I grab the pen on my desk and hold it out for her. A zing races through my hand, into my arm, and straight to my groin when her fingertips brush mine.

"Th—thanks," she says, dropping her gaze to the papers. She flips to the last one, signing on the dotted line.

I heave a sigh of relief, only to have a new terror claw its way to the surface when she hands the papers back to me.

Here goes nothing...

"Well, now that's out of the way ..." I shuffle the papers into a pile and set them aside. Then, I take a seat, shifting in it uncomfortably. "I guess I better fill you in on what *more* Nocté does."

Lily

I'm hanging onto the edge of my seat, wondering what on earth Club Nocté does that requires an NDA.

And please, for the love of all that's holy, don't let it be something illegal. I don't think I could handle that.

Before London can get another word in, there's a loud huff in the doorway behind me.

"What *the fuck* are these?" Myles walks back in, holding a bright pink stir stick with a phallus at the end.

I smother the smile before it erupts from my lips.

So, that's why London was buying those.

London blinks innocently. "I don't see the problem. You wanted stir sticks. I gave you stir sticks."

"*These,*" she spits pit, stepping further into the room and waving the penis-ended stick at his face, "are *not* funny. And they're not stir sticks."

He cracks another smile, obviously enjoying riling her up. "Nope, you're totally right. They're dick sticks."

Myles narrows her eyes, still pointing the phallic object at him. "Rude, Saint. *Rude.* I don't even like dicks in real life. What am I supposed to do with these?"

He shrugs. "I dunno. Maybe put them in drinks?"

"I can think of somewhere else to put them," she huffs through tight lips.

"Why do you call him Saint?" I ask, interrupting their hilarious back and forth with the question that's been plaguing my mind since the last time she interrupted.

Instead of answering me, she jabs the stir stick in my direction. "Do *you* think this is funny?"

"I mean ..." My eyes widen of their own accord and I hold back a barely veiled laugh. "I don't—"

She drops her arm and her head lolls back. "*Christ on a cracker.* You do."

I have to press my fingertips to my lips to stop myself from laughing.

London, on the other hand, has the world's shittiest grin on his face and he's two seconds away from breaking out a guffaw.

"Laugh it up, funny boy. Laugh it up. Paybacks are a bitch," Myles says, but the fire in her rebuttal is starting to lose its edge. With a heavy sigh, she turns to me. "And to answer your question, I call him Saint because *usually*"—she turns to glare at him—"he's the guy that always comes through. Like a *Saint.*"

My heart actually full-on squishes. London was always that guy for me, too.

"It also helps that it's the start of my last name," he deadpans.

Myles shrugs, her face expressionless now. "That's fair."

"It's also less syllables than London. Or St. James," I offer.

Myles raises her arm and jabs the stir stick at me again. "See, she gets me. I mean, she's clearly delusional about *some things*"—she waves the pink stick in the air like a wand—"but she gets me."

"Stop delaying the inevitable and get back out there," London says, shooting her a pointed stare.

Again, she drops her arms and her shoulders slump. "Make it stop."

"Now," he presses, his eyes widening as he tips his head toward me.

She swaps the way she's holding the stir stick in her hand, then slices it through the air with it like it's a butcher knife.

"*Go,*" he grounds out.

Without another word, Myles spins on her heels and exits London's office. When she's gone, I slowly twist around to face him, my left eyebrow arching.

He grins triumphantly. "What?"

"So, *that's* what those stir sticks were for?"

He finally lets himself laugh as he leans back in his chair. "I love Myles, but I swore to myself the next time she forgot to order stir sticks, I was gonna make a point of it."

His laugh is infectious and after a few seconds, I find

myself joining in. "She looked genuinely put out by those."

"Oh, trust, there is no putting out where Myles is concerned," London fires back. He pulls up short as if he realized what he was saying a second too late.

My cheeks heat and I blink rapidly. I hadn't given a single thought to whether or not she and London were a thing—but maybe I should have.

"Are you two—" I begin, pointing between him and the empty doorway.

His dark blue eyes darken further. "No. Not even a little bit."

I glance down at my hands now resting in my lap. "Oh. I thought I just—"

"I'm not her type, if you know what I mean," he offers, his voice low and serious now.

"Really?" I ask, glancing back up.

He nods. "Oh, yeah. Didn't you hear the comment about her not liking dicks?"

"Sure, but I thought she meant assholes—because who likes those?"

He shakes his head. "Nope, *actual* dicks."

"Huh," I say, my mouth dropping open. "I never would have pictured that."

"You picture that sorta thing often?" He quirks an eyebrow.

"I mean—*no*. Not that I wouldn't. Or that there's anything wrong with ... That's not what I—" My entire body goes rigid and my blood pulsates, hammering in spots that really need no extra awareness.

His laughter returns and he stands up, then walks over to his door and shuts it. "I hope you don't mind, but I'm gonna lock this to keep out any more distractions."

I nod, shifting in my seat, and thankful for the redirection.

When he returns, instead of having the desk as a barrier, he pulls the chair next to me around, so it's facing my direction, and he takes a seat. I shift slightly so I'm facing him, too.

After a few seconds, he reaches out, placing a hand on my knee. Instantly, it feels as though my entire leg is on fire as his touch ignites a chain reaction in me.

I suck in a breath, trying not to freak.

"What I'm about to tell you, very few people on the whole planet are aware of," he whispers.

I blink hard, trying to focus on his words and not his touch. "Okay."

His eyebrows knit together and he takes a deep breath. But his hand is still on my knee and I don't think I can remember how to breathe.

"Remember those rooms on the upper level? The VIP rooms?" he begins.

I nod. "Yes."

His eyelashes flutter wildly across his cheeks as he drops his gaze to where his hand touches my knee. After a beat, he finally whispers, "They're meant for hookups."

I narrow my gaze. "Hookups? Like ... *a sex club* kind of thing?"

He winces slightly. "Not exactly. But sorta."

"Are sex clubs even legal in Wisconsin?" I respond, trying to wrap my brain around what's happening.

"There's no money exchanged for what happens here. So, yes. What happens in the VIP rooms are legal," he says, meeting my gaze. His eyes practically burn a hole straight through me.

"Okay," I breathe, not fully comprehending what's going on. "Why did I need to know this?"

Because let's face it, I kind of wish I didn't.

London's tongue snakes across his lower lip and he inhales through his nose. "Because the event you're going to be planning is for the *Upper Tier.*"

"Is that what you call the people who—" I begin, not able to bring myself to say the rest.

He nods.

London is the manager of a sex club.

The thought barrels through my head and does strange things to my insides. I don't know whether to be repulsed or turned on—or mortified that I'm even considering those as my only options.

It furthers his reasoning behind choosing those stir sticks, honestly.

"Like I said out on the main floor, the Upper Tier is invite-only. There are rules to the *club* and how it works," he says, easing into this conversation gently, by the sound of it. "Not everyone off the street can join. And because there's no money involved, people can't buy their way in, even if they find out about it."

"If there's no money in it, why do it?" I ask, trying to

understand the motivations of a nightclub that also operates as a hidden sex club.

His eyebrows tug in as he considers his words. "Honestly, no one really knows except for the owner. We just follow his rules and keep things above board."

"Hmmm." My head's spinning and I almost forgot about his hand on my knee until he pulls it back.

"Are you okay?" he asks, watching me closely. "You know, with all of this so far?"

"I mean, I can't say I was expecting this—" I begin. *Understatement of the year, Lily.*

He huffs quietly. "I doubt many would."

I snicker in agreement. "So, if people can't buy their way in, how do they get an invite?"

"That's above my pay grade," he responds, leaning back. "We just know that everyone in the Upper Tier has been recently cheated on by their partner. From what I understand, the club is a way to ... *get over it,* I guess?"

"Have you—" I say before I can stop myself.

His eyes widen, but he finishes my thought. "Been involved in the Upper Tier?"

I nod.

"No. I didn't even know about it until I'd been manager for two months," he says, laughing under his breath.

"Wow," I whisper, dropping my gaze to the floor.

"I know this is a lot to take in. But I needed you to understand the dynamics before I give you the assignment." He reaches out, hooking his index finger under my chin and lifting it so I have to look at him.

I inhale, letting my lungs fill up so fully that my shoulders rise and fall. "Tell me about the event."

He shifts in his chair, clearly uncomfortable. "From what I understand, Noah—*the owner*—wants us to create some sort of dinner for the Upper Tier. There are a few of them who haven't utilized the services their invite offers and he thinks by creating something different, he might be able to get them"—he narrows his eyes—"*excited.*"

"So, this needs to be like a what? A sex party with food?" I ask, my voice coming out an octave higher than necessary.

"He didn't really specify. I think he's leaving it up to us to design the event. The only thing he wants for sure is some element of food."

"H—how many people are in the Upper Tier?" I ask, surprised I'm able to even come up with intelligent questions when my mind is still reeling.

"They always come in pairs so no one is singled out. Right now, there are twenty-two people," he answers.

That's easy math. "One couple for each VIP room."

A grin plays at the left side of his lips. "Not exactly."

I narrow my eyes.

"So, one of the rules of the club is that you only get *one night* with one of the other participants. Or *multiple* participants," he shoots me a pointed look.

I blink at him confused. But the longer I stare, the more obvious his statement becomes.

"Oh," I blurt out.

He nods, then chuckles, lightening the mood. "There's a lot of that in the Upper Tier."

Again, my face flushes.

It's so weird to be having this type of conversation with him. When we were kids, the closest we ever got to some sort of sex talk was whether or not it was weird to have *'boy parts.'*

If he notices, he doesn't say. Instead, he continues, "If at any point the participants want a night *two* ... Well, they're out of the Upper Tier and free to explore more with each other and new people are brought in."

"So, this is literally a one-night stand club," I say.

Again, a grin plays at his lips, drawing my attention to them. "You could say that."

"*Nocté,*" I say the word like it's a prayer.

Suddenly, it all makes sense. The double entendre.

London narrows his eyes and tilts his head.

I glance up at him and explain, "Nocté is Latin for night. I thought it was just a cute name for a nightclub. But now..."

"Ah," he says, nodding. "The definition has expanded."

"Yeah. You could say that."

"So, does this mean you're still with me on this?" he asks, his dark blue eyes surveying me.

Those words stir inside my belly, making me feel lightheaded and a little giddy.

I blink at him for a second, letting all that I've just learned settle in my brain.

I definitely understand the need for the NDA now.

I mean, if word got out...

I bite my lip, realizing the ramifications of taking this job are bigger than I anticipated.

Is this even a good idea?

I'm not sure that Seth would approve—and truthfully, the semi-awkwardness of being around London again after all these years was bad enough without it also being a sexually charged event.

Yet ... there's a part of me that *really* wants to do it.

The idea that I could design an event that marries the two sides of my personality—my event coordination and the Dirty B in me—feels sorta ... *right.*

And to be able to plan it with London? What could be better than that?

But oh, god ... What if my sister Angie found out?

I'd never hear the end of it.

Besides, she knows how close London and I were as kids and back then, she always thought I had a crush on him.

I look up, staring straight into his expectant eyes. "I'm sorry, London. I know you want an answer, but I'm gonna need to go home and think about it."

CHAPTER 11

London

"Didn't I tell you this place might freak her the fuck out?" Cal chides, leaning against the side of my Escalade and crossing his arms over his chest.

We're an hour away from opening, so the two of us snuck outside before the chaos kicks in.

I sigh, raising my eyes to the sky. There is a scattering of wispy clouds, but for the most part, it's free and clear. The temps are gradually getting warmer, but even in the upper forties, the wind has its moments of bite this side of the lake.

"How did she word it?" Cal presses when I don't say anything.

I look over my shoulder at him and shrug. "She wants to think about it."

"Did she say how long?"

I shake my head. "Nope."

"Fuck."

I huff. "Right? Maybe I should start planning it myself now."

Cal rotates so his shoulder is leaning against the truck as he faces me. "What, like assume the answer is gonna be no?"

"Maybe?"

Truthfully, I'd rather plan for the worst, even if I'm wishing for something vastly different. If I can prepare for disappointment, I can handle it.

Cal watches me for a moment and his scrutiny starts to make me feel uncomfortable.

"What do you think her biggest concern is?" he finally spits out.

"How the hell should I know?" I ask with a shrug.

Deep down, I wish I did know. I used to know her so well that I'd be able to read her thoughts just by a look. But now, everything is so different.

He raises his right hand and rubs at his chin. "I mean, it's her job to plan events. Nocté is a paying client—and I bet the money is nothing to sneeze at, considering. She's clearly not a prude, either."

My eyes dart to his. "How do you figure?"

"Didn't you say she meets weekly at Dirty Books?" he fires back.

"I mean, yeah," I say, even though my head is shaking back and forth.

His eyes narrow. "Do you think she has a thing for you, too?"

"What? *No,*" I say, snickering under my breath.

The thought is absolutely absurd—even if it does something weird to the pattern of my heartbeat.

"I'm just thinking if we knew what her objections were, we could convince her they're no big deal. You know?"

"Why does it matter to you?"

Cal pushes off the truck and stands in front of me. "It doesn't matter to me. It matters to *you*. And considering how much you take care of everyone else around here, I figure you might need someone who's got your back."

My brows furrow and a lopsided grin makes its way to my face. "Thanks, man."

He reaches out and slaps my shoulder. "Hey, don't mention it."

An idea pops into my head and I stand up, patting my front pockets.

"You goin' somewhere?" Cal asks, eyeing me suspiciously.

I nod. "You gave me an idea. Think you can cover for me for an hour?"

Cal shrugs. "I mean, if Myles asks me where you went, I'm not gonna lie. That chick's scary."

I huff a laugh. "You don't have to lie. Just tell her I'll be right back."

He tips his head and takes another step back. "Will do. Good luck."

"Thanks," I say, as I hop into my vehicle and fire it up.

I wave at Cal and he turns to make his way back to the building.

My pulse kicks into high gear by the time I hit the bridge over Lake Superior. This is probably a crazy idea and to be fair, I totally recognize it. It doesn't mean I won't follow through with it.

I might not know Lily very well these days, but I know someone who seems to have a strong pulse on her. The only question is whether or not I'll be able to convince Quinn to persuade Lily to say yes.

My gut says *'piece of cake.'*

Quinn was willing to help me get Lily to dinner last night and he seems cool with me hanging out with her. He wants her happy—just like I do.

When I pull up to Dirty Deeds, I've convinced myself this will truly be a walk in the park. In fact, I should be back to Nocté in no time.

The streets are more busy than usual—probably because it's a Friday night—and I have to wait a minute just to get out. However, when I open the door to Dirty Deeds, Quinn isn't behind the counter, like I anticipated.

My eyes scan the store, but there are only three people. Two guys in the back and a woman who's making her way this way. Her pink hair is split down the middle and braided on either side of her head

"Can I help you find something?" The woman asks. She has a tattoo of a thorny rose etched up her forearm and a curious expression on her face.

"Uh, yeah. Is Quinn here?" I ask, looking past her, half-expecting to see him pop up between the shelves.

She shakes her head. "Not today. He has the day off."

My face falls. "Oh."

He mentioned something about taking his mom to the hospital today.

Shit, now I wish I would have driven him home. At least then I'd know where he lives.

"Is there something *I* can help you with?" she repeats, but this time, she puts more seduction into the way she asks. She even twirls one of her braids in her finger.

"Uh—*no*. I just need Quinn," I say, blinking hard.

"Oh," she says like she just had an epiphany. "*Shame.*"

I ignore the revelation she must have just had, seeing as it's inaccurate and I don't care. "You don't happen to have his address, do you?"

"Sorry, we aren't allowed to give out personal info on our employees." She shrugs.

"Shit," I mutter, but nod. That would have been too easy. "Thanks."

I walk out of the store and stand on the sidewalk with my hands in my hair.

What was I thinking? Just because I work most days of the week doesn't mean everyone else does.

This was a stupid idea.

Cursing under my breath, I start walking to my vehicle.

"London?"

I stop in my tracks and spin on the spot.

Lily's friend—the senator-looking woman—is

standing outside Dirty Books. Her hand is on the door but she lets go of it when I turn around and walk in her direction.

"Hi, uh—" I begin, then narrow my eyes, unable to recall her name.

She waves my indiscretion away. "Anastasia—but everyone calls me Tasia."

Relief washes over me and I smile. "Hi, Tasia. Sorry, there were a lot of names thrown at me last night."

"I can imagine." She grins. "So, back again, huh? You're becoming one of our regulars."

While her words say one thing, her pointed stare is telling me something very different. I shift from one foot to the other.

"Yeah, I was, uh—looking for Quinn. But it appears he has the day off."

She eyes me suspiciously for a moment but nods.

"Any chance you might be able to give me his address? I know he lives on East First, but not sure which number. I should have driven him home last night, then I wouldn't have to track him down like this," I say, feeling self-conscious enough to babble.

"What did you need to talk to Quinn about?" she asks, sidestepping my question like a pro.

My eyebrows tug in and my mouth opens, but no sound comes out.

She takes a step closer, her teal shirt flapping in the breeze as she crosses her arms over her torso. "Is this about Lily?"

I blink hard, not sure what to say. On one hand, she's

also friends with Lily, but on another—she's one intimidating woman. I'm not sure which one of those elements to lean into.

"Yes," I blurt, opting for the truth. The last thing I need is for her to hunt me down, or turn Lily against me.

"Good," she says, seemingly pleased. "I was hoping it would be. Quinn's in 703."

I exhale a big breath, contemplating what she meant by her first statement. "Thanks. I appreciate it."

We stand there, squaring off on the sidewalk for a beat.

"Well, I should—" I say, pointing toward my vehicle.

She nods but doesn't make a move to leave. I take that as my cue, so I turn to head toward the Escalade again.

"You know ..." She begins before I reach it. When I spin back around to face her, she drops her hands and sighs. "Quinn isn't Lily's only friend. If there's something you need—maybe I could help?"

This was a turn of events I didn't see coming. And I'm not entirely sure how to navigate it. Would it be better to ask for her help? Or continue with my quest to find Quinn.

Tasia must sense my hesitation because she takes a step closer. "Look, from her current best friend to her former, I think we could help each other. But if you don't want my help." She raises her hands and starts to turn around.

Current best friend?

My heart takes a leap into my throat and I look up

and down the street. Before I consciously think about it, I'm nodding.

"So, what's on your mind?" she asks.

I release a pent-up sigh. "Did Lily tell you she was considering an event planning gig working with me?"

Tasia shrugs. "Of course."

I nod, feeling the need to pace. "I'm worried I might have scared her off."

She narrows her eyes. "Why would you think that?"

I screw up my face, trying to search for the line between the truth I can tell her and the things best left unsaid. "The event Nocté needs to plan is going to be challenging—and she wants to take time to think about it—*which I totally get.*"

I look up into her intense brown eyes as she watches me.

"Lily isn't a frail little flower. She's capable of rising to *challenges*," Tasia says sternly.

I wave my hands between us. "No, I didn't mean to imply she couldn't. It's just—I *really* want her to do this. But she wants to think about it."

She tips her chin in understanding.

"What should I do?" I ask, my words coming out softer than I wish they would.

Tasia takes a beat to think before she responds. "If Lil needs time to think about it, there's a good reason for it. But don't assume the answer is going to be no. She's been going through some shit"—she locks her gaze with me—"and it's been messing with her."

"Is there anything I can—"

She shakes her head and cuts me off, "London, she's happy to see you. She's happy that you're back in her life, even if she's not sure what that means just yet. But ..." her gaze drops to the ground and she bites her lower lip like she's trying to stop the next few words from coming out.

"But?" I press.

Her brown eyes rise to mine and there's a significance to the look she gives me. "But if she means anything to you, don't let her get away."

"I won't. I can't—"

"She has enough people in her life who treat her as an afterthought," Tasia continues. "Make her feel like a priority and she'll forget any of the reasons she was worried."

I take another deep breath, feeling like her words bring more than just support—they bring inklings of hope.

"She's always been a priority," I say, jutting out my chin.

She nods. "Then I wouldn't worry."

A smile finds its way to my lips. Despite missing Quinn, I still found a way to feel better about this whole thing. While Lily and I may have drifted apart since we were kids, she certainly found a way of surrounding herself with people who care.

"Lily's very lucky to have you in her life," I offer, reaching out and placing a hand on Tasia's upper arm. "Thank you for looking after her."

"She's my girl." Tasia grins.

"Ditto."

With that, I turn back to my vehicle and check my watch. I've been gone a little over an hour. There's a chance Myles hasn't quite noticed my absence and I'd like to keep it that way.

"Thanks again, Tasia," I say as I open my door.

"No problem," she calls back.

I hop in, start the engine, and grab my phone so I can add Quinn's address to it before I forget. Then, I set my phone in the cupholder and shift into gear.

The drive back to Nocté takes about twenty minutes, but the entire thing is a blur as I play over Tasia's words in my head.

She has enough people in her life who treat her as an afterthought.

My instincts tell me that's a jab at her husband Seth.

If Tasia's not a fan, maybe that could play to my advantage?

I shake my head.

What in the hell, London? She's your friend.

What difference does it make if her best friend doesn't like her husband?

However, my heart nearly claws its way out of my chest when my phone dings, and I see it's a text message from Lily. But I'm almost afraid to open it.

Instead, I wait until I've found a spot in Nocté's lot to dare a glance. After a few deep breaths, I flick open my phone and tap the messages app. Then, like a coward, I hover over her name, praying it's good news.

When I've gathered my courage, I tap on it.

I'm in.

Relief, exhilaration, joy. They all mix and I drop my phone onto my lap and my head to my headrest.

She's gonna do it.

Hell, *yes!*

Now, we just need to figure out how to make this work.

CHAPTER 12

Lily

My brain has been consumed with ideas for how we could create an incredible experience for Nocté's Upper Tier.

Truthfully, it's crazy, but I've been buzzing since I heard about the assignment. The mere idea of it has sparked my creativity and excitement in a way I haven't felt for a really long time.

Maybe ever.

I mean, there aren't many events like this one, that's for sure.

It's a bit taboo, a little bit secretive ... *and totally enthralling.* We're creating something for a group no one really knows exists.

How freaking cool is that?

It's like a secret society—right here in the Twin Ports.

My only hesitation remains anchored to what Seth might think. He's never been much for sex—or even interested in trying anything new. Our love life has been as vanilla as it comes—and that's only when we've indulged.

It's just never been a high priority for him. His thing has always been travel and for a while, I really loved that about him.

But after years of coming in second and feeling like my needs have never really been met, I don't know how to approach the subject. As it is, I've never even told him about the Dirty B's book club. I didn't know how to bring it up and I highly doubt he'd care to even know about it since it has nothing to do with breathtaking views and hidden locations.

However, I have a feeling that if he found out I'm going to be working an event for a sex club, he'd still have a heart attack.

At least, that's the story I've been telling myself.

Then Tasia called and helped me work through it. I was able to see this has nothing to do with him. This is *business* and I'm a big girl.

Seth doesn't tell me the ins and outs of his job. So why do I feel like I should be doing it for him? It's not like I'm *participating* in the event. I'm just planning and executing it.

Granted, there's the *slight* issue of London.

I've mentioned him in passing to Seth, but he was always in the context of a distant childhood memory. There was no mention of the sexy, adult version he's become because I had no idea. Now that he's here, in my present, it *feels* different somehow.

As much as my logical mind knows he's *my friend,*

there's this crazy part of me that stirs awake whenever he's around. I blame it on my dormant sex life and the fact that I've been alone more than with Seth in the past year.

Even knowing all of that, I can't seem to find the strength to stay away from London and this world he's surrounded himself in.

Something in me needs this. I can't explain why.

I pull into the Nocté parking lot and kill the engine on my Rav-4.

It's been a while since I was in Superior. Hell, other than a few days ago, it was probably when I turned twenty-one and went bar-hopping downtown.

So, seven years, give or take.

My friends at the time wanted to go to Superior because the bars stayed open longer than in Duluth. Funny how that sort of thing matters when you're twenty-one. Now, if I'm up past ten, it's a miracle, and the idea of partying until two in the morning is absurd.

My inhalation is shaky as I try to breathe deeply through my nose. I don't know why this is so nerve-wracking. It's not like this is my first gig. I've literally planned hundreds of events over the years, but it still feels monumental. One thing's for sure, I need to get a grip. I can't go in there acting like I'm nervous as hell.

At least I was able to make the journey on my own this time. That has to be saying something, right?

I grab my briefcase, exit my vehicle, and make my way to the massive concrete structure. If you didn't know

Nocté was a nightclub, from the outside it looks like another warehouse on the side streets of Superior.

Simple lines, dark gray exterior paint. Hardly any windows—probably to suppress the light show that goes on inside. The only thing that stands out is the bright neon sign on the side of the building in the form of Nocté's logo. But without context, even that could go unnoticed.

It definitely makes me curious about the owner—Noah, I think London said his name was.

Why did he start the club?

What's with the Upper Tier? Why was that created?

Was he cheated on once and this is his way to overcome it? Or was he the cheater who's trying to find forgiveness?

Does he have a vision for the club's expansion? He must since he wants the Upper Tier more engaged.

It would make it a lot easier to design this supper event if I knew the endgame, or what made him tick. As it is, I'm going off of what London knows and that isn't much.

I reach out, pressing the intercom button beside the back door. Waving into the camera, I fully expect to have to wait for Myles to come let me in. However, the door buzzes and the lock clicks back.

Smiling to myself, I give one more wave to the camera and walk in.

I find Myles behind the bar—her usual station, it seems—and make my way over to her. There's something about the confidence she exudes that makes it easy to approach her. It's a good quality to have in a bartender, that's for sure.

"Hey, you," Myles says as I walk up and place my briefcase on the bar. She eyes it, then raises a well-shaped brow. "Very official today."

I grin back at her. "Yeah, well … I'm here on official business."

She nods, a ghost of a smile playing at her lips.

I grin back, then take the opportunity to look for London. He's nowhere in sight, but one of the larger booths on the edge of the dance floor has paperwork spread across it.

"He'll be out in a minute. He said something about needing a damn pen that works before he stomped off," Myles offers. When I turn around, she's rolling her eyes. "Want anything to drink while you wait?"

I shake my head. "No, I'm good. But thank you."

She shrugs off my response and turns to a box on the counter behind her. Then proceeds to stock the various bottles of alcohol along the mirrored wall.

London walks out from the back offices and my breath catches. His hair is disheveled and his eyebrows crowd together. He's clearly worrying about something.

However, his outfit is extremely put together—a nice dark blue button-up top that I bet brings out the blue in his eyes if I get close enough—and a pair of faded denim with rips in all the right places. His sleeves are rolled up, showcasing his tattoos and I have to divert my gaze when I realize I'm staring.

My heart kicks up a few notches and it's suddenly way too warm in here.

"Hey, you're here," London says, walking up to the bar. "I didn't hear you come in."

"Kinda hard when you're running back and forth fifty times," Myles mumbles under her breath.

"What was that?" London asks, glancing in her direction.

"Not a thing," she says, plastering a fake smile on her face.

London takes a deep breath, shaking off her words, and turns to me. "Are you ready to do some planning?"

"I think so," I admit, grabbing my briefcase. "You?"

"As I'll ever be," he says, extending his left arm out to suggest we move to the big table. He presses his right hand to the small of my back, gently urging me to take the lead.

I step out in front of him, acutely aware of the point of contact between the two of us. As hard as I try to focus on my forward momentum, it's impossible thanks to his touch, and I miss the first of two steps that drops us down to the main floor.

Because who in their right mind would put the bar level slightly higher than the main floor? Don't they know drunk people have to traverse these floors?

My briefcase goes flying and I lurch forward, my life flashing before my eyes. Or maybe I just wish death was imminent.

Because someone kill me now.

Horseman of Death, where you at?

"Whoa there," London says, his voice suddenly beside my left ear. It causes all of the hairs on that side of my neck to stand on end.

His hands wrap around my waist, pulling me upright and closer to his body than I have any right to be. Yet, for the briefest of moments, I can't help but revel in the way he feels and the warmth radiating from his hands and body.

"You, uh, really should do something about those steps. They came out of nowhere. Talk about a hazard. I mean, I can only imagine what kinds of drunken escapades happen thanks to the ridiculous placement. Your insurance has to be through the roof. Truly, there must be nightly calamities with those bad boys," I babble, trying to right myself and deflect from the fire racing straight to my cheeks.

London chuckles, releasing me to pick up my brief-case. "Surprisingly, it's not often. But at night, the lights are low and the steps are lit up. So maybe that helps."

"Oh, well, yes. That would definitely help. Big flashing lights definitely change the game. Am I right? I mean, you'd think with the lights on full blast right now I would have noticed them, but *whoo*—so not the case. It's like they're just begging to be tripped over. Maybe the psychedelic carpeting did it. You know, like hypnotizing me to continue on to my death?"

Stop talking Lily, for the love of all that's holy.

I fan myself, trying to alleviate the humiliation. "A— *anyway*. I'm alive. All's well that ends well. Back to business?"

A smirk tugs at the corner of London's lips and he holds out the briefcase to me. "Would you like me to file an incident report, Lily?"

His tone is playful and I can tell he's having far too much fun witnessing my demise.

I swallow hard and tug on my shirt. "No, I'm fine, thank you very much."

With a huff, I slide into the booth and place my briefcase on the table in front of me, all the while wishing I could crawl under the table and vanish from existence.

London slides into the booth from the other side and scoots around until he's sitting right next to me. For some reason, that makes it so much harder to breathe.

Get yourself together, Lily.

This is *London*. He doesn't care if you completely mortified yourself.

"So, I was thinking we should set a theme first," London suggests, breaking me from my internal dialogue.

Relief floods me and I turn to face him. "Yeah? I was thinking the same thing. I have a few ideas—"

"Hey, London," a woman who looks suspiciously like a blond version of Angelina Jolie says as she walks by. Her voice is wispy and it's clear she's got a thing for him.

London bristles, but doesn't even look up at her. "Hi."

"Oh, are you working on that top-secret event? Anything I can help with?" she asks, stopping at the table and bending forward so her boobs squish together and nearly fall out of her black top. She hasn't even sent any indication that she sees me sitting here.

"Nope," he responds.

I clear my throat and attempt to stand so I can shake her hand. But the table extends too far into the booth space. Instead, my hip knocks into the table and it tilts slightly, forcing Ms. Big Boobs to drop with the motion.

Half-standing there like a moron, with my arm extended to her, she gasps and steps back like I just stabbed her in the bosom.

"Sorry," I blurt, holding up my hands as I sit back down.

This day is not going well.

Anyone know the number to the nearest graveyard?

I'm definitely digging my own hole at this point.

When I finally get enough courage to glance at London, he's full-on grinning at me. I bite my lip, so confused.

"What in the actual hell?" Big Boobs spits out, her chest heaving.

"Rebecca, we're trying to work here. I suggest you do the same," London says, turning back to me and totally shutting her out. "You know, Lil, why don't we take this upstairs so we can focus?"

Elation floods through me, knowing that London wants to take us away from the immediate vicinity of this woman and her boobish advances.

She was practically throwing herself at him and he couldn't care less.

I don't know why that makes me so giddy, but it does.

Well, until reality hits me.

I mean, let's be real.

I'm totally fine getting away from her, but going upstairs—*to the Upper Tier's lair*—there's something about the idea that screams *'Danger, Will Robinson!'*

It's where the *sexiness* happens.

But it's also where the event will happen.

"I—sure," I say, fighting an internal battle that won't end well. "Lead the way."

CHAPTER 13

Lily

"Do you want to see the rooms?" London asks when the elevator door opens.

"I mean, I guess? Yes, it would probably be the way to go. But it feels weird. Does it feel weird to you?" I ask, my insides suddenly feeling like they've been struck by lightning.

He laughs. "I wouldn't really say it feels weird. No one is here, so they're just empty rooms. Now, if they were *occupied* ..."

"*Total* weirdfest," I say, giggling like a lunatic at the thought.

God, could you imagine?

Yes, yes I could and it's making my nether regions heat up. *Not good.*

London shakes his head. "Come on."

He leads the way, walking down a dark, exotic-looking hallway. The wallpaper is a deep red velvet with black embellishments. Everywhere I look, there are draped fabrics, different textures, plants, and sensual paintings or prints. Some of the paintings are so provocative, even they make my pulse race.

Despite myself, I stop in front of one. It's a large piece, easily five feet by seven feet. It depicts a couple in the act—the woman on top, the man embracing her protectively. The colors are bold, giving it an abstract and colorful vibe. You can still tell they're people, but it's blurred just enough that it doesn't matter who the people are. There's something about it that draws me in.

After staring for a moment, I realize it's the passion it portrays. The need the two embody and ... *it's incredibly hot.*

"Do you like it?" London questions, standing beside me.

Swallowing hard, I nod. I'm pretty sure my voice would betray me at this point.

"I do, too. It's one of my favorites," he admits, his voice lowering an octave.

I want to ask him to elaborate. I want to learn what he likes about it. But somewhere in the back of my head alarm bells are ringing. I shouldn't want to know this about him. It's none of my business.

I turn to him, fanning myself. "Well, this place certainly inspires the hanky-panky. I don't understand why the Upper Tier needs any more encouragement."

"Many of them have never used their invitation. I think that's why Noah wants to lure them in. We've been running this side of the club for months now and he wants them to see Nocté as more than *just* a sex club, you know?"

I nod, breathing heavier than I was before. This place—its vibe makes my head spin and my libido kick in. If I had been invited, I think I'd have a hard time staying away.

Which would be problematic, considering it caters to one night stands.

Granted, I'd never want the life experience that brings the invite, either. Being cheated on, it's the worst feeling in the world. I only had it happen to me once—*when I was seventeen*—and it sucked.

But it does make me jealous that Nocté is a club that's only meant for that type of clientele. Something in me would love to experience it without the emotional turmoil all of that brings.

If there was a club like this for normal couples...

The thought of bringing Seth here, or to any place like it, stops me in my tracks.

What am I thinking?

That would never, *ever* happen.

"Come on. I'll show you the first couple of rooms. They're all pretty similar. Then we can set up in the lounge area."

London guides me to the first room, using a keycard he had in his pocket to unlock the door. He steps aside, allowing me the space to enter the room first.

To say it's breathtaking is an understatement.

It's a sexual oasis.

The bed is massive and obviously the main feature of

the room. It's covered in a variety of pillows of various textures and sizes. The dark red bedspread flows to the ground, looking like an invitation all on its own. There are two large cushy chairs on the right side of the room and a large black X propped up in the corner.

"What's that?" I ask, stepping into the room. It has iron loops on all four corners and I'm pretty sure I know what they're meant for. But I can't stop myself from asking.

London follows my gaze, then clears his throat softly. "A Saint Andrews Cross."

He doesn't explain any further than that and I'm glad he doesn't. I can look it up later when I'm not totally embarrassed by what I find.

As it is, my mind is whirling, wondering how many people have used this room and what kinds of acts have occurred.

Goosebumps flash across my skin and I inhale sharply. "You know, I think I've seen enough. Let's go to the um"—I lick my lips, suddenly parched—"let's go to the lounge now."

"Sure." He turns to face the door and I rush past him, needing to be out of the room and in a place less sexually charged.

"Which way is it?" I ask, suddenly desperate to be in a normal location. I start pointing in random directions.

London grabs hold of my arm and tugs. "This way."

When we reach the lounge, it looks more like an enormous living room. It's full of lush couches and chairs with pillows and interestingly shaped seating.

There are a couple of coffee tables, so I take a seat on one of the couches and drop my briefcase. I try to settle my pulse but it's extremely difficult.

Come on, Lily. This is a job. *You are working.*

No reason to get all bent out of shape.

London takes a seat next to me and places his hands on his lap. "Everything okay?"

"Oh, yeah. *Sure.* Right as rain. Why?" I ask, my voice coming out in a squeak.

His left eyebrow twitches upward. "You seem kinda wigged out."

"Psh," I mutter, swiping the air. "Totally *not* wigged."

Yes, yes I am.

This is the last place I should be when I'm already hot and bothered. I can foresee another night with Enigma coming up.

"Well, should we decide on a theme?" London suggests.

I nod, reaching for my briefcase and pulling out the suggestions I have prepared for just this occasion. "I've already done some brainstorming. What do you think of these?" I hand him the paper.

He takes it from me, his eyes floating over the page. His gaze narrows a couple of times before he sets it in his lap and looks up at me.

"Any of those seem like a fit?" I ask, biting my lip.

He leans back, placing his arm on the back of the couch. "I mean, I like the idea of a masquerade ball or the jungle theme. I'm not sure they're quite right though. Especially if we're trying to incorporate food."

"True, the jungle theme was a little out there. I thought it would be fun to bring in some elements that pull them out of their normal Minnesota or Wisconsin weather. You know? Nothing screams sexy more than being in a hot, sticky climate where your clothes cling to your body and you strip down to the bare essence," I respond, trying to justify the concept for some bizarre reason.

He inhales sharply, shifting in his seat. "True. I like that concept, but not jiving with the jungle. It feels too *'welcome to the wild'* if you know what I mean. Some of the invites are going out to people who haven't been here before, so we need it to be more inviting for this event. More *intimate*."

I glance up at the word intimate, catching what I swear is heat hidden in his eyes.

He likes things intimate.

I don't know why that does things to my stomach, but it's ready to drop out of my body again.

Blowing out a breath, I whisper, "What about a sensual garden? We could still bring in beautiful plants and flowers—ones that have a romantic, aphrodisiac vibe like orchids and Asiatic lilies."

A slow grin breaks his features. "I like the sound of that."

"Which part?" I ask, feeling like there was a hidden meaning in his answer.

"All of it," he says, but after a second he whispers,

"But especially the lilies. It's like your calling card, letting everyone know you were a part of the event."

My cheeks warm and I glance down at my lap. "That's not what I was—"

"I know. Lily. I like it. That's all," he says, placing his index finger under my chin and lifting up so I look at him. "What else?"

I think about that for a second. What could make it more intimate?

Then, the idea comes to me. It's like a rush of energy and my entire body feels like a live wire.

"We could incorporate blindfolds or masks," I say. He opens his mouth to respond, but I hold out my hand to cut him off. "Hear me out. These are people who have never been here. They're nervous. They're hurt by love. What if they start the night totally shrouded."

"What about the food part?" he asks skeptically, his eyes searching mine for the answers.

"It could all be finger foods. Things that are easy to pick up and feed each other with," I say, excitement building in me. "Strawberries dipped in chocolate. Watermelon. That sort of thing."

"It's an interesting concept. They'd have to connect on a deeper level. We could have them circle the room so they have a few minutes with everyone there. Or we could pick their match for them for the night. It could even force them to lean into a bit of trust if the people around them are the ones feeding them. Would they be able to take the masks or blindfolds off? It kind of negates the lush garden vibes if they don't," he asks, the excitement sparking in his eyes mirroring my own.

I nod. "I was thinking the same thing. They have to get through dinner and dessert before they can take things off. But only if they want to."

"If we can instigate the right vibe, it sounds incredibly sexy," London admits, his voice gruff.

A sly grin floats to my lips. "Isn't that the point?"

He holds my gaze for what feels like forever. There's something unspoken hidden their depths and it takes everything in me not to fidget.

Finally, he nods. "I like that. I like it a lot."

A rush of pride and excitement flow through me. But something shifts in the room, and the way he regards me —it makes me feel lightheaded.

There's a hunger in his expression and for the life of me, I can't remember why that could be bad.

His eyes fall to my lips and my breath hitches.

Like two magnets, we begin drawing together.

"London, Noah's on the line. He wants an update on the event when you have a sec," Myles calls out from the doorway.

The two of us jolt apart.

Without even waiting for a response, Myles turns and vanishes.

My soul, on the other hand, has left my body.

I sit there mortified at myself and horrified at what I *think* nearly happened.

"Sorry, Lily. I need to take this call," London whispers, blinking away any signs of what he was thinking, or feeling, before. "He probably wants to know how the planning is going. We've done good here. Do you want to hang out with Myles for a few minutes while I fill him in?" London asks, as he gets up from the couch.

I nod quickly, the hypnotic spell vanishing. "Sure. Do you want me to join you?"

He shakes his head. "No, he has pretty specific contact protocols. But I appreciate the offer."

"Oh, yeah, okay." I nod, surprised at how that makes me feel. Like I'm still just an outsider—despite being asked to plan some pretty intimate details of this event. I raise my eyebrows and press my hand to the tops of my thighs. "I could use a drink anyway."

An adorable lopsided grin appears on his face and he nods. Then, he makes his way out the door and down the hallway that leads to the elevator. I close my eyes, breathing slowly to release the tension, then follow after him.

"Well, I, uh—feel pretty good. Don't you?" London questions, turning to face me while we wait for the elevator to open.

I nod, glad that he's ignoring whatever just happened back there. I don't know that I could handle it if he wanted to talk about it. "Definitely. We accomplished a lot. I mean, after the way today started, I'd be pretty happy just having a theme. But this is better."

He laughs softly. "Yeah, we definitely had a colorful start to today."

I raise my eyebrows and sigh. "Understatement of the year."

The elevator door dings and then opens. We step in it together and London presses the button to bring us to the main floor.

"We make a good team. Even after all these years," he says, turning to face me. His dark blue eyes hold so much in them as he stands there. It's like the decades he's experienced are trying to find a way to express themselves through the boldness of his irises.

There's something in the way he looks at me that still makes me feel *seen*.

Truly seen.

The door dings and opens, making my insides jostle.

A curious expression flits across his features before he turns to the door and swipes his arm out. "Shall we?"

"Yeah, okay," I say, inhaling sharply.

He waits for me to exit first and when we reach the point where he needs to veer off, he leans in and whispers, "I'll be right back. Promise me you won't leave before I can say goodbye."

I nod, doing my best to smile at him and not relay just how freaked out I am.

He grins back, brushing a strand of hair behind my ear. The sensation zings through me and I suck in a breath.

"Be right back." He drops his hand and takes a step back.

Then, he's gone, making his way to his office on the other end of the building. I watch him for far too long before I realize I should head over to Myles if I don't want to call attention to myself.

There's a strange tension growing in the pit of my stomach and I know it has everything to do with him.

London makes me feel things that I didn't know I could feel. Hell, I probably *shouldn't* be feeling.

Pushing everything aside, I walk to the bar and set my briefcase on the floor. Then, I hop onto one of the stools.

"So, the two of you seem to get along," Myles says, giving me some serious side-eye as she wipes the insides of a glass with a towel.

Despite myself, I can feel the blood rush to my face. "Yeah, it's always been that way. London's great."

Myles nods, keeping her eyes on the glass. "He really is. I just wish he'd realize it."

My eyebrows tug in and I find myself leaning closer to the bar. "What do you mean?"

Her eyes find mine and for the first time, I notice she has two different colored irises—one blue and one more of a hazel color. It's not quite green—not quite brown.

"Your eyes ..." I practically whisper, mesmerized.

She shrugs, setting the glass down. "Yeah, it's called heterochromia. I was born with it."

"That's so cool."

She grins and picks up another glass. "Well, it was annoying as fuck as a kid."

I sigh, then nod. "I can relate."

She tips her chin my way. "Cleft lip, right?"

I nod. "Palate, too."

"Was it painful? You know, going through the surgeries?"

"Well, I don't really remember the big ones. I wasn't

even a year old. So ..." I shrug. "But the ones to rebuild my jaw, those were not fun. I had them done once my adult teeth had all come in."

"Ouch." Myles shudders. "And I thought normal puberty was a pain in the ass."

"Right?" I agree. "Sorry, I didn't mean to go off the rails. You were saying something about London—that he doesn't realize he's great?"

She chuckles under her breath. "Yeah, that asshole is always trying to help out. He'll go out of his way to make sure everyone's happy, but the guy can't ever look out for himself. You know?"

I shake my head. "I don't really know him. Not anymore, anyway."

"Oh, yeah. I forgot. You guys seem so natural together—it's like you've known each other forever," she says, swapping out for another glass.

"Well, you're not wrong. We have known each other for a long time. But we had this big estrangement when his family moved."

"You didn't keep in touch?" Again, her eyes meet mine.

"No. My family wasn't a fan of technology. I grew up barely knowing how a computer worked. So, when London's family took him away, the only computer time I had was at school."

"He never called? You never called him?"

I shrug. "I mean, I guess I would have. But I didn't even know his new number. When he lived in Duluth, we were neighbors, so it was easy to just track him down.

You know?"

Her cheeks mound and she nods. "Well, you found each other again. That's pretty damn special."

"Yeah, it is," I whisper, smiling to myself.

"Want something to drink?" Myles asks, nodding to the beers on tap.

My brows crease and I nod. "Can I have a Shirley Temple?"

"Whoa, might want to ease off the hard stuff," she laughs, setting to work.

Feeling lighter, I watch her work and wonder about all of the years I've missed in London's life.

What was it like after he moved?

Did he like his new school—his new neighbors?

Has he ever been in love?

I want to unravel it all.

As if reading my mind, Myles says, "You know, when Saint first started here, I didn't know what to think of him. I mean, he's this big guy with tattoos and a surly attitude. I figured he'd be a pain in my ass. If for no other reason than because I'm gay. Guys who look like him usually come with backward ideas. But he never did. He's always been just ... *chill*." She pauses, laughing softly to herself as she hands me my drink. "Well, when he's not giving me dick sticks, anyway."

A slow grin creeps over my face and I lean in to take a quick sip. "That was pretty good."

She shakes her head. "Asshole."

"But a lovable asshole," I counter.

"Oh, for sure. I mean, this one time—shit, it must

have been one of his first weeks here—I was swamped with drink orders. I think it was a holiday weekend, too. My backup bartender had called in sick and the club was rammed. Total clusterfuck. Even though Saint typically stays in the office, or makes the rounds to keep an eye on the patrons, he saw I needed help," she begins, shaking her head. "The guy's not even a bartender, mind you—but he decided to help me mix drinks."

"Jesus, not this story," London groans as he steps up beside me.

I nearly jump out of my skin at the sound of his voice. I hadn't even heard him approach, I was so enraptured, trying to find another piece to the London puzzle.

"Well, now I *have* to hear it," I say, bumping London with my shoulder.

He sighs heavily but there's a glint of humor in his eyes.

Myles laughs and sets the glass in her hand down. "Well, at first, I was just appreciative that I wasn't slinging drinks alone. He was able to keep up with the beers and I did the mixed drinks and whatnot."

"That's putting it nicely. She basically ordered me to only touch the bottles with tops still on them and pour on-tap beer," he huffs.

"Hey, I let you pour wine, too," she says, rolling her eyes and sticking out her tongue. When she turns to me, she continues, "Turns out that was wise."

I lean forward, planting my clasped hands under my chin. "Go on."

London pinches the bridge of his nose. "Christ, I should never have left you alone with Myles."

"Too late now," she retorts, shooting him a big grin. "So, when things seemed to be dying down a bit, Saint here was incredibly sweet by offering to cover me so I could take a fifteen-minute break. It had been *six hours* of nonstop pouring drinks and I desperately needed to pee."

"None of us needed to know that," London cuts in.

"Uh-oh, I think I see where this is going," I say, shooting a sideways glance toward London. He rakes his hand over his face in response.

"Well, wouldn't you know it, a rowdy group from a bachelorette party came in shortly after I left. I think they planned it, but I can't be sure. Of course, they were flirting all over *Mr. Hot Tattoos* here, asking him to make all sorts of sexual drinks." She locks eyes with London and smirks. "Granted, he didn't know how the hell to make a *Slippery Nipple* or *Sex On My Face*. Shit, I don't even think he knew they were drinks until that day. Did you, Saint?"

"Wish I coulda kept it that way," he mutters, shaking his head and staring at the bar in front of him. "Coulda gone my whole life without knowing most of those existed."

"Oh, no," I say, hiding my giggles behind my hand.

"Oh, that's not the worst of it," Myles continues with a head shake.

London raises his eyes to the ceiling but doesn't say anything.

"Saint here—being the *angel* that he is—went on to

give the ladies a stern conversation about sexual harassment."

"He didn't," I blurt out breathlessly.

"Oh yeah," Myles says with a nod and eyebrow raise. "He totally did."

"To be fair, they weren't acting like they were talking about *drinks*," London says, scratching at the back of his neck.

Myles shakes her head. "So, I come back to find London giving this group of drunk women the shake-down and I had to shoo him aside, apologize and tell them that he was new, and make their drinks. Then—"

"You can leave this next part out. Seriously," London cuts in, narrowing his gaze.

"You *cannot* leave it out," I retort, placing my hand across London's mouth and turning back to Myles.

"Oh, don't worry, *I won't.*" She grins from me to London, who pushes my hand from his face. "So, after the fiasco with the drinks, Saint decides he's going to bring their drinks over and apologize to them."

"Well, that was sweet," I say, reaching out and patting his arm.

London, on the other hand, is making throat-cutting mannerisms and shooting daggers with his eyes at Myles.

Her grin only broadens. "I, of course, think nothing of this. He's a burly man, capable of bringing over a tray of drinks to some hot women. Right?"

I bob up and down on my seat, excited to hear what craziness befell him because you know it's gonna be good. After the start of my day here, it'll soothe my weary soul to hear about his escapades.

"It would have been fine had one of them not tried to grope me under the table," he interjects.

"One of them groped you?" I twist to face him, my eyes wide.

Myles scoffs. "Oh, bullshit. That's just his story to save face."

"Says you. My man parts were violated," London counters.

For whatever ungodly reason, I find myself thinking about his man parts. I twist back to Myles, hoping he doesn't catch the fire burning in my cheeks.

Myles narrows her eyes, watching him for a moment before continuing, "So, anyway ... He gets to their table, the tray of drinks in hand"—she pauses for effect—"and proceeds to dump the entire thing—we're talking fifteen plus drinks here—across the entire group of horny women."

"Noooo." Again, I hide my giggles behind my hands.

"Laugh it up," London says, reaching behind the bar and pouring himself a shot of whiskey.

"To say I was *not* pleased was an understatement. I had to remake the entire tray of drinks," Myles chuffs, grabbing the bottle back and swatting at his hand. "On the upside, two of the ladies were soaked through and I got a pretty good view of some hard nips because of it."

"Along with everyone else," London mutters, shaking his head.

The color in his cheeks does him some good and I

can't help but laugh at the utter predicament. It definitely rivals my own earlier.

"The women were all good-natured about it. Hell, they still gave him a great tip." Myles picks up a new glass and starts wiping it.

"I felt like a complete ass. Needless to say, that was the first *and last* time I offered to help out at the bar. For obvious reasons," London says, flipping over his shot glass and standing up.

"Eh, it was an accident. And makes for one hell of a good story now," Myles responds with a laugh, grabbing his glass and washing it out.

"That it does," I say, nodding in agreement.

"Cleary, no good deed goes unpunished," London retorts.

"That's why I prefer *Dirty Deeds,*" I fire back, spouting off the rest of Dirty Deeds' tagline. However, when I realize how that could have sounded, I stiffen in my seat.

London's eyebrows rise and Myles just blinks back at me.

Then, with a slow smirk, London says in a low rumble, "I prefer Dirty Deeds, too."

Something about the gravel in his voice and the way he says it sends a chill straight down my spine—and then it travels further south. I shift in my seat and bite my lip.

God, that confession should not have sounded so hot.

CHAPTER 14

Lily

"What are you doing? I have a store to run, you know?" Tasia says, trying to get out from under my forced hand.

Instead, I ignore her complaints and continue to push her into the back room of Dirty Books. I'm having a freak out moment and I need someone to help me clear my head. She was the easiest to find—and also the one with the most level head.

When we're far enough away from the door, I stop moving.

"Tash, I need help. I—" I drop my hands from her shoulders and take a step back.

Tasia twists around. "What is it? What's going on?"

I twist my hands in front of my body. "I don't know. I'm just so freaking confused."

She quirks an eyebrow, her eyes tracking my movements. "About?"

I take a deep breath, unsure what in the hell to say.

How do I tell her that I keep noticing London in ways I really shouldn't? Or that the more time I spend with him, the more I question my life—my *marriage.*

"There's this vibe..." I begin.

"With?" Tash prods, trying to help me along.

"London," I whisper, pleading with my eyes for her to understand.

She narrows her gaze. "Did he do something? Do I need to kick his ass?"

"I think... I think I almost kissed him," I blurt out, then cover my mouth with my hands.

"What?" Her eyes nearly bug out of her head.

Great.

"London—I almost kissed him." I throw my hands up in exasperation. "At least, I think we almost ... I mean, there was a moment when it seemed like maybe ... ? We were upstairs and there were these paintings and—"

I stop talking, realizing how precariously close to the rules of the NDA I was tip-toeing to.

"Hold up." Tasia shakes her head and raises a hand. "You went to your first official day on the job and almost kissed your boss?"

"He's not my boss. He's my—" I freeze. I was about to say best friend, but that's no longer true. Besides, Tasia would kick my ass if I said that because she's been my best friend for what feels like forever.

Her scowl deepens.

I run my fingertips over my right eyebrow. "I'm freaking out here, Tash."

"Lily, you know I love you. So, this is coming from

that place, okay?" She gives me a pointed stare, then continues, "What about Seth?"

"I *know,*" I groan, feeling like I was just kicked in the gut.

"Do you have feelings for London?" she presses.

It's my time to pin her with a stare. "Of course, I do. We were so close as kids. But I don't—"

She levels me with another hard look. "The next words out of your mouth better not be a lie."

I snap my mouth shut.

Was I going to lie?

I don't even know anymore.

Tasia steps forward and places her hands on my shoulders. "Lil, you already know how I feel about you and Seth. But only *you* can decide how to proceed with your marriage. However, don't fuck around. That's not cool. If you're done, be done. But make it clear. Don't fuck with his heart."

I shake my head. "I wasn't—"

"You *are.*" Again with the pointed look.

"Fuck," I mutter. "I don't know what I'm doing."

"That much is obvious."

Tears threaten to spill over as I take a deep breath and raise my eyes to hers. "What do I do?"

Her expression turns sympathetic. "Honey, you're the only one who can answer that."

I huff out a humorless laugh. "I can't."

"You'll have to. You owe it to everyone to figure it out," she whispers, pulling me into a hug.

"Maybe I shouldn't be working with London ..."

Tasia snickers. "And how does that feel?"

Like a jab to the heart.

A kick in the shin.

Like all oxygen has left my body.

"Awful," I answer honestly.

She nods as she steps back. "I figured as much. Look, nothing has to be figured out this red hot minute. You haven't cheated. Nothing happened. So, go home. Take a bath, drink some wine, and think about things. At least all this alone time you seem to have can offer you that. Ask yourself if you want to stay with Seth. If so, why? If not, would you rather break up so you can pursue London?" I make a move to speak but she places her hand over my mouth and continues, "If so, *why?* Just play out the thoughts and see which one feels right."

She removes her hand from my mouth and I take a moment to consider her advice.

"Yeah, that feels ... *right*," I whisper, taking a deep breath. "I should think about it all."

She pats me on the shoulder and smiles. "Good. Now, get out of here so I can do my job."

I heave a sigh, my head still swirling through the day's events. "Okay, thank you, Tash."

She spins me around and forces me back the way we came. "You know I'm here for you."

"I know." My words are barely a whisper as I move automatically toward the storefront.

When we reach the checkout counter, Tasia moves toward the register and I head for the door.

"Lily," she calls out, making me pause. "For what it's

worth, I like London. At least, what I've seen of him. I just don't want to see the two of you fuck things up because you're not thinking with the right heads."

"Yeah, me, too." I shoot her a lopsided smile and walk out.

The light breeze coming off of Lake Superior is enough to keep the late May afternoon from being overly warm. If anything, it's trying hard to remind anyone on the hillside that winter still owns this town, even if summer is inevitable.

I walk over to my Rav-4 and get inside, letting my head rest back on the seat.

Dammit. Tasia is right.

I need to go home and have a good, long think. I'll break out my pro-con list and figure my shit out.

I can't believe how close we came to ...

Had it not been for Myles' interruption, I'm not sure what would have happened. All I know is I had no thoughts whatsoever of pulling away. And that scares the hell out of me.

I *should* have pulled away.

Resolving myself, I sit up straight and turn the engine on. The traffic home isn't terrible and by the time I pull into my driveway, I'm so ready to brainstorm myself out of this conundrum.

Rather than park in the garage, the way I normally would, I pull up next to the house and leave the car on the driveway, so I'm closer to the door. I grab my purse and keys and make my way to the house, deep in thought.

There's so much apprehension swirling around a ball of what feels like ... *hope?* Excitement? I'm not sure what I'm even feeling. All I know is I need to sort out this knot of confusion.

I unlock the door and step inside the foyer of my two-story Victorian ready to grab a bottle of wine and start with that hot bath Tasia recommended.

I drop my keys and purse on the small stand beside the door and bend down to take off my shoes.

Out of the corner of my eye, movement catches my attention and I spring upright.

My heart hammers in my chest and I grab the nearest thing—*an umbrella*—so I can defend myself.

I take a few tentative steps forward, ready to knock out my would-be assailant with my weapon.

When I catch a glimpse of a shadow, I pounce forward with my umbrella raised like a sword.

"What are you doing?" the man says, flicking on the light switch.

"Oh, *oh*—" I scream, pull the umbrella back, and clutch it to my chest.

An amused expression flits over my husband's face as he tentatively steps forward, takes the umbrella from me, and sets it beside the door. Then, he chuckles softly. "A bit jumpy, I see."

"Seth—" I blink hard, forcing my insides to calm down.

Did I know he was coming home?

I search my memory banks and come up completely empty. Nope, no mention of coming home. In fact, the last thing he said was something about a new stop he pitched to his editor and he'd be home later than anticipated.

"Hey, honey. Where have you been?" Seth asks, ignoring his near-death experience as he steps forward and wraps me in his embrace. Then, he presses a kiss to my temple.

My heart is still thumping unevenly in my chest as I return his hug and lean into him. He smells like Seth—a combination of the forest and Old Spice. His scent is something I've gotten so used to over the years.

"I was working," I say too quickly, feeling the need to justify my absence, even though there's nothing to justify. I *was* working.

He steps back and smiles. "That's great, sweetie. New gig?"

I nod. "Yeah. The first day, actually."

"Awesome news. Well done." He reaches out and runs his hand along my arm.

"Thanks," I respond, smiling weakly. Normally, I'd be compelled to fill him in on the type of event, but the words get stuck in my throat.

"Looks like we have two things to celebrate tonight," he says, taking me by the hand and leading me to the kitchen.

I take a deep breath, unsure if I should be grateful he changed the subject or not.

"Two things?" I question, following after him.

The kitchen smells like Chinese food and I can see

why when we enter. There are takeout containers scattered across the kitchen counter.

Seth leads me to a stool at the breakfast bar and plants me on a seat.

"Let's talk about it over dinner. Hope you're hungry," he says, proceeding to open the takeout boxes and grabbing two plates. Without even asking what I want, he piles food on both.

In the past, I would have thought it was endearing, but he just filled my plate up with spicy chicken—something I have never enjoyed.

He passes me my plate and some chopsticks, then takes a seat next to me.

"Thank you," I respond on autopilot, setting everything down. Then, I turn to face him so he can continue to explain this celebratory mood.

"I'm starving," Seth says, digging straight into his chicken.

Trying hard not to freak out, I turn back to my food and pick out the bits I'll actually enjoy. When I've eaten the only edible bits, I set my chopsticks down and turn to him.

He glances over his shoulder and notices my plate. "You're not eating."

I shrug. "I'm not all that hungry. I want to know what's going on."

There's no point in telling him I'm not a fan of the chicken. It's been said a hundred times before and he just doesn't take any notice.

A broad smile brightens his features and his light

blue eyes—a blue that's much lighter than London's—dance with excitement. Part of me wonders why on earth I would even notice or compare them.

"You finally get your wish," he says after a beat.

I narrow my eyes, confused. "What wish?"

"No more traveling." He shrugs one shoulder. "Well, not far, anyway."

I shake my head. "What? What do you mean?"

"I was offered a position with a new startup here in Duluth that's featuring the scenic North Shore and all that can be done here. There will be an app *and articles.* They want to turn it into this really big—"

"A *startup*?" I ask, cutting him off. "Isn't that risky?"

"What do you mean?" he asks, shaking his head. His light eyebrows tug inward as he assess me.

I inhale, trying to wrap my head around what he's said. "I mean, what happens if they don't work out? Most startups fail. Look at how hard it's been for me."

"Then I go back to Ted and beg for my job back." He chuckles softly. "I'm sure it'll be no big deal. In fact, he's happy for us. He knows how hard it's been to be separated so much."

This is something we've talked about forever. It's the only thing that made sense because I can't plan events on the road. But he can write from anywhere—*obviously.*

But a part of me never thought it would ever happen.

Seth loves the open road. He loves the mystery of finding a new place and exploring it. It's practically encoded in his DNA.

"I mean, that's great." I shake my head, trying to chase away my worried thoughts. "It's just..."

He narrows his eyes a bit and drops his chopsticks onto his plate. "I thought this is what you wanted. Why aren't you happy?"

I open my mouth to speak but no sound comes out.

This *is* what I wanted.

Isn't it?

CHAPTER 15

London

Myles knocks on my office door but doesn't wait for my response before barging in and plopping down into one of my office chairs.

Mental note: I need to start closing my door. Maybe lock it, too.

"What the fuck is going on between you and Lily?" she fires off before I can even say hello.

My gaze flits from my computer screen, where I've been desperately trying to focus on my workload before Lily arrives, over to her.

Salty straight out of the gate, I see.

This is going to be interesting.

"What?" I ask, leaning back and grabbing my neck.

She scowls at me. "You heard me. What's going on between you two?"

Myles's question hangs in the air for a few moments, leaving me feeling both exposed and more than a little defensive.

It's true—there's a strong connection between me and Lily and as much as I hate to admit it, it has nothing to do with our childhood friendship. But that's not something I want to get into with Myles—not when I've decided to make it my mission to ignore it.

"Nothing," I say, shaking my head. "We're friends."

"Ehhh," Myles begins, giving me some serious side-eye. *"Are you though?"*

I raise my gaze to the ceiling. "What are you getting at, Myles? I have work to do."

"I've been going over it in my mind since yesterday and I swear—I walked in on something," she replies.

I drop my gaze back to her. My mouth is suddenly dry and my palms start to sweat because I know the exact moment she's talking about.

Fuck.

I thought she missed that.

My pulse pounds in my ears as I try to come up with an explanation for what Myles might have seen.

"I don't know what you think you saw, but there's nothing going on. She's the event planner for—"

"Yeah, yeah. I know what the official excuse is," she responds with a swipe of her hand. "But I'm catching a vibe and I need to get to the bottom of it."

"Why?" I ask, blinking hard and trying to ignore the panic clawing its way up my spine.

She kicks up her feet, letting her combat boots thunk onto my wooden desk. Then she interlocks her hands behind her head. "Because my life is boring and I demand to be entertained."

"Nice." I pinch the bridge of my nose.

"And also," she pulls her feet back and leans forward, "so you don't make a mess of things."

"Christ," I mutter. "I told you, there's nothing—"

"Oh, buddy. Lie to yourself all you want, but there's *definitely* something."

I shift under her scrutiny and my gaze drifts to the hallway beyond her. Where's Cal when I need him?

Actually, what the hell am I talking about? He'd be right there cheerleading with Myles and trying to pull the truth from me.

"You know she's married, right?" Myles questions, her voice low and serious.

My eyes flit to hers. "Of course. Why does everyone keep asking that?"

She holds my gaze for far longer than I'm comfortable with. Finally, she says, "If she means anything to you —*and I know she does*—tread carefully."

I exhale slowly before giving her a single nod of understanding. Then, trying to steady my voice, I offer, "Look, whatever it was you think you saw, it was nothing, okay?"

Myles stares at me as if trying to read something in my expression that will give away the truth. Finally, she sighs heavily and slumps back in her seat.

"Fine," she mutters. "But I can tell you this—if anything is going on between you two, you need to be careful or it could make things super awkward around here. Clear?"

Again, I nod, ignoring the twinge of guilt that pings

through me because it feels like I'm lying to her. However, digging into the truth wouldn't do any good either.

"Crystal clear," I say softly before turning back to my computer screen and focusing on work again.

I know what Myles is saying and it's not something I needed reminding of—I am all too aware of the risk of letting anything happen with Lily. It's a slippery slope, and if I'm not careful, I could end up ruining both our lives.

I want to think it was the atmosphere upstairs. The upper tier has such a sexual vibe that it can get to the most steadfast of people—even when no one else is there doing unspeakable things.

It lives and breathes in the spaces up there.

I've even noticed it.

But that doesn't mean Lily and I can't still be friends and work together on this event. Right?

With that thought in mind, I exhale slowly and rub the back of my neck. I need to keep things professional between us, no matter how difficult that might be.

She's off-limits.

Myles' voice breaks into my thoughts as she stands up from her chair and taps the edge of my desk with the tip of her middle finger. "Just remember what I said, okay?"

I look up at her and nod slowly in response.

She gives me a curt tip of the head before walking out without another word. I watch her until she disappears beyond my office door before leaning forward and running my hands over my face in frustration.

A tiny part of me wishes I'd never bumped into Lily.

It was easier having her be a hypothetical in my head. But now, here she is—*real and tangible*—and all I want is to be closer to her—and to stay as far away as possible—all at the same time.

It's hard not to feel something for her when we have so much history between us. It's a past that has been dormant for far too long. And that onus is on me. I get that.

Even now, it's like we're on the same wavelength—and it just feels so natural when we work together. Like no time has passed since we last saw each other, and that scares me a little because it means that despite everything, we're still intricately connected.

I take a ragged breath and try to push these thoughts out of my head and refocus on the task at hand. After all, Lily will be here soon and I need to get my other work finished before then.

With a deep breath and a renewed sense of determination, I sit up straighter in my chair and turn my attention back to the tasks at hand.

I make quick work of reviewing and signing off on documents for the upcoming event that Lily and I will be working on together.

My thoughts only stray once or twice.

Thank fuck.

Eventually, though, I rein them all in and finish up the work that needs to be done before Lily comes in with her usual enthusiasm and puts a smile on everyone's face.

My phone dings, drawing my attention to it. When I

turn it over, my stomach flutters more than is masculine when I see Lily's name across the screen.

Swallowing hard, I open my phone and read her text.

> Sorry, London. I can't make it today.
> Long story.

Shit, that's short and to the point and it jabs at the insecurity already plaguing my mind since Myles stopped by. I type up a quick response.

> Everything okay?

The dots dance across the screen, showing me she's typing. Then, they vanish. I watch my phone, clutching it and waiting for her response. A few long minutes, and a couple of vanishing dots later, her text finally comes in.

> I'm processing.

The lump that's settled itself in the center of my torso gains some added weight. Is this because of what almost happened between us? Is she having second thoughts about working on this event now?

I knew I'd nearly crossed a line. Had Myles not burst in, I have no doubt in my mind, I would have kissed Lily. And I kicked myself all night long. It was rash and stupid and—why I decided I need to keep things strictly professional from here on out.

I'd hoped that with the way we'd parted yesterday,

she was going to let things slide, too. Hell, maybe she hadn't even noticed.

Fighting back the dread creeping into my body, I type back, trying to keep it simple and not jump to conclusions.

> That doesn't sound good.

What I really want to do is race over to her house so I can talk to her, tell her how sorry I am, and how nothing like that will happen again. It takes everything in me to stay seated at my desk.

A few minutes roll by and just as I set down my phone, assuming she's done talking about this, my phone dings again.

I flip it over and read her response.

> It's not bad. Just … Crap, I don't know.

My brows pinch tight and I sit up straighter, typing back.

> Is this about yesterday?

I stare at the words for a few minutes, wondering if I should ask this question that's burning in my mind. Weighing the pros and cons, I finally hit send and hold my breath.

Her response is almost instantaneous and takes all the air out of my lungs.

Yes.

"Fuck," I mutter, pushing away from my desk and shoving my phone into my pocket.

I've screwed up royally in the past—*but this* ... This feels worse than all of the others. I can't even tell you how long I've been imagining what it would be like to have Lily back in my life and I've fucked it up within the first month.

Great going, London. Truly, stellar work.

I make my way to the bar, where Myles is busy putting up the new stock of bottles on the glass shelves behind the bar.

Bellying up, I admit, "I need a drink."

Myles turns to me with a raised eyebrow. "Aren't you supposed to be meeting Lily in an hour?"

I shake my head. "She's not coming."

"Really?" she says, drawing out the e for far too long.

I level her with a glare.

There's no way I'm getting into this with her again. I just need something to take the edge off so I can go back to work without every thought being about Lily.

Of course, that doesn't help me now because all I can think about is what would have happened if Myles hadn't come in when she did.

What now then? Is this going to jeopardize our whole working relationship and leave us unable to function together professionally?

Myles takes one look at me and sighs heavily before reaching for a bottle in the mini-fridge beneath the bar.

"Here, this is all you get," she says, cracking open a bottle and placing it in front of me. The contents are effervescent and escape out of the top the moment the cap is removed.

Yet, one look at the bottle and I know it's not beer.

Carefully, I lift up the bottle and twist it in my hand. "What is this?"

"Kombucha. Enjoy," she responds without looking up.

I narrow my gaze and make a face when I sniff it. "What in the hell is *that*? And why does it smell like feet?"

She shrugs. "Probably because it expired last year."

I slide the bottle across the bar. "Then why would you give this to me?"

She narrows her gaze and leans forward on the bar. Then she hiss-whispers conspiratorially, "It's what all the *would-be* adulterers get."

I hold my hands out and snort. "For the hundredth time, I'm not going after Lily."

Myles rolls her eyes as she pulls away from the bar and continues stocking bottles. "Don't care."

"What in the hell does that mean?" I retort.

This is the last thing I need right now.

Over her shoulder, she says simply, "It means—I don't know. Maybe you *should* be."

Fucking hell.

After the talk earlier, I was not expecting that.

CHAPTER 16

Lily

My phone dings and I pull it from my pocket. Somehow, despite blowing him off earlier, I'm insanely hoping it's a text from London.

It's not.

It's a text from my sister, Angie.

> Hey, sis! I heard Seth's finally packing in all the traveling. Yay! You must be thrilled! We should get together for coffee soon. Let me know what works.

I stare at the text, wondering why I ever tell my mother things. It's apparent, she doesn't know how to keep what I tell her between us.

Now, I need to respond to Angie and I have no idea what to say that won't set off alarm bells in her over-achiever brain.

She's right. I *should* be thrilled. I *should* be over the moon.

Instead, I've been consumed by an irrational panic. More than once in the past few days, I've had to lock myself in the bathroom just to control my breathing.

Not my finest moments, let me tell you.

Seth has been home for three days and I haven't been back to Nocté since he arrived. I don't know what to say to London—or how to tell Seth about the kind of event I'm working on with him. Rather than dealing with it, I've pretended none of it exists.

Great going, *I know.*

It's just ... I don't know what to do.

And now, with Angie finding out about Seth's job change, her impending judgment weighs on me, as well. Ever since she became a marriage counselor, she's tried using my relationship with Seth as one of her case studies. I've been able to dodge her advances, for the most part. However, if she found out my marriage is on shaky ground, she'd have a field day and go hog wild with her suggestions and advice.

I don't think I could take that right now.

Especially since I'm not even sure if I *want* to fix things anymore.

God, how terrible is that?

Since Seth's returned, not once has he tried to have sex. We've been apart for months and ... *nothing?*

I mean, don't get me wrong, I'm kinda glad I haven't had to navigate those feelings, but at the same time ...

Why doesn't he want me?

My heart constricts and cracks a little.

Not once did I feel like the man was undressing me with his eyes.

He's my *husband*. Shouldn't he be doing that?

Instead, he just slipped back into a routine like a roommate, while he works on getting his new job lined up.

I mean, that's great, but ... *really?*

I shouldn't compare, but there were moments—*flashes really*—where I could sense a palpable vibe from London. It was like he was struggling to hold himself back from saying or doing something we'd both regret.

I shouldn't love that feeling.

But I kinda do.

It makes me feel—*beautiful*.

Desired.

Hell, *seen*.

I didn't realize just how much of that was missing from my life until he crashed back into my orbit.

I pinch the bridge of my nose and whisper, "Get it together, Lily."

Rather than respond, I leave Angie on read and shove my phone into my pocket.

At least I've been able to slip away from Seth for the night to attend the Dirty B's—something else I haven't explained to him. He's down at some laser tag venue, researching for an article. So, his absence this evening has allowed me the breathing room to carry on with my Thursday night routine without having to discuss it.

Besides, if I didn't get to book club, Tasia would

hunt me down and start asking questions. She already knows too much thanks to my freak-out earlier this week.

I open the door to Dirty Books, anticipating Tasia at the front counter. Instead, I hear voices in the back, so I lock the door and follow the cacophony.

"It's been great. Seriously, if I would have known giving up sugar would make me feel so alert, I would have done it ages ago," Carlie says, her face animated and green eyes sparkling. "I still have to set up an appointment with a personal trainer, but I'm totally dreading that."

"Why?" Tasia asks, then nods in my direction. "Hey, Lily."

Everyone turns to face me, waving or broadcasting their welcomes. I wave in return, then take a seat next to Carlie and Tasia.

Carlie smiles at me, then turns back to Tasia. "It's been ages since I worked out. I'm going to die, for starters. And, well, look at me." She sweeps her hands in front of her person.

Tasia's eyebrows tug in. "What about you?"

Carlie rolls her eyes. "Ugh, you're sweet. But knowing my luck, I'll trip over myself and end up in the emergency room. Or I'll get paired up with some buff muscle head guy who'll take one look at me and think *what a slob.*"

Vivian's head swivels to Carlie. "You're not a slob. You've got killer curves, woman. Own them. If you get a beefy guy, he'll be the one struggling with the massive boner you'll give him every time you do squats. Make sure you bend and snap on the way up. Really gets their gears turning."

Carlie's cheeks gain some color and she blinks at Vivian, clearly shocked. That's saying something, considering she writes sexy scenes for a living.

When everyone looks at Vivian, she just shrugs. "What? If I had an ass and boobs like that, I'd be flaunting the hell out of them."

Anna turns to her with her expression deadpan. "You flaunt yours all the time." She points at Vivian's teal halter top that's barely holding her breasts in place. "Case in point."

"Awww, Chang, I didn't know you cared," Vivian counters, then hoists her boobs up higher so they practically spill over the top.

Anna rolls her eyes and returns to her phone.

"So, you're late. I was worried you weren't coming," Tasia says, turning to me. "Everything okay with London?"

Again, one by one, all eyes turn to me.

I shift in my seat.

"Things are fine," I mutter, glancing at the coffee table with five empty wine glasses.

Shit, it was my week to bring the booze.

"Oooh, I sense goss," Vivian says, tucking her legs up into lotus position on the loveseat.

Anna pokes Vivian's extended knee with her index finger and pushes it back to Vivian's side.

"There's no goss. I'm fine. We're fine. Everything's *fine*," I protest. But my voice squeaks at the end and I'm not entirely sure it pressed home the point I was trying to make.

All eyes remain on me—even Anna's.

I blink.

They blink.

I clear my throat. "So, uh, I forgot the wine." I stand up. "I should go rectify that."

Without waiting for a response, I march myself through the store and back to the front door. Unfortunately, I don't even get to the handle before my arm is tugged backward and my feet come to a halt.

"Lily, what's going on? It's not like you to be late—or forget your week for wine," Tasia says when I spin around to face her.

Instead of answering, I step forward and drop my forehead to her shoulder. "Seth's back," I mumble.

She grabs my shoulders and holds me in front of her. Her brown eyes search mine for a moment before she says, "You're not happy about this."

It's not a question, it's a statement. That's how well she knows me.

"He's back and he's home. And he's *staying*," I moan, raising my gaze to the ceiling. "This is all I've wanted for years but now that it's here..."

"It's not what you want." Again, she finishes my thought—and it's not a question.

I swallow hard but don't respond. If I say it out loud, it makes it real.

"What did you decide about London?" she asks, still watching my every move.

I exhale. "I haven't seen him since Monday."

"What?" she fires back, nearly choking on her spit, by the look of it. "I thought this event is supposed to take place next month."

"It is," I respond, trying not to groan. "I just—I was going to do what you recommended, but when I got home ..."

"Seth," she finishes.

I nod.

"Well, shit."

"Yeah. *Shit*," I whisper.

She lets go of my shoulders and brings me into a hug. "I know you know this already, but you can't hide forever. You need to get back on the job. And if you can't handle it—"

I pull back, horrified at the direction she's heading down.

She shakes her head. " Okay, so no quitting. *Good*. Well, then you need to get your head out of your ass and get back to work."

"I know," I mutter. "I just couldn't face him. Not yet ..."

"He needs to know this isn't about him. I mean, it's *not* about him, is it?" she asks.

I shrug. "I don't know how to act around him. I don't know how to explain to him that my husband's back and it's messing with my head more than it should. Or that I'm confused every time we're in the same room. I want this job—hell, I *need it*. But if I'm honest, I just want to be around him. I'm so ..."

She nods as if she expected all of that. "Well, none of it's going to get resolved tonight. So, instead, we're going to talk about dirty books and drink wine. Forget heading out. I have a stash in the back."

"Really?" I respond, surprised.

She grins. "Yup. Granted, I bought it in case Vivian ever flaked out. Never thought it would be to save your ass," she huffs, nudging me with her hip.

I let out a soft laugh and run my hand over my face. "God, I suck."

"You don't suck. You're just trying to find your worth."

My gaze flits to hers.

"You deserve more than the life you've been living, Lil. We've talked about it hundreds of times. I bet Seth hasn't even made a move since he's been back," she says. When I don't say anything to rebut her, she nods tersely. "Thought so."

In the past, I would have argued on Seth's behalf.

He's tired from all the travel.

He needs a few days to get back in the flow.

He's got a lot of people to catch up with.

But now, I don't even want to.

I just want to feel whole.

"Come on. I'll steer the conversation away from your drama and back to Vivian's. Did you hear? Jordan wants to bring in another woman so he can watch?" she whispers, grabbing me by the shoulders and guiding me back to the alcove.

"What? No. How did I miss that?" I ask, my voice dropping into conspiratorial territory.

"Apparently, he hasn't been as '*into her lately*' and he thinks it'll be hotter to watch her make out with another girl. I doubt it will stop there. Between you and me, I think all these trips to Tahoe are so he can get it on with other women without Vivian finding out," she declares.

I turn to her. "You think?"

She shrugs. "Can't be sure. Just waiting for the signs to get a little more obvious."

I nod slowly as that sinks in—the idea that Jordan might not be as into Vivian as he used to be. I never would have thought Vivian's relationship might be having troubles. By the way she always talks about it, things have always been hot and heavy.

I've been insanely jealous of how free the two of them are sexually.

If *she's* even having trouble keeping her man satisfied, what does that mean for the rest of us? Are we all doomed to have unsatisfying relationships?

The thought makes me sad.

I don't want to live my life devoid of connection and intimacy.

But that's exactly what it feels like I've created.

Tasia's right, I need to get clear on what I want— *what I'm worthy of.*

First, it means moving forward. However tentatively that might be.

So, tomorrow, I'll be back on the job with London.

I need to face my fears head-on.

Starting with him.

CHAPTER 17

London

T his is stalker-level shit.

Yet, I can't even feel bad about it.

After my talk with Myles, it got me thinking ... Is she right? Should I be making a move on Lily?

Not in a sexual advance kind of way, but what if I told her how I've been feeling? How much she means to me. How much she's *always* meant to me ...

Would that change anything?

I've gotten the impression her relationship isn't the greatest. Her friends have all but steered us together. Quinn and Tasia, specifically.

What if I just had an open and honest conversation with her? Laid it all out there?

At least that way, everything is out in the open. If she doesn't feel the same—well, then I can move on. Right?

So, here I am, standing outside Dirty Books, and waiting for Lily to come out.

I need to talk to her. I need to feel everything out.

And if nothing else, I need to convince her to come back to work.

She's canceled on me three times now and I'm not gonna let there be a fourth. We have a job to do, and goddammit, we're going to do it together if I have my say.

If she doesn't feel the same way about me, then I'll find a way to convince Lily that what happened—*what nearly happened*—will never happen again.

I flit my gaze between the two storefronts, wishing Quinn was working tonight. Instead, I was told he had the night off again.

So, instead of having someone to banter with and take my mind off the ridiculous level of jitters I've got about standing here, I'm stuck in my head and counting the seconds.

If Cal knew what I was about to do, he'd have one hell of a field day. He knew before I did how much I liked Lily.

I run my hand down my face just as the door to Dirty Books opens and five tipsy women barrel out.

Standing up straight, I push off my vehicle and lock eyes with Lily, acutely aware of the fact that I don't have Quinn as a buffer this time.

Her eyes betray a quiet turmoil, making my chest feel like it's been taken over by an enthusiastic woodpecker.

She's dressed in a pair of faded denim jeans that hug her form just right. However, it's her maroon shirt that captures my attention. With her hair up in a ponytail, the neckline invites the gaze, while concealing as much as it reveals.

God, she looks good.

I take a deep breath. It's now or never.

"Lily, do you have a second?" I ask, making my way to her.

The rest of the group huddles around her, all eyes on me.

"Lookie who's here, Flower. It's tall, dark, and gorgeous," Veronica—*no, Vivian*—croons, eyeing me up and down like I'm a Porterhouse steak.

I shift uncomfortably.

The Korean woman—can't remember her name— jabs Vivian in the stomach with her elbow.

"London—" Lily says, her mouth slightly agape. "What are you … ?"

Her question lingers between us as I glance around the group of women.

I tip my head toward the other end of the street. "Care to join me for a sec?"

Tasia turns to Lily. "Do you want me to come with you?"

"No, it's fine." Lily's exhale makes her shoulders drop and my heart goes right along with it.

Something's not right.

I can feel it.

Whatever it is, it isn't going to be good news.

As Lily steps toward me, the four remaining women huddle together, all eyes on the two of us, as we walk down the sidewalk toward the corner of the block.

When we reach the end, I turn to face her. The turmoil in her eyes carries a hint of curiosity now.

I clear my throat. "Lily, I—" Blinking rapidly, I try to grab hold of the words that will help her understand how I'm feeling.

I don't want there to be confusion—or weird vibes. I want us to be on the same page.

She shakes her head. "London, I'm sorry. It's been a difficult week. I know I should have talked to you sooner. Things have been weird and I just didn't know how to bring it up. Then, when I didn't bring it up, it made it harder to say anything at all. You know?"

Confusion clouds my mind and I hope she's not upset at me. "Bring what up?"

Lily glances down, some strands of her hair falling in front of her face in the motion. After a moment, she glances back up and levels her stare on a long exhale. "My husband, Seth, is back home. He took a job in Duluth to be closer—*to me.*"

Understanding kicks me straight in the balls.

The distance she put between us this week wasn't about the near kiss.

It's about the heart of her marriage.

She wants to be with him. And now he's back.

"Fuck, Lily, that's great," I sputter, trying to muster up the energy to be happy for her.

She narrows her eyes, watching me for a moment.

Reaching out, I plant my hands on her shoulders and pull her in for a quick hug. I want it to speak for me so she knows I get where her priorities are, despite wanting to dig a hole and hide myself in it.

She hugs me back.

See, nothing weird here.

Totally friend zone. I'm cool with it.

Only, my body doesn't get the memo and things stir below the belt the second she settles her body against my chest.

With a sharp inhale, I release her and take a step back.

Space—*space is good.*

Her eyebrows are still knit together when I chance a glance in her direction.

She doesn't look happy. Not at all.

"What's wrong?" I ask, suddenly concerned.

"You're okay with it?" Her voice is strained and her words come out slowly, tentatively.

I nod, then swallow hard. "Of course. I'm sure it wasn't easy having him travel so much."

"It wasn't," she whispers, her gaze dropping to the ground.

"Well, I can see why you've needed to take some time the past few days," I say, pulling on the back of my neck. My face heats and my jaw clenches.

Of course. She's been *busy* with *her husband.*

Jealousy courses through my veins, the intensity of it taking me by total surprise.

Though *why* it's a surprise is beyond me.

Hell, I should get my head checked out. I've clearly lost it.

Yes, London. They've been ... *catching up.*

Get with the program.

I try desperately not to think about all the times they've had sex in the past three days, but my stomach bottoms out despite myself.

"You know, I'm glad that's all it was. I was worried you—" I shake my head. "You know what, never mind. Glad it's all good. I'm gonna—" I point to my truck.

Without saying anything else, I stalk toward my vehicle in a total daze.

Her husband is back.

She's been with him all week.

Him.

While I knew she was married, there was something about the fact that he hardly even lived with her that made him feel like he wasn't real. That's stupid, I know.

I feel all eyes on me as I walk to my vehicle, but all I can think about is how I need to get away. Far, *far* away.

I need to sort myself out and I can't do it here.

"London," Lily calls out.

I halt in mid-stride and turn to face her, trying to plaster on a sincere smile.

She levels me with a look. "I'll see you tomorrow. At Nocté."

I fight back the sharp inhalation of relief that claws its way through my lungs. Then, I force a smile, tip my head in acknowledgment, and finish walking to my truck.

In my rearview mirror, I watch Lily walk back to the others as I drive off.

Then, I drive on autopilot, refusing to think—or hell, breathe. Instead, I go numb.

What did I expect to happen?

She's married. Of course, she'll be with her husband.

It's not like I have some sort of claim on her, just because I saw her first.

"Fuck," I ground out, slamming my hand on the steering wheel.

For a brief moment, I entertained the notion of telling her how I was feeling just in case she might be feeling the same. I knew I should have gone with my first instinct.

I should have stuffed this all down and let it lie.

Goddamn Myles and her stupid ideas.

I knew better.

When I pull into Nocté, I shut my Escalade off and sit there, staring out the window for what feels like forever.

The parking lot is packed and the music from inside can be felt even from here.

What in the hell am I going to do?

I shake my head and pinch the bridge of my nose.

I'm gonna do the only *thing I can do. I'm going to be her friend.*

That's what she wants—what she needs.

And I'd rather have her as a friend than not at all.

Rolling my eyes at myself, I shut off the truck and get out. There's no sign of Cal, but I'm sure he's here somewhere, watching.

He better damn well see the look on my face and know to stay away.

When I open the back door and walk inside, the music blares and the base rattles the walls.

There was a time when I loved the nightlife. I loved the sound of the club.

Tonight is not one of those times.

I just want to go home and figure out a game plan for how I'm going to deal with tomorrow.

At this point, Myles will be knee-deep in slinging drinks and Cal will be coordinating with the rest of his security team. So, I slip quietly into my office and close the door.

Then, I flip the fucking lock.

Leaning forward, my forehead thumps against the door.

What a shitshow.

Somehow, I've got to convince Lily I can do this. I can be just friends with her—even if that's the last thing I actually want.

Suddenly, an idea pops into my head.

I grab my phone and without questioning it, I type out a message. It's stupid, but it might just do the trick to ease the tension and show her I'm all in as friends.

Before I can talk myself out of it, I hit send.

Then, I hold my breath, waiting to see what she'll do with that.

CHAPTER 18

Lily

I tip my Uber driver and meander to my back door, slightly tipsy and insanely frustrated.

How did I read London so wrong?

I was so sure there was something ... I mean, we almost kissed. Didn't we?

Tears prick in my eyes and I blink them away, angry at their existence.

This is so stupid.

I shouldn't be upset that he's happy for me that my husband is back and he's here to stay. Hell, *I* should be happy for me.

But I'm not.

This is so many shades of fucked up.

As I walk through the house, it's clear Seth isn't home yet. All of the lights are off and the house is quiet. It's the vibe of the home I've come to know—and nothing like the strange energy it's taken on since Monday.

Wandering aimlessly, I end up sitting on my couch in the dark. I can't even be bothered to turn any lights on for fear their light will shed more judgment on me.

Suddenly, my phone buzzes in my pocket.

Sighing heavily, I tug it out, expecting to see another text from Tasia. She's made it her mission to stick her nose in my business.

Instead, it's a text from London.

My heart rate picks up and I shift on the couch so I'm sitting upright. With my index finger hovering over the notification, I steel myself.

What could he want?

Is it about work? Is he telling me not to bother coming tomorrow?

God, I hope not.

My ribs feel like they're collapsing with the thought that he doesn't want me back.

Quickly, I tap on the notification. My facial recognition unlocks the phone and I stare at his message.

> Sock puppets are an underrated art form.

I blink a few times and read it over and over.

It's the most random text I've ever received in my life and I don't even know what to do with it. So, naturally, I have to respond.

> Uhm, okay?

Almost instantly, the dots dance across my screen as

he types his response. I lean back, waiting. A confused, lopsided grin floats to my face as his next text comes in.

> I saw a sock puppet in a store today and it made me think of the legendary performances we put on as kids.
> Thought you should know.

I pull my feet up on the couch, tucking them beside me as I type back.

> Legendary? You and I remember them very differently. :P

When we were seven, London and I started putting on short sock puppet shows for our parents. I have no idea which one of us started them—*probably him.*

However, if there's one thing I've come to understand by attending a weekly book club, it's how story structure works. London and I had no clue how to create a cohesive story when we put those shows on.

Naturally, our parents thought they were the funniest things ever. So they became a weekly occurrence for a while.

> Come on. They were epic. Ooohhh…
> Should we add a sock puppet show
> to our event? LOL!

Relief floods through me. He still expects me there tomorrow. Shaking my head, I giggle out loud. Then, type back quickly.

> Oh, yeah. That's definitely what we
> need to get everyone in the mood.

His response dots appear, then vanish.

My eyebrows tug in as I watch the screen, waiting for him to continue typing.

When they start and stop again, my insides feel like a live wire.

Did I say something wrong?

I go back and reread the messages. They were all fun and light-hearted until I brought up the reason for the event.

Way to go, Lily.

I swallow hard, wondering if I should text him again to try to diffuse the tension. If I was reading him wrong, then he's probably trying not to lead me on.

Stupid.

"What are you doing in the dark?"

I yelp, throwing my phone over my shoulder. It bounces off the wall and ricochets off my ankle before landing face-up on the floor.

"Dammit," I mutter, groping my ankle with one hand and a fistful of my shirt above my heart with the other. My eyes sting with the sharp pain that shoots up my leg.

Seth chuckles from the doorway. "Dang, I wish I'd been recording that. It would have made a great TikTok."

I narrow my eyes and glare at him. The throbbing in my ankle is anything but funny at the moment.

He shakes his head. "Sorry, I thought you heard me come in. I was talking to you from the kitchen."

I blink at him, still holding tightly to my ankle. "No, I didn't."

My phone lights up and buzzes with an incoming text. Swallowing hard, I glance at it and back to Seth.

"Do you need to get that?" he asks, tipping his chin to my phone.

I shake my head, feeling the roar of my pulse in my ears. "No."

Get it together, Lily. There's nothing wrong with what you were doing. You were just talking to your old friend about sock puppets. No funny business there.

I reach down, snatch my phone from the floor, and set it face down on the coffee table in front of me.

Seth shrugs it off. "Okay, well ... I'm going to take a quick shower and get to bed. I have to meet my boss early in the morning to go over this laser tag article and get my next assignment."

"Oh, okay." I nod, relieved. "I'll be there soon."

"Okay," he says, laughing under his breath as he turns and makes his way to our bedroom.

I lean back, pressing my body into the couch cushions. My eyes drift closed as I take a deep breath to steady my nerves. The dull thud in my ankle reminds me of my phone and the fact that London's text finally came through.

The sound of the shower running gives me the nerve to lean forward and pick up my phone again.

I tap on his message and glance around quickly before taking a peek.

> *gasp* Lily, are you saying my sock puppet renditions aren't sexy?

My eyelids slam shut as another laugh bursts from me. I can honestly say the *last thing* his sock puppet performances conjure in my mind is sexiness.

I type back.

> Definitely not. LOL! Where's your head, man?

He types back quickly—no delay this time.

> How would I know? But if you find it, can you send it back?

Smiling now, I type back.

> *packages head with terrible idea & ships it to London*

I giggle into my hand, trying not to be too loud. The shower has shut off and I'm pretty sure Seth has gone to bed.

> Well, shit. That was brutal, Lily. Here I thought it could bring something old-school to the event.

I shake my head.

> I think we need to stick with what we've already planned. ;)

Suit yourself. *shrugs*

> Are you pouting?

wipes tear away No.

> *rolls eyes*

LMAO

I laugh, feeling so much lighter than I have for ages. It's so easy to talk to London this way. So, I tell him.

> It's weird. It feels like I've known you forever.

Lily, you *have* known me forever.

> You know what I mean. :P

Not really.

I suck in a breath and try to release some of the tension from my shoulders.

> I mean, I don't know much about you now. But it still feels like I do. I should stalk your social media so I can get more grounded.

No researching me.

My mouth pops open. *Rude.*

Why not?

You might not like what you find.

raises eyebrow slowly Oh, really?
Are there bodies buried somewhere?

Erm… No comment.

Pft.

Ah, hell. You're not getting any more
than that, Sherlock.

We'll see. *raises eyebrow and cracks
knuckles*

All this eyebrow-raising and you
haven't even said which one. I can't
visualize properly.

It's more mischievous not knowing.

Hmmm. It must be the left one,
then. LOL!

You might be right.

Most people can't raise their right
eyebrow properly. So, I'll take my
chances with the left.

I can technically do both. *switches*

As if he can see me, I switch which eyebrow I'm
arching back and forth like a wave.

That's not fair. I can only do the left
with a little arch on the right.

If you could see me, you'd be
laughing. I'm trying to get my right
eyebrow to arch. Instead, I'm cursing
your name.

Bwahahaa! I wish I could see that!

In the words of a Goddess friend of
mine, "Pft."

I stare at the word for far too long. *Goddess.*
Not just friend. *Goddess.*
I swallow hard and type back so it doesn't seem like
I'm hung up on his words.

LOL! Are you picking on me, sir?

Oooh, didn't know there was any
other way to be? *raises devilish
eyebrow*

narrows eyes Hmph.

An epic rebuttal. *raises eyebrow &
slow claps*

Eyebrows are my thing. You find your
own, dammit. :P

I glance at the clock on my phone and my jaw drops open. I've been sitting here texting for the past couple of *hours*. It felt like minutes.

Also… Holy crap! It's after one in the
morning. As much fun as this is, I
think we better go to bed.

Why?

pointed stare Sleep.

Sleep? What is this you speak of?

It's this newfangled thing where
everyone goes unconscious for like,
eight hours, or something. It's all the
rage.

Eight hours!? WTH?

shrugs So I hear.

I don't believe it. But I'll let you get to
it. ;)

Okay. Night, London.

Night, Lily. <3

I stare at the way he signed off, trying not to read too much into things. But I can't help it.

He used a heart.

My own stupid heart trips over itself.

As I exit our conversation, I find myself over on Facebook, searching his name. There's a profile on there that seems like it might be his, but there are no pictures of him that are public, so it's hard to tell. The main profile picture is just a telescope.

I make note of the profile name: LondonStJames94. Then, I head over to Instagram and type it in.

The same profile image is there, too. However, the profile has a few public pictures.

One by one, I scroll through them, trying to figure out if the profile is his. The most recent images are night shots. Images of the moon, stars, and the Northern Lights.

Then, I lock in on one that triggers a smile.

It's a picture of Myles sticking out her tongue at the camera. Her hair is bright pink and longer than it is now.

Bingo.

I continue scrolling through the images, stopping on one of London and the waitress—Rebecca? They're in a booth somewhere. A restaurant, maybe?

He's smiling at the camera but there's something off about it. Like it doesn't quite reach his eyes.

Rebecca, on the other hand, is dressed in a black tank

top that accentuates her white skin as her ample cleavage pops and her boobs practically spill out of it.

I open the image and read the caption.

"Date night with my girl."

Jealousy sweeps through me when I realize they were an item.

The date on the photo is from five months ago. With the way he treated her the other day, I doubt they're still a thing. However, that doesn't stop me from tapping her tagged name and hopping over to her profile.

Hers is a billboard of bimbo. It's nothing but boob shots and duck faces.

I shudder, but obsessively continue to scroll, searching for any evidence of London on her timeline.

She posts much more frequently than London, so I have to scroll a bit before I stumble on something that makes me stop in my tracks.

London is laying on what looks like to be a bed. He's totally shirtless, and his left arm is raised up and over his eyes, like he's embarrassed by the photo. Or doesn't want any one to know it's him.

But I'd know that smile anywhere now.

While the question of why he's half-naked in a photo of hers makes my skin crawl, my eyes zero in on his muscular chest.

I know he has tattoos now—tattoos I would love to know the meaning of. But this newly discovered one makes my breath catch in my throat.

Tattooed right over his heart is a single flower.

A lily set in stars.

My mouth goes dry and I blink back tears.

Pressing my hand to my mouth, I click off the phone. For the longest time, I sit there in the dark with the image of his tattoo burned into my retinas.

So many questions float through my mind like it has a revolving door.

What does it mean?

Am I reading too much into this?

Why a lily if not for me?

Lost in a daze, I finally untangle my legs and walk to my bedroom. It's only when I get to the edge of the bed and hear his soft snores that I remember Seth is home.

Undressing and putting on my full set of pajamas, I slip into bed as quietly as I can, staying as far to my side as possible.

God, I'm in so much trouble.

CHAPTER 19

London

"Take it the fuck down," I ground out through clenched teeth. *"Now."*

Rebecca flinches slightly at the venom in my words. I'd feel bad if it wasn't the third time I've asked her to remove the shirtless photo of me from her Instagram feed.

Until now, there wasn't any sort of urgency but the last thing I want is for Lily to stumble on it.

She'll freak out.

As it is, it's taken four days just to get her back to work after the almost-kiss and her husband coming home.

The last thing I want is to push her away again because I have a tattoo symbolizing our connection.

Christ. That's something she definitely doesn't need to know about. Hell, I'm just glad I noticed the photo, so I could scrub it before she has a chance to find it.

After last night's late-night texting conversation with

Lily, I did a sweep of my social media platforms. Just in case she decided to do some sleuthing. There were two posts with ex-girlfriends on my feeds—both of which have been deleted.

That's how I found out Rebecca still hadn't taken down the image she took the night we broke up.

God, I was so fed up with her shit that evening. She came over to try to salvage things but I just wanted to be left the fuck alone. I had closed the door in her face and laid down on my bed, only to realize she'd followed me and snapped the photo.

She said it was so she could remember me. Then I found it on her Insta feed like we'd had a romp that evening and I was post-sex happy or some shit.

Please, as if that woman could draw out any kind of happiness. Post-sex or not.

When she still hasn't made a move to grab her phone, I widen my eyes and spit out, "You know what? You're fired."

That startles her more than my tone.

"What? Why?" she gasps.

"Sexual harassment. You never got permission to post that image and I've repeatedly asked you to remove it," I fire back. I'm not in the mood to play games or deal with her constant innuendos. I've let that go on long enough because I felt sorry for her.

She yanks her phone from her back pocket, scrolling through her Insta feed until she gets to the image in question. Her finger hovers over the delete button when she turns it to me.

"Fine. Here," she says, tapping the screen.

The image vanishes, so I pull out my phone and double-check that it's no longer there.

It's not.

"About fuckin' time. Now, get the hell out of here," I growl, turning to leave.

"Wait—" she calls after me. "You're not serious. You're firing me? I did what you asked."

I spin on her, getting right into her space. "You should have done it the first fuckin' time, Rebecca. I want you out of this club. Why I've dealt with your shit as long as I have is beyond me. You're lucky I don't send this up to Noah."

Fear strikes her eyes and she takes a step back, pouting.

I don't care, though. I just don't have it in me.

So, I turn away from her and head to my office to cool down.

Honestly, I'm not even really all that pissed that it took this long. I'm more upset that Lily could have stumbled on it.

I sit down at my desk and rest my face in my hands.

"Well, that was quite the show."

I glance up to see Myles in the doorway. Her arms are crossed as she leans against the frame.

"Don't start," I warn.

She holds up her hands. "Hey, it's about time you kicked her ass out. I'm just wondering what the catalyst was."

I shoot her another annoyed look, but Myles being

Myles, she doesn't read the room. She walks in and takes a seat.

"Don't you have work to do?" I ask, fully aware my tone is anything but friendly right now.

"Are you kidding? With her on the rampage before she leaves? Hell no. If you get to hide, so do I," Myles retorts, crossing her left ankle over her right knee as she leans back.

"Why are we hiding?" Cal questions, slinking into the room and taking the seat beside Myles.

"Christ," I look to the ceiling and mutter under my breath.

Myles jabs a thumb in my direction. "Saint here finally gave Rebecca the ol' heave-ho. Emphasis on the *ho.*"

My expression deadpans when I glance in her direction.

"About damn time." Cal laughs. "If I had to watch her batting her heart eyes at you much longer, I was gonna have to invest in barf bags."

"Nice," I say, making a face and flicking him off.

Myles reaches out and taps Cal's forearm. "I'm trying to get him to admit that his feelings for Lily finally got him to boot her out. Wanna help?"

Cal leans forward and places his elbows on his knees. "Is that so?"

Deny.

Deny.

Deny.

I shake my head. "Psh. Nah, that's not it. You're both *way* off base."

"What is it then, pray tell?" Myles asks, folding her hands over her knee and giving me a smug-as-hell grin.

"If you must know," I begin, raising my eyebrows, "she took a photo of me shirtless and posted it on her Insta feed without permission. I've asked her numerous times to take it down and she still hadn't done it. I was fed up."

Myles' eyes are about to bug out of her head.

Gotta admit that makes me feel kinda powerful.

Yeah, lose that smug grin, lady.

Men are sexually harassed, too.

"Wow," Myles sputters. "I thought for sure it was about ..."

Cal holds up a hand, forcing Myles to stop talking. "Hang the fuck on."

I narrow my eyes. *Shit.* This isn't gonna be good.

Myles turns to him, her expression full of expectation.

The bastard that he is, Cal just leans back and grins, eyeing me the entire time. "So, you're saying you *just so happened* to be flitting through your ex's Insta feed and realized this?"

"I knew that she ..." I scratch the back of my head. "I mean, I was kinda ..."

As if in slow motion, Myles turns to face me, total recognition dawning in her damn different-colored eyes. "You were scrubbing social feeds." Her mouth pops open as humor glints in her eyes. Then she points forcefully at me and barks out a laugh. "I fucking *knew* it."

I itch the side of my nose. "After all of the shit she's been pulling, it was time."

"Bullshit," Cal snickers.

"It had nothing to do with L—"

A knock on my door frame pulls my attention and the brown eyes peering back at me makes my stomach flip flop.

I stand all too quickly and finish my sentence as if I intended to greet her all along, *"Lily."*

Cal and Myles also turn around to view the visitor in the doorway.

"Rebecca let me in," she says looking extremely uncomfortable as she glances around the room. "Is—I hope that's okay?"

"Oh, yeah. Sure," I say, shaking my head 'no' even though I'm saying yes.

What the hell kind of mixed signal is that?

I itch at my temple.

Fuck, tell me she didn't hear any of that previous shit.

"Well, I guess that's our cue," Cal says, nudging Myles on the shoulder.

"Looks like," Myles chirps, dropping her foot and slapping her thighs before standing up.

"I didn't mean to scare you two off," Lily says, taking a step into the hallway.

"Nah, I gotta get back to work," Myles responds,

slapping Lily on the shoulder. "If Rebecca let you in, it means the coast is clear."

She continues down the hallway without even a second glance in my direction. *Thank fuck.*

Cal, on the other hand, jabs his index and middle finger toward his eyes, then twists his wrist to point them at me.

He's watching me.

Message received.

Fucksake.

Once he's fucked off, I walk around my desk and point to one of the vacated seats and point. Then I lean against my desk and cross my ankles.

See? Relaxed. *Totally cool.*

Lily grins softly, clutching her briefcase to her chest like a shield. Tentatively, she walks into the room and takes the seat closest to me.

"So," she begins, dropping her briefcase to her lap.

"So," I repeat. This is almost becoming our thing.

She inhales a deep breath and bites the side of her lip.

The movement draws my attention to her mouth.

Her plump lips flash with color and look insanely kissable.

Shit.

Clearing my throat, I opt to take a seat on the other side of the desk.

When there's a desk between us, she sighs and opens her briefcase. "I know I've been MIA. I'm really sorry about that, London. I know I should have—"

I hold up a hand and cut her off. "Don't. It's not necessary, Lily."

She shoots me a look that says she disagrees. "At any rate, I don't want you to think I completely blew you off." Her forehead scrunches together and she shakes her head.

What was that all about?

Before I can ask, she continues, "A-anyway, I've been contacting my vendors, getting quotes for the event. I think you'll be really pleased."

She clicks open her briefcase and pulls out a stack of papers. Then, she closes the case, setting it on the seat beside her.

"What's this?" I ask as she hands the papers to me.

"The quotes."

Of course.

I set them on the desk and pick up the first one. It's a quote for the food—and it's coming in well under budget.

"Nice," I say, setting it aside and shuffling through the others.

Every single one of them is coming in under budget. Not just slightly, either. Somehow, she's managed to plan it all for thousands less than anticipated.

She's a goddamn miracle worker.

Noah's going to be impressed.

"These are awesome, Lily. How did you do this?" I ask, my surprise and awe hard to hide.

She runs her hand over the back of her neck. "I know

a lot of people in this business. I just pulled in some favors."

My eyebrows pull in. "Favors?"

She giggles. "Nothing nefarious."

I narrow my eyes.

"Seriously. I use their services frequently. It's more of a loyalty discount than anything," she says, picking at her nails.

"Well, shit, this is—" I say, shaking my head. "Noah's gonna love you."

She beams back at me and relief washes over her stance as her shoulders drop. "You think? I was really worried that my absence this week was—"

I stand again, setting the papers on my desk. "No, he's going to be thrilled. Really, what you've done here is impressive."

Everything inside me is screaming at me to walk around the desk and hug her. Let her know Noah's not the only one who's grateful.

I am too. She's saving my ass with this one.

Lily grins, pressing her hands between her knees. "Good. I was worried I messed things up."

"You should never have been worried. I knew we'd manage. But this"—I tap the papers—"this puts us steps ahead."

"It does?"

I nod. "Of course. We can skip ahead to getting everyone on board."

"Are you sure? I mean, I can get more quotes so you can compare and contrast—"

That does it.

I walk around the desk and stand in front of her. "Lily, I trust your judgment here. If you're happy going with these vendors, then so am I."

A beautiful shade of pink floods her cheeks. "Oh," she breathes.

"So, now that we have all of that settled, what else do we need?" I ask, needing to redirect the energy a bit because it's suddenly very charged.

Does she notice it, too?

Her forehead crinkles as she thinks. "I mean, not really. We have the theme and with the vendors in place, it's really all I need. Although, I wish—"

She twists her lips to the side, the rest of her sentence held hostage.

"You wish?" I prod, wanting desperately to know what she wants.

After a few moments, she exhales. "I really want to impress the Upper Tier—and obviously you and Noah. I wish I knew what they're already used to experiencing. You know? Like, what do they already enjoy and how can we next level it?"

Again, her cheeks flush. My eyes flit to the way her chest rises and falls—like she's nervous and excited at the prospect.

"Tonight's Friday, you know," I say before I can stop myself.

Danger.

Danger.

She narrows her eyes and then her eyebrows tip up in the middle. "I mean, I'm aware. What's that got to—"

"Wanna see what a normal night in the Upper Tier is like?" I ask, my heart hammering in my chest.

I shouldn't be doing this, but hell, I'm gonna anyway.

I want to see how she responds to the Upper Tier.

"What?" she asks, breathlessly. Her cheeks flush and her eyes sparkle with excitement. "You mean ... While they're—" She points upward.

The way her voice squeaks is so damn cute.

Getting her flustered just might be my new favorite pastime.

Smirking, I shrug. "Yeah, why not? Consider it research." I reach out for her hand. "Come on."

CHAPTER 20

Lily

"I sn't it a little early?" I ask, my voice a hushed whisper as we walk down the hallway toward the club's dance floor. My heart is thumping hard and I'm fairly certain it's about to flutter away.

I want to understand how the club works by seeing it in action—but for some reason, seeing how it works also makes me incredibly nervous.

Well, that, and having London be the one to show me.

He checks his watch. "Nope."

Confused, I bite down on the side of my lip. He notices and stops walking to turn to face me.

"Do you remember what it looked like upstairs?" he asks, quirking an eyebrow.

Taking a deep breath, I nod, but that doesn't help ease the confusion.

"There are no clear rules for when the Upper Tier can use the space. That was deliberate. While yes, the majority of them come later in the evening, there are a few who like their afternoons ..." he offers, shooting me a knowing look. "Fridays are a favorite."

I can't help it, I shake my head. "It seems so weird. Like dirty deeds should be done under the cover of night or something." Heat rushes to my cheeks and I glance down.

"There aren't any windows upstairs, Lily," he says quietly. "It's perpetual evening up there."

My eyes widen and I raise my eyes to his. "Oh, right. I totally forgot about that."

London laughs, grabbing hold of my hand and tugging me along behind him. Surprised by the sudden contact, I stare at the way our hands are joined. Butter-flies erupt in my belly, yet, for the life of me, I can't bring myself to let go. Instead, a part of me actually revels in it.

"While it's not a big deal for *this* event, knowing how some of them use the space might end up being an important fact to remember. Especially if you help us host another event down the road," he says over his shoulder as he drops my hand and enters the main dance club area.

"Right, right," I mutter, surprised by the sudden sense of loss when his hand is no longer connected to mine.

The DJ is on the stage, getting ready for the night and I wave as we walk past. He smiles back and waves in return. We haven't been introduced yet, but I make a mental note to do so when I have the chance.

"What are you two up to?" Myles calls out from across the bar.

"Research," London responds without even glancing her direction.

His rushed pace makes me wonder if he's nervous or excited to show me how things work.

Does he think this is weird? Is he just trying to get it over with?

"Is there a theme today?" I ask, trying to keep my mind off of what we might see when we get upstairs.

"What do you mean?" he asks, turning a quizzical expression in my direction.

"Like, does the Upper Tier just come in and see who else is there? Or are there rules to when they come in and how they behave?" I ask, searching his eyes for some clue on how he's feeling.

A lopsided grin appears on his face. "There are basic guidelines. Food and drinks will be available anytime after noon. The rooms are all open for use—unless a door is closed. Then that one is off-limits. However, if it's left open and someone's in there, others are free to join in."

"Join in," I blurt out. Again, heat rushes to my cheeks and I pat them down.

London smirks. "Yeah."

Breathing out, I fan my face and nod without another word.

No words necessary.

Hell, I don't know if I could find words anyway.

"Unless there's a planned event, which isn't often,

the only rule is the one you already know. They get *one night*. If any of the participants want a second one with a specific person, they're free to explore a relationship outside of the Upper Tier," he says, scanning his security card and punching the button on the elevator to go up.

"What's with that rule?" I ask, unable to help myself. "You'd think if you want more engagement, you'd just let them—" I can't bring myself to finish my thought.

He shrugs. "Truthfully, I don't know why Noah has that rule. He's not overly forthcoming about his reasons behind Nocté."

I let that sink in for a moment, then nod.

The doors to the elevator ding open and London holds them for me to go first. When I'm inside, he follows after and presses the button for the next floor up.

"If everything's open by noon upstairs—how does the Upper Tier get in there? Aren't the doors to this area closed until after five?" I ask, circling my pointer finger around the space.

"There's a door on the outside. In fact, that's the only way the Upper Tier can get in," he responds, turning to face me. "This elevator is for staff only."

"Oh," I breathe, the wheels in my head turning.

"Come to think of it, I'll need to get you a badge with RF access," he says, pulling on the one dangling from his neck by a lanyard with a small bungee cord.

As the doors to the elevator start to close, I hold out my hand to keep them open.

"Can you show me? The Upper Tier entrance, that is. I'd

like to experience it the way they would. It will help me figure out the best way to cater the experience," I murmur, excited to view things in the way a newly invited person might.

His eyes search mine for a moment and he shrugs. "Sure."

He reaches out, holding the doors and ushering me through. Rather than head in the direction of Myles and the bar, he takes me through a side door that opens to the outdoors, and a portion of the parking lot.

The sun is setting and the air is cooling now that evening approaches.

We follow a sidewalk around to the back of the building. If I wasn't following him, I wouldn't even think there was an entrance back here. The sidewalk is unkept with weeds growing up through the cracks. There are no flowers or gardens, or anything enticing me toward an exclusive club entrance.

I make a note to fix this before our event.

When we round the corner, the back of the building faces a grove of trees that separates Nocté from other businesses and provides a little bit of cover.

Unfortunately, the door is also extremely boring. It's just a metal door to the back of the building. It almost blends in.

I shake my head. *No, this won't do.*

London reaches out with his keycard and the lock to the door clicks back. He reaches out, opening it for me as he points to the staircase inside. "Head on up."

My eyebrows raise. "This is it?"

London's face falters as if he's trying to decide if I'm being serious.

"This is a sad entrance, London." I take a step inside, peering up the metal stairs and gray walls that have been scuffed—most likely from drunken escapades. It's absolutely the most boring welcome ever.

"It's not where the magic happens," he counters.

I deadpan when I turn to face him. "I know that, but first impressions matter. This impression is terrible. We're going to have to fix it."

He chuckles. "Well, you have plenty of room in the budget now. I'm sure we can come up with something."

I nod. "You're damn straight. This is ..." I shake my head, "*sad*. Just sad."

"Glad we have that decided. Now, if you'd like to continue," he suggests, pointing up the stairs.

I sigh, setting off up the stairs with our footsteps echoing off the bare walls. "No music, either? Nothing playing as they enter this new space to set the ambiance? I mean, it's almost as if a guy got this whole thing started."

"A guy did." He laughs.

When we reach the top landing, I still can't believe how terrible this impression is. "I know, but we can do better."

He tips his head and grins. "I look forward to it."

The door at the top of the landing isn't locked, so he reaches out and simply opens it. I walk through, taking in the way the space invites a person to continue deeper into the area.

There are large, sweeping red curtains that drape

from floor to ceiling, almost as if we're entering a circus tent. The lighting is dramatic, just like the main hallways of the space and the other areas I've already seen.

"Well, this is better," I say, walking beyond the curtains into the area I'm already familiar with. I'm already calculating where I'll put the flowers and plants and hide some speakers.

"So, we meet your standards once we get into the space. Good to know," London teases.

I turn on my heel. "You already know I like this space. But wow—" I shake my head. "*Terrible.*"

A lopsided grin lights up London's face and it takes my breath away. My eyes travel to his chest, where I know his tattoo is, and I divert my gaze by spinning around. "So, uh—it's kind of quiet in here."

There really should be some background music playing to set the mood throughout the whole space. No wonder people aren't as engaged as they could be.

"Yeah, it is," he agrees, tilting his head, listening. "Come on. We'll check things out. Just stay close. It'll be best to stick to the sidelines. If people are here, you won't want to inadvertently get mixed up in the festivities."

He starts walking toward the main hallway.

My eyes widen as I follow him. "Yeah, no. That would be ..."

I mean, I want to see how things work, but I sorta don't know how to, either. Like, how do you witness something like that without being a total creep? And I certainly don't want to inadvertently get mixed up in things.

"Normally there is staff up here. I'll have to check with Cal. We should have at least one from his security team, as well as the servers. They must be in the kitchen since it's so quiet," he says, tipping his head that direction.

"See, I told you. Too early." I grin sheepishly.

He stops walking and narrows his gaze. "I'm sure that's not it. Besides, I got a notification that someone had arrived on the security app. They must be in a closed room."

"Isn't there, I don't know, a hidden room or something where we can see things from a distance?" I ask, running my hand along the back of my neck. "You know, without interrupting anything?"

His eyebrows lower as he spins to look at me. "That would be illegal, Lily."

"Oh, right." I shake my head, embarrassed. "I'm just—"

"I know. It's weird," he says, wincing slightly.

"Kinda, yeah."

He glances down the hallway.

"Well, it looks like whoever's here has their door closed." He points to the end of the hallway where one of the doors is shut.

We turn and start heading back the way we came. Truthfully, I'm kind of relieved. I don't think I was mentally prepared for what I might be shown anyway.

When we make it back to the intimate dining area, I turn to him and say, "Well, I don't know if I should be disappointed or—"

I don't even get the rest of my sentence out before a naked woman runs past us, squealing in what I can only assume is delight. I double-take, noticing she's got a long, furry tail hanging off her backside, but for the life of me, I have no idea how.

She takes up residence in the living room area, directly across from us, without a care in the world. It's like we're not even there.

London, however, moves quickly, boxing me up against the wall as he presses in close. "Here's your chance. But since you don't have a badge letting the participants know you're part of the staff, I suggest you pretend you're with me."

"Wh—what?" I sputter, unable to remove my eyes from the woman as she bends over the arm of one of the couches.

Suddenly, a burly, naked man wearing a mask—it's an animal of some kind, but I have no idea what kind in the low light—stalks toward her like he's on the hunt. He's built and he knows it, as he prowls forward slowly, his eyes never straying from her backside.

My eyes widen when I realize his massive erection is glistening in the low accent lighting—clearly having already seen some action.

"Holy shit," I breathe, unable to tear my eyes away.

"Put your hands on my back," London commands, his voice low and urgent.

Doing as he says, I put my hands on his back, tugging on his shirt and bringing him even closer. The proximity to him makes my head spin and the intensity of his cologne doesn't help one bit.

Add on top the sight in front of me, and I'm all kinds of messed up as my pulse skyrockets and my libido kicks in.

I shouldn't like this—I shouldn't want to see more.

I shouldn't enjoy having London this close.

Yet, here I am.

London lifts his left hand to the side of my face, pressing in close so I can look over his shoulder.

With his lips under my left ear, he whispers, "Get a good look now. When they've engrossed in the act, we'll slip out. Trust me, you don't want to get cornered by Xavier. He'll assume you're new and he's running out of contenders."

I tear my gaze away, peering into London's serious gaze.

"He's been here a while," he whispers. "And he's persistent."

I shudder, returning my gaze to the scene in the room across from us. The woman is still bent over the couch, her legs spread as Xavier kneels between them. He flips her tail, so it rests up her back, then he smacks her ass, only to rub his hand over the mark.

After a few times doing this, he bends in, sweeping his tongue from her clit to the bottom of her tailpiece. She lets out a guttural sound that makes my legs weak.

"H—how does she have a tail?" I whisper, totally awestruck.

London swallows hard and his voice is slightly strangled when he says, "It's a butt plug, Lily."

His chest rises and falls and I can't help but notice how rigid he's gone.

Heat rushes from my core, across my chest, and up into my cheeks. "Oh."

I should know this…

Why didn't I know this?

Clearly, I'm going to have to have a word with Tasia.

Xavier's tongue goes to town on the woman and her moans are now so loud I'm actually turned on by them myself. It's clear, even from here, that Xavier knows exactly what he's doing to her and she's enjoying every minute of it as she plays with her breasts.

Then, as if I couldn't get more turned on, he reaches down and strokes his cock.

"I think we should go—" I say, diverting my gaze when Xavier stands up and positions himself at the woman's entrance.

Tears spring to my eyes and I try desperately to keep myself in check.

Between London's closeness, which is all kinds of confusing, and all that's happening a few feet away, the weight of my nonexistent sex life comes crashing down.

I've never had that kind of sex—let alone in a place like this.

How in the hell am I meant to create an event that will turn these people on when I'm so ridiculously inexperienced?

What the hell was I thinking?

CHAPTER 21

London

My head and body are spun into a whirlwind of confusion.

When Xavier and his conquest for the night came in, things got so sexually charged, that I thought for sure Lily would bolt.

Instead, she stayed.

I also thought for sure she'd notice the way my body had sprung to life.

Christ, I was so hard, it was painful.

It wasn't because of the others, though.

It was Lily.

The way she clung to my body after my command. The way her breath hitched and she took shallow sips of air as she watched them—like full-on *watched* them.

Christ, it was fucking hot.

Yeah, in that moment, I realized the stupidity of bringing her up here when she's off limits. I knew better, yet, like a complete moron, I did it anyway.

But then...

When tears filled her eyes, I knew I'd fucked up big time. *Again*.

Friends.

I swore I could just be *friends*.

Yeah, good luck with that.

Biggest lie ever told.

"I think we should go—" she whispered, her voice wavering.

That was all it took to break the spell.

Springing into action, I take her hand and guide her away from the action and to the staff elevator. She follows behind me, allowing me to hold her hand the way I had earlier—another stupid move, but I can't seem to help myself where she's concerned.

I can tell she wants to run—to get as far away from me and this situation as possible. So, when we're inside, I punch the button to go up one more level. I don't let go of her hand, either. Hell if I'm going to break that connection if she lets me do it.

As the elevator closes and starts its climb, she doesn't say anything. Instead, she clutches at the front of her shirt with her free hand, her breaths coming quick and fast.

"Lily," I whisper, turning to her.

The elevator doors ding open to the roof of the club. Streams of sunlight stretch across the sky as it sinks behind the trees, brightening the small enclosed space we're in.

She blinks back her tears and shields her eyes. "Where are we?"

I pull her over to the gas fire pit and the Adirondack chairs we sometimes use for breaks, or to get away from the commotion, and force her to sit. Then, I pull another chair around to face hers and take a seat.

"Are you okay?" I ask more urgently, ignoring her question, so I can focus on my bigger concern. She has a tendency to shut me out when she gets freaked and there's no damn way I'm letting that happen again.

She sighs heavily and raises her eyes to the sky. Her chin quivers and I reach out, tipping it back down so she has to look at me.

Her lips twist to the side and she shakes her head. "I was"—she swallows hard and levels a stare—"that was very *eye-opening,* London."

I breathe out, surprised by the relief that floods through me that she's opening up. "I'm sorry if that was out of line. I thought—"

"No, that's not ..." She shakes her head again. "I mean, it was an eyeful, that's for sure." With her right hand, she fans herself and blows out a puff of air. "It just made me realize I might not be the right person for this job."

Panic stabs me straight through the chest. I scoot to the edge of the chair until our legs touch, then I place my hands on top of her knees. "What are you talking about? Don't be ridiculous. You've been fantastic—"

She eyes me skeptically and the look is so painful it forces me to stop talking. Her jaw works back and forth and I can see the storm brewing in her eyes. She wants to open up more but she's not sure if she should.

Come on, Lily. You can trust me.

Holding my breath, I repeat it like a mantra in my head.

After a few moments, her gaze falls to where my hands rest on her knees and tears slip past her lids and streak her cheeks. "Things ... they haven't been great with Seth and—" A humorless laugh slips past her perfect lips.

I can't help it, I feel physically sick at the mention of her husband's name.

This is about him.

Of course, it should be. She misses him.

"I'm sorry, Lily," I whisper. It's all I can manage because the realization has sucker punched me and taken all the oxygen from my lungs.

She takes another deep breath and slowly releases it past her lips. Her gaze moves to the sunset as she rolls her teeth over her bottom lip. "He and I don't really... God, this is so embarrassing."

Watching her closely, I fight internally with myself. I want to be there for her, I really do. But I don't really want to hear about her relationship. Not when ...

Lily shakes her head and her eyes glisten when she locks them with mine. "I'm sure this is TMI, but I don't really have much of a sex life." She drops my gaze and winces. "Haven't for a long time. So, after witnessing all of that, I'm feeling very inadequate and naïve right now. How am I supposed to up the ante for the Upper Tier when they already operate on a completely different level?”

I blink hard and her words hit my chest like a bag of bricks.

She doesn’t have a sex life?

All I can think about is … *why?*

If she were mine, I’d have a hard time keeping my hands off of her.

Hell, I’m having a hard time with that now.

“Lily,” I begin, trying to keep my tone level and my feelings out of it. “You don’t have to be on the same level as the Upper Tier to plan a great event.”

She shoots me a *get-real* expression. “I didn’t even know what that tail was all about—and my *best friend* owns an adult toy shop, London.”

I smirk at her, trying to lighten the mood. “Okay, you got me there.”

The tiniest of grins floats to her face and she pushes me in the shoulder playfully. I surprise her when I grab her hand and hold it over my heart.

Her eyes widen, but she doesn’t try to break the connection. Instead, she stares at where our hands rest. Right above my tattoo for her—the one, *thank god,* she doesn’t know about.

“Listen to me, Lily, and listen closely,” I say, wanting her to know how serious I am. “You are the *perfect* person to plan this event. Whatever you lack in under-standing, I’ll do my best to fill in the gaps. We’re a team.”

Pulling her hand from mine, her cheeks flush, and I

want to know desperately why. It's the sexiest thing I've seen in a long time.

"What is it?" I ask. "What were you thinking about?"

"Nothing," she whispers as the color of her cheeks deepens.

"I beg to differ," I tease. "You know you can't lie to me."

She chuckles softly as she rubs at the tops of her thighs. "That was a long time ago. We're not kids anymore. A lot has changed."

"Oh, are you saying you lie to me often now?" I quirk an eyebrow.

"Well, no," she begins, but her voice is strained—tentative.

I narrow my gaze. "Spill it."

She huffs a laugh. "You're just so different. So ... sexually confident. I wish I had that."

My heart trips over itself a little with that compliment, not gonna lie.

Leaning forward again, I look her dead in the eye and say, "I don't know what the deal is with your relationship and while I don't really want more details, I need you to know it's not *you*."

Her breath hitches and she squeaks, "What does that mean?"

Don't do it, London. *Don't...*

"Whatever the reason for your ... *dry spell,* it's not about you. If you ask me, Seth is an idiot," I say before I can stop myself. "You're beautiful, Lily. Inside and out. If your husband doesn't recognize that and take advantage of the gorgeous woman he has in his life, it's his damn loss. Did you ever think that maybe you deserve better?"

The air is charged between us and I know she feels it, too. But then her chin quivers and her eyes fill with tears again.

"Shit, I wasn't trying to make you cry." I reach out, brushing them from her cheek when they spill over.

"It's not you. It's just ..." Lily's eyes are full of sorrow as they take me in. She places her hand over the one I have against her face. Leaning into it, she sighs and closes her eyes.

Watching her, I want desperately to take this ache in her heart away. I wish she could see herself through my eyes.

"I'm so confused," she confesses, her chest rising and falling heavily when she opens her eyes.

That makes two of us.

"What are you confused about?" I ask, rubbing my thumb across the corner of her mouth.

My eyes drift to her lips—*those beautiful lips.* I smile, tracing the tiny lightning-shaped discoloration across her upper lip. It's nothing more than a faint battle scar—a reminder of the kid I was best friends with and all that she's been through.

God, she's beautiful.

Lily swallows hard, her eyes dropping to my lips as energy zaps between us.

I don't know what this is—or what's happening. But it's like I've left my body and someone else takes over. Someone who takes what he wants.

To hell with it.

In slow motion, so slow that she has plenty of time to stop me—*please stop me*—I bend forward with one thing on my mind.

I *have* to kiss her.

Right before I reach her, her breath hitches again. That tiny intake is my new favorite sound, I swear it.

I brace myself as I gently press my lips to hers because I'm acutely aware it's going to ruin me.

When she stiffens slightly under my touch, my heart is on the verge of shattering into pieces. Then, just when I think I've totally misread this situation, her hands float to the back of my neck and she pulls me closer, kissing me back.

A groan escapes the back of my throat as I deepen the kiss, sweeping my tongue across her lower lip. God, she's so soft—*like silk.*

When she moans, then opens her mouth to give me access, it's the best fucking feeling in the world.

My tongue sweeps inside, tangling with hers, and fuck me, she tastes like bubble gum. A fitting flavor that symbolizes her seductive blend of innocence perfectly.

The tip of her tongue flicks at mine and suddenly, my hands are in her hair and hers are in mine. She hops into my lap, pulling herself closer as she presses her upper body to mine.

I've never felt anything so good—*so monumental.*

This was how it was always supposed to be.

Lily and me.

She was always meant to be *mine.*

The door to the elevator dings, startling us both and forcing us to spring apart.

"What the hell—?" Cal asks, his eyes wide and hand on his walkie.

It feels like the wind's been knocked out of me. Between that earth-shattering kiss that was just getting going and the spike of adrenaline from Cal's interruption, I can't seem to catch my breath.

My eyes dart from Cal—*who looks too fucking amused for his own good*—to Lily.

Panic floods her features and I reach out to her, trying to reel her back in.

"Oh, shit. Oh, *fuck*," she gasps. Her hands fly to her hair as she walks around to the other side of her chair and starts to pace. "What have we done?"

CHAPTER 22

Lily

London stands quickly, his hair a tousled mess and face as flushed as mine feels. His lips are swollen and *oh, my god.*

If I look anything like he does...

I tug on the ends of my hair, trying to straighten it as if that's going to help anything right now.

I pretty much have a scarlet letter painted on my chest.

London turns to his security guy and practically shouts, "What in the hell are you doing up here, Cal?"

"I should ask you the same question," Cal responds, shooting us both a pointed stare.

Heat creeps up my neck and my cheeks burst into flames.

If there was any question before, there isn't now.

He saw everything.

How could he not? I was practically attacking London's face.

My stomach rolls and I think I'm going to be sick.

God, I'm so messed up.

When London glares in return, Cal continues, "Got an alert for activity on the roof. Came to check it out because, you know, it's *my job*. The one you *hired* me for."

"Well, it's just us. You can go now," London fires back, his chest heaving and eyes wild.

Cal holds London's gaze for a beat, then turns ever so slightly to face me. "You good, Lily?"

Nodding, I swallow hard.

But, the funny thing is, I don't know why I nodded.

I'm *not* good. I'm soooo far from good it's left the planet. *Good* is off orbiting the rings of Saturn at this point.

I start inching toward the elevator.

I need to get out of here.

I need to think.

To come up with a plan ...

To get the feeling of London's, hands, body, *kiss* out of my goddamn mind.

To ...

"Lily, don't move." London commands, holding one hand up to me and another to Cal like he's a conductor of an orchestra. I stop moving out of impulse. "Cal—" He widens his eyes and jabs his index finger toward the elevator.

Cal shrugs, raising his hands to the sky, and turns on his heel. When he reaches the elevator, he turns around and says, "Don't do anything else stupid."

When the doors to the elevator close with Cal inside, I cover my hands over my face and sink to the ground.

God, I've messed up.

So bad.

Never in a million years would I have thought I could do something like this.

What kind of horrible person kisses another man—*a man who isn't her husband?*

Angie will have a field day if she finds out.

I'll be strung up like the floozy I am.

Before I know it, London is standing in front of me.

"Lily, look at me," he whispers, pressing his warm hands to my shoulders.

Taking a deep breath, I drop my hands and fight back the tears threatening to reemerge—but for an entirely different reason this time.

All oxygen leaves my lungs and my heart thumps unevenly in my chest, pressing home its point with each beat.

Tramp.

Traitor.

Adulteress.

When we lock eyes, his expression softens. Then, he pulls me closer, kisses the side of my head, and wraps his arms around me. Arms I shouldn't want to take comfort in.

But I do.

I should leave.

This shouldn't feel like home ...

But it does.

So I sink into his embrace, letting the tears fall.

He doesn't say anything at first. He just holds me and runs his palm over the back of my head as I cry.

My world is imploding. *I can feel it.*

If I'm honest, my world has been imploding since the moment London came back into my life.

Longer, actually.

There's no going back now.

Not when I've done the unthinkable.

I'll have to tell Seth.

I'll have to …

"This is on me, Lily," he whispers. "I never should have … If you didn't want me to— I'm so sorry."

I pull back, wiping at my face. "No. Don't do that."

"Do what?" he asks, genuine confusion written across his handsome face.

"Shoulder the blame," I respond with a tight throat.

"I kissed you, Lily. This was me, it's all me. Please, don't—" he says, trying to convince me—or maybe convince himself—that I wasn't as much to blame.

"Don't you get it? I wanted it, too. But I shouldn't want—" I shake my head, my eyes slamming shut.

I should be stronger than this.

I knew I was treading a dangerous line but I had to push my limits.

And here we are.

"You deserve to be happy, Lily. I said it earlier and I meant it. You *deserve better.* You deserve so much love and joy, and plenty of mind-blowing sex, if that's what you want …" he sighs heavily, then shrugs. "Truth?"

My lip quivers, but I nod. "Truth."

"Do I regret the kiss? No, I don't. I probably should, but I don't. Consider me an asshole, but I'd do it all over again. Hell, I want to now, even though I know we shouldn't," he says, clenching and unclenching his jaw. "I know you're married. I get it. But ... you're not imprisoned. You still have choices."

I watch him fight with himself, his eyes as tortured as I feel.

"Do I wish you'd choose me?" he says softly.

My breath catches in my throat and I wait for him to answer that question.

He reaches out, brushing another tear from my cheek. "Lily, I'd be lying if I said no. So, do I wish you'd choose me? Hell, yeah. *I do.*"

My heart practically leaps out of my chest when I look into his intense blue eyes. The eyes I've known for so long. The only eyes who've ever looked at me the way he does. Like I'm the most beautiful woman on the planet.

"You do?" I gape at him.

"Of course," he whispers, running his palm along my jaw. "I *always* have."

I exhale, unsure what to do with that kind of confession.

My mind races through all of the major events of my life since he left. It was like everything I did was just me going through the motions. School, college, *getting married*. In retrospect, all of the color in my world faded away the day he was no longer by my side.

"What are you thinking about?" London asks, breaking through my internal chatter. His expression is so serious, that it makes my heart trip a beat.

Tears well in my eyes when I confess, "I think I always have, too."

A huge grin breaks across his features and he frames my face with his hands. "Lily, that's great. That—"

"But, I can't—I can't do this, London." I break from his hold and drop my gaze, no longer able to look into the intensity of his eyes. It's like looking into the sun. "I'm not that kind of person. I never should have let things get this far."

Silence expands between us and when I finally venture a glance, the expression that greets me breaks my heart into pieces.

"So, you're not …" his voice is barely above a whisper and he reminds me of the child I used to know. He swallows hard. "Are you saying you're not willing to …"

"I don't know—" I blurt out, swallowing hard. "I'm confused and I need some time to sort things out."

"Oh," he whispers, his shoulders dropping. "I understand."

Despite his words, his face tells a very different story.

"I'm sorry, London. I need to go." Before I can talk myself out of it, I stand up and rush to the elevator.

He doesn't try to follow me or call me back.

I don't know whether to be thankful or sad about that fact.

Instead, I focus on the elevator and making sure I hit

the right button. Then, I slam my eyes closed so I don't have to face his devastating expression.

When the door closes, the tears start falling.

I want to believe London.

I want to believe I have choices.

That I could choose him.

I want to believe we have a future.

That we could find some kind of a life together.

But the fact is, I'm still married.

And until that changes, I can never, *ever* let something like this happen again.

No matter how desperately I wish it could.

CHAPTER 23

London

I'm going to be sick.

Physically sick.

Right here on the roof of the club.

My world implodes as I watch Lily flee the scene as fast as she can—and there's not one damn thing I can do to stop her.

She needs time to think.

Of course, she does.

I just rocked the foundation of what she believed she was capable of. I could see it in the shock and horror in her eyes.

She may have wanted that kiss as much as I did—but she's the only one whose life could be destroyed because of it.

How things went sideways so fast is beyond me.

I've got emotional whiplash if I'm completely honest.

Nothing in the world has ever felt as good as that kiss.

But thanks to my inability to keep my lips to myself and Cal's shit timing, I may have just pushed Lily over the edge.

Why the fuck didn't I learn from the last time?

We didn't even kiss and all hell broke loose.

What did I think was going to happen?

You wanted to show her how desirable she really is.

Lot of good that did.

"Fuck," I groan, slamming my eyes shut.

For the longest time, I stare out over the edge of the rooftop, watching the last tendrils of light fade beyond the horizon. When the sun has finally vanished, I take a deep breath and turn toward the elevator.

There's no point in staying here.

I'm not going to be any good to the club tonight.

Before I reach the elevator doors, my phone buzzes in my pocket and my heart nearly trips over itself with the hope that it's Lily.

> Hey biotch. I've had to deal with my mother and grandmother for the past two weeks. It's been hell. HELL, I tell you. I need to hang out with someone who doesn't have a vagina. You in?

I stare at the text message, totally confused. The number doesn't have a contact attached to it.

Is this some sort of drunken text to a wrong number?

Out of sheer morbid curiosity, I type back my response.

> Who is this?

The bubbles appear and a second later, the response comes in.

> What do you mean who is this? Who else would call you biotch?

> Sorry, that was snippy. See what I mean?

> Also, it's Quinn, FFS. 😜 And before you ask, Lily gave me your contact info ages ago.

I can't help it, I shake my head and snort a laugh.
Of course, it's Quinn.
And *of course* Lily gave my contact details to him.
While hanging out with Quinn tonight would never have crossed my mind, he might just be the one person in this fucked up world who won't make me feel like absolute shit about what just went down. Plus, I could use his brand of humor right now.
I type back quickly.

> Sure. I'm in. Where do you want to meet?

It only takes a few seconds to get his response.

> Grandma's in Canal Park. I need onion rings and a Long Island iced tea, STAT.

That makes two of us.

Inhaling deeply, I nod and type back.

On my way.

Before I can even put my phone back in my pocket, his response comes in.

Thank fuck.

I chuckle humorlessly as I cram my phone back into my pocket. Quinn might think he's the one who needs this, but I have a feeling, he's gonna be in for a rude awakening when he hears what I have to say.

Unfortunately, first I gotta face Cal and tell Myles and let them know I'm heading out for the night. Myles isn't going to be pleased.

And yet, I can't find it in me to change my mind.

When I reach the main level of the club, the music is already thumping and the crowd is screaming and gyrating to the rhythm.

Thankfully, Cal's nowhere to be seen—something I'll have to deal with another day. *Goodie.*

I grab my keys and wallet from my office and make my way to the bar.

When Myles notices me, her gaze narrows suspiciously. "If you think you're going to help me, you got another thing coming, Saint. Fuck off."

I shake my head. "Nah, I'm heading out."

The muscles on the side of her jaw twitch. "Say what now?"

"I'm not feeling great. I'm gonna head home," I say, not wanting to get into things with her. I'm not a moron, she'll find out eventually, but for now, ignorance is bliss.

"Does this have anything to do with Lily racing out of here?" she fires back.

Very astute.

I shake my head. "Just don't feel well."

She eyes me up and down, then gives a curt nod, and shoos me with her free hand. "You do look like shit. Get away from me. I don't want it."

"Are you gonna make my drink or what?" Some guy asks, leaning over the bar.

Like a viper ready to strike, she turns her attention to him. "Oh, I'm sorry, you wanted a drink?"

He shrinks back from the venom in her words.

She flicks her fingertips at him. "Let's see your ID."

"Are you shittin' me?" he responds, looking incredulous.

Myles juts her chin out and crosses her arms.

"Fucksake," he mutters, clearly smarter than he looks, as he fishes out his wallet.

I press my palm to her shoulder. "See ya tomorrow."

"If you're still sick, you can stay the hell home," she retorts.

Rather than fight her about it, I just nod and leave the floor. I don't go through the main doors—there's a crowd still vying to get in. Instead, I hit the back door and make my way to my vehicle as quickly as I can.

I still half expect to get cornered by Cal, but I don't.

Yay for small miracles.

Making my way from Superior to Canal Park takes less than fifteen minutes but the entire drive I'm on autopilot. Instead, I keep replaying that kiss over and over.

It was a damn good kiss. My body still tingles from the memory of it.

When I pull into Grandma's parking lot, I catch Quinn standing by the entrance looking disgruntled. It takes a few passes to find a spot in the lot, thanks to being the first Friday in June.

By the time I walk up to him, he's leaning a shoulder against the building and staring at his phone.

"Hey," I mutter, then shove my hands into my pockets.

Quinn glances up and his shoulders drop. "Finally, a friendly face. Do you know there's a *forty-minute* wait for a table? Like what in the love of all that's holy am I meant to do with that?" He shakes his phone at me. "I have to watch my phone because they'll text me when our table opens up. God, I hate tourist season." Just then, his phone buzzes, and his face lights up. "Oh, never mind. Our table's ready."

I shake my head, chuckling under my breath.

Yeah, this is exactly the distraction I need right now. Otherwise, I'll be obsessing over Lily and what she's thinking ... What she's *doing*. All she's going through.

Following the server and Quinn, we get seated in a booth in the main area.

"You are about to be my new best friend, er—" Quinn pauses, squinting at the server's name tag. "*Tom.* Great name, by the way."

Tom narrows his eyes. "Uh, okay."

"So, I'll skip the small talk. I need onion rings with a side of ranch and a pitcher of Long Island iced tea yesterday," Quinn fires off.

Tom's expression gives his amusement away as he nods and passes over a menu to each of us. "And for you?"

"We'll share," I say, glancing down at the menu. I'm gonna need a burger or something to soak up the copious amount of alcohol I plan on drinking.

With a curt nod, Tom walks off and I look over the burger selection.

Quinn glances at his menu briefly, barely even enough to take any of it in, then sets it down. "Do you know what it's like to help your grandmother downsize her house full of a *'century's worth of memories?'"* He uses air quotes for the last part of that sentence.

My eyes widen. "Can't say as I do."

"It sucks. I don't recommend it. Zero out of five stars," he says, his gaze floating around the restaurant. His shoulders slump and he sighs loudly. "Where is my damn drink?"

"I'm sure it wasn't so bad ..." I respond, setting my menu down.

He shoots me a look of annoyance. "Not only did I have to help Mammy chuck out years of worthless artifacts that *no one,* including my nonexistent children, will ever want, but I had to do it under the watchful eye of my mother—who, by the way, had a colonoscopy right in the middle of this shit show. Wrong choice of words?" He makes a face. "Eh, no. It's pretty much spot on."

Tom the server walks up with a pitcher of Long Island iced tea and our onion rings. He pours two large glasses for us and Quinn snatches his with the kind of agility I've rarely witnessed.

"Thank the lucky stars above and all that's holy," Quinn mutters, reaching out and taking three onion rings next.

Tom eyes Quinn and chuckles. "Do you both know what you'd like to eat? Or is this everything?"

I glance at Quinn and hold out a hand suggesting he goes first.

"Smokin' ghost burger, please," Quinn says, dipping an onion ring in a vat of ranch dressing. He takes a bite and moans loudly. "With more onion rings and ranch, please."

Tom laughs again, taking note. "And you?"

"I'll have the bacon cheddar burger," I say, passing over the menu. "Fries for me, though, please."

Quinn gasps as if I've offended him and his entire family lineage—including his Mammy, mother, and nonexistent children. "You're going to have *fries* when you're in Grandma's? Where were you raised? A barn?"

We lock eyes for a minute and I'm acutely aware I'm not getting through this dinner without ordering more onion rings.

I turn to the server. "Make that onion rings."

"Wise man," Quinn mutters, returning to his stash and taking another bite.

"Great, I'll be back in a bit with those," the server says, leaving us with our mound of onion rings and booze.

"What I was thinking saying yes to two weeks with the matriarchs of my family is beyond me. I must be a glutton for punishment," Quinn mumbles, taking another big swig of his drink. "Soooo good."

"I'm sure they both appreciated your help," I offer, snagging one of the enormous onion rings and taking a bite.

He jabs his index finger toward one of the tubs of ranch. "Seriously, dip it in the ranch. Life as you know it will never be the same. It's orgasmic."

My eyebrows flick upward. "Not sure I need to orgasm in the middle of Grandma's restaurant."

Quinn's left eyebrow arches. "There can never be too many orgasms."

I press my lips into a thin line. *So* not going there.

For the next half an hour, we make small talk, neither of us really touching on anything too important until our burgers arrive. Then, we spend time devouring them.

I have to admit, Grandma's burgers are damn good. It's been years since I had one.

We're both two Long Island iced teas in when Quinn leans back in his seat and groans loudly. "Why did you let me eat so many onion rings?"

"Yeah, there was no *letting* you do anything there,

man. That was *all* you," I laugh, then reach for the pitcher and pour us both another drink.

My brain is starting to feel good and fuzzy. *Just what I was hoping for.*

There's a good chance I'll be getting an Uber tonight.

"So, you've been awfully quiet," Quinn says, shoving his plate away from him. Then, he even grabs a napkin, opens it, and spreads it over the remaining onion rings.

I twist my mouth to the side. "Just, not much to say."

He narrows his gaze. "Uh, huh."

"What?" I shrug. "I don't."

He tilts his head to the side, appraising me like it's the first time. "You haven't said one thing about Lily this whole night. Not *one.*"

Just the mention of her name makes my damn body spring to life and my heart thud against my ribcage like a trapped bird.

When I don't say anything, he bolts upright, his eyes widen, and he hisses, "Oh, my god. Something happened. Spill it. Right the fuck now."

My breath catches and I reach for my drink, taking another long pull.

Quinn practically leaps out of his seat. "*London.*"

I flick my gaze to his and swallow hard. Now or never.

"I kissed Lily."

His hands fly to the neck of his shirt like he's clutching his pearls. In a low, breathy voice, he whisper-shouts, "*Whaaaaat?*"

I lick my lower lip, and I swear I can still taste her. *Fuck me.*

Quinn's on the verge of hyperventilating as he fans himself. "I'm over here, spouting off about getting rid of my grandma's horrifying teddy bear collection and dealing with my mother's watery bowels, and this whole time you *kissed Lily?* You absolute bastard," Quinn fires back. "Why are we even friends?"

I laugh. "If it's any consolation, it just happened tonight."

His mouth drops open and he looks like a goldfish as it closes and opens back up. "No, *London.* That *doesn't* make me feel better. It should have been fresh in your goddamn mind. You should have been chomping at the bit to share this news with me. Hell, why are you here? You should be with her. You should be—" He pulls up short. "Why *aren't* you with her?"

My gaze drops to the table. I reach out and grab my glass, downing the rest of my drink. "It was a mistake."

"The *fuck,*" he sputters. "I've been waiting with bated breath for this moment. She deserves so much more than what she's settled for. Tell me everything."

I shake my head. "Can't."

He gapes at me.

"I just ... *can't.*" *Not without a signed NDA and permission from Lily.*

"She freaked, huh?" Quinn guesses.

"Something like that." I reach out for the pitcher, only to realize it's empty.

I look around the space, hoping to see the server.

"This is ... *monumental*," Quinn continues. "Do you know what this means?"

"She's going to avoid me for the rest of our lives?" I offer.

When I look over at him, Quinn's scrutiny makes me shift back into my seat.

"London, I gotta know something—" he adjusts in his side of the booth so he's sitting up straighter and holds my gaze. "Be straight with me. I mean, I know you're straight, obviously. That's frustrating, by the way."

I stare at him from under my low eyebrows.

He waves me off. "You know what I mean."

I breathe a heavy sigh and drop my eyes to my empty drink. "Yeah, I know."

He reaches out and places a hand over the top of mine. "Do you love her?"

My mouth goes dry and my stomach drops. Like, full-on plummets to the floor.

Do I love Lily?

The answer hits me like Cupid's stupid arrow straight to the chest.

Of course.

I've loved her since we were kids.

I inhale sharply, wishing my fuzzy brain could suppress it. Because ...

Dammit, Cal was right. I've been pining for her all along.

But now, I love the incredible woman she's become, too.

Slowly, I nod. "Yeah, man. I do."

A mischievous twinkle glints in his eyes. "I was hoping you'd say that."

"Why?" I ask, wishing I could stop the aching in my chest.

"Because it's time you stop dicking around and win her over."

Trollop. Harlot. Floozie.

I jab my thumb into my right eye socket, trying to will the pounding in my head to subside. Sleep was elusive and I know it's all my fault. It was my penance for my indiscretion. Especially since I couldn't bring myself to tell Seth about what I'd done.

Instead, I've been stuck in this incredibly uncomfortable place between hating myself and feeling like I need to do something. I need to make a move to ease this tension.

My only problem is ... I don't know which move is the right one.

So naturally, I've thrown myself into work. I've been at *Bean There, Done That* coffee shop for hours, working on the event for Nocté with the hope that I can pass the rest off to London and his team, then back away.

Until I find the courage to tell Seth about the kiss, I have no business being in the same room as London.

I don't trust myself.

The caterer is set. The florist is locked in and the party decorators have sent their invoice.

At this point, the only thing left is to get the invitations out—something I'll be handling personally, so I can add some personal touches. They'll go out tomorrow. Then, it's in the hands of the Upper Tier.

Truthfully, it's better if I'm not there during the event. After witnessing—*what I witnessed*—I don't think I could handle it anyway.

I glance up from my laptop, my eyes scanning the familiar coffee shop. The occasional clink of a spoon against a mug and the soft murmurs of conversations around me are comforting sounds that momentarily ease my turmoil.

Coming here used to be my office of choice. It reminds me of simpler times.

Lost in my thoughts of the past, the chime above the door snaps me back to the present. I'm about to get up to order another coffee when I double-take at who jangled the bell.

Angie.

Her long, dark hair is sprinkled with hints of golden highlights and cascades gracefully down her back. Her skin is slightly more sun-kissed than mine, showing traces of laugh lines around her hazel eyes—the mark of a woman who's experienced more of life's highs and lows. Her vibrant energy immediately fills the room, and though she's older, there's an undeniable youthful spirit about her.

A pang of jealousy hits me that she can live her life so happily when I'm an absolute mess.

Then, the guilt hits.

If she finds out my marriage is crumbling …

Angie's eyes light up when they land on me. She waves dramatically and alters her course, making her way towards me.

"You look like hell," she quips, setting down her oversized handbag on the seat across from me with a thud. "One caramel macchiato, coming right up." She winks and heads to the counter.

I lean back, trying to force the panic clawing its way up my throat to settle back down. Instead, I blink hard at my sister's back, trying desperately to think of talking points that won't have anything to do with the mess I've made of my life.

When she returns, two mugs in hand, her face is more serious. "Okay, spill. What's going on with you? You've been absent for days now. You think I haven't noticed?"

I try to smile, though I can feel it's not reaching my eyes. "Just work stuff."

She narrows her eyes, apparently not buying my feeble attempt at evasion. "Lil, it's me. Don't play coy." Taking a sip, she leans back and waits.

I swear, that discerning stare is a tool she received from Mom.

Trying hard not to squirm under her scrutiny, I shake my head and shrug. I don't trust myself enough to not voice what's been really going on.

"Fine, don't talk. But let me give you a little piece of advice," she responds, setting down her cup and leaning in closer. "Whatever has you so twisted up in knots … You're going to want to get it out."

"What are you talking about?" I breathe. It's like she can read minds.

She shrugs. "I've counseled enough people to know when a secret is eating a person up. Don't let it fester, Lil."

My mouth gapes open.

"How's it been having Seth back?" she prods gently, taking a demure sip.

Oh, she's good.

Suddenly parched, I reach out and grab the fresh macchiato she brought for me.

"That bad, huh?" she asks, tilting her head to the side.

I blink feverishly. "How'd—"

"Other than a decade working with marriages?" She shoots me a 'give me a break' kind of expression. "Lily, things haven't been going well with you and Seth for years. I thought you'd come to me sooner or later. But man, you're one stubborn lady." She chuckles under her breath.

"I mean, I—" I shake my head, trying to rattle loose the revelation that Angie's known my marriage has been slowly falling apart.

"Remember when we were kids, and we would play house?" she cuts in, catching me off guard yet again.

"That was a long time ago," I whisper, unsure where she's taking this.

She levels me with a stare, then shrugs. "Eh, maybe, but you haven't changed a whole lot."

"What does that mean?" I question, my eyebrows tugging in of their own accord.

She surveys me again before continuing, "Lily, you always wanted an equally matched partnership. Someone who would share your passions and at the very least, be there to talk to about all the crazy deep thoughts in your head. Someone who gets you and shares who he is with you. Seth's never been that guy. He's a gypsy at heart and he's not going to change."

I suck in a breath. "He wasn't always like that."

I'm not sure why I feel the need to defend him, but I do.

A memory sneaks its way to the forefront of my mind. It was our second anniversary, and we didn't have the money or the time to plan anything elaborate. Honestly, I had braced myself for a quiet night in—perhaps with some takeout and a movie.

But Seth had other plans.

I remember stepping into our apartment to find every single light turned off. The only illumination came from a pathway of tea-light candles leading from the entrance to our balcony. I followed it, my heart in my throat, trying to guess what awaited me at the end.

As I stepped out onto the balcony, I was absolutely shocked. Seth had transformed it into a makeshift rooftop diner.

There was a small table set up with a checkered table-cloth, a vase with a single rose, and our best set of plates and glasses. Jazz music floated up from a small radio, and in the middle of it all stood Seth, wearing the most ridiculous waiter's outfit. I have no idea how he put it together.

"Bienvenue, mademoiselle," he had said with an exaggerated French accent, pulling out a chair for me.

That night, we dined on microwaved TV dinners, but it felt like the most exquisite five-star meal, simply because of the effort he had put in.

I remember laughing so hard that night, our shared jokes and banter lighting up the tiny space more than any candle ever could. It was a night where our love felt boundless, where every little imperfection added to the beauty of our relationship.

"I know. He was good to you in the beginning," Angie agrees, a ghost of a smile floating to her lips.

"What does any of this have to do with playing house?" I ask before I can stop myself.

The corner of her mouth quirks. "You were always married to London. Did you know that? Every. Single. Time." She smiles at the memory, but the comment hits me like a ton of bricks. "If I'm honest, I always thought you two would end up together. Well, until his family moved to Colorado, anyway."

She did?

I swallow hard, the weight of the revelation crashing down on me. "I did that? I don't even remember it." My cheeks flame and I adjust in my seat.

"Oh yeah. Sometimes, I wonder what he'd think if he knew that. Then again, he always seemed as infatuated with you." She chuckles, taking another sip of her coffee. "Look, I know you haven't asked for it, but here's some sisterly advice—with a mix of marriage counselor in there. Don't stay in a marriage that makes you unhappy. Life's too short for that shit. If you need to move on, do it."

"But I thought you'd want me to stay. To figure out a way to fix things. To ..." My words peter out as I sit there dumbfounded.

She takes a deep breath and reaches out, placing her hand over mine. "Lily, sometimes, giving up and walking out is the only thing that will allow the right thing in. You've been trying to make this work for years and it's commendable. But you gotta do what makes you happy, sis. Sometimes, a relationship runs its course."

Her words bounce around in my head.

Sometimes giving up and walking out is the only thing that will allow the right thing in.

Is that what's happening here?

I raise my eyes to her. "What happens if ... the right thing is already knocking?"

Angie sits up straighter. "Have you met someone?"

I roll my teeth over my bottom lip and slam my eyes shut. "No. I mean, yes. Ugh, I'm so confused."

When I open my eyes, hers are wide. "Lily, you have to talk to Seth. Staying in this place—it's like purgatory. No wonder you're so distant lately."

I nod. "I know."

She stands up and walks to my side of the table. Then, she tugs my hand so I stand up and collapse into her embrace. "I'm here for you Lily. Please, don't be afraid to talk to me. I'll help you in whatever way I can."

Tears prickle in my eyes and take a step back. Never in a million years would I have expected this conversation. She's left me with more to think about than I could've ever anticipated.

"If you need someone to talk to—or a place to stay—just say the word." Angie pats my upper arms, then smooths her palms over the back of my triceps.

Lost in thought, all I can do is nod.

"Look, I gotta run. I've got a session in fifteen minutes. But remember what I said, okay?" she whispers, taking a step back.

I nod, my body suddenly starting to shake. "I will."

She smiles softly, then turns to the table and picks up her coffee. In one quick move, she downs the rest of the contents. Before she walks out, she says, "Call me in the next day or two. I want to know how it goes."

I stare wide-eyed at her.

"Lily, promise me," she fires back.

"Okay, okay," I promise.

She nods resolutely. "Love ya, little sis."

With that, she spins around and is out the door before I have time to process the way my life has just been upended.

First, by my own making. And now, through the conversation with my sister.

Can I do this?

Can I really let Seth go so I can have a chance with London?

Is that even right?

What would others think?

Even though the thought of what others might think makes my stomach clench, there's a small part of me that feels a sense of relief in it.

In finally letting go of what's not working.

And, of course, there's London himself.

Absently, I sit down in my chair and shake my head.

Angie always thought I'd end up with London ...

What would she think if she knew the other man *was* London?

Suddenly, my phone buzzes.

I pull it out of my pocket in a daze. My eyes lock on the sender and my heartbeat stutters.

Seth.

Swallowing hard, I close my eyes and give myself a moment to calm down.

Then, I open the text to read it.

> Can we talk tonight?

My heart lurches but I type back before I can talk myself out of it.

> Yes.

Angie's right.

Maybe it's time.

CHAPTER 25

London

I knew she'd avoid me today.

That's why I'm not bothering to go in to work. Instead, I'm letting Myles think whatever sickness I came down with yesterday is still plaguing me today.

The club will be fine without me for two days.

Besides, I'd be useless there, anyway. There's no way I could focus.

Not after everything that's happened.

As it was, last night, I tossed and turned, never getting any real, restorative sleep. When I did manage to doze off, I was immersed in dreams where Lily's lips were on mine and she *wanted* to be in my arms.

Where she was *my* wife.

Not someone else's.

Now, it's noon and I feel like hell.

I blame Quinn and those damn Long Island iced teas.

And the shitshow I've made of things.

I shake my head and make my way to my kitchen. It's not anything fancy, but at least it's got a modern vibe, unlike a lot of houses in the Twin Ports. I stalk over to the fridge and open it, swiping a beer from the back, then make my way to the deck chairs out back.

I've barely managed a few steps when I shiver.

It's still a bit chilly, even for June.

As I settle into my chair, I shudder against its bite, approving of the punishment it seems fit to dole out.

My gaze drifts out over my backyard, illuminated by the mid-day sun. The leaves are a vibrant green, betraying the vibe the lake winds are putting out. If I shut off my other senses, I could almost believe it was summer.

I set down my unopened beer on the small table to my left, then reach into my pocket. I pull out my phone, checking the notifications for the hundredth—*thousandth*—time.

The hope that Lily would have texted me has begun to dwindle, so I shove that idiotic part of me back down as I open my phone and tap on YouTube.

I maneuver to my favorite playlist and press play in the hopes it can take my mind off of things, if only a little bit.

Stuck In My Head, by Blü Eyes is the first to play.

It's such a fitting song, I almost laugh out loud. *Almost.*

I reach for my beer, crack it open, and take a deep draw in the hopes it might numb my mind.

For a while, I just sit there, listening to the music, sipping my memories away, and staring into the trees beyond. The breeze blows, continuing to prove that summer comes not because of a date on a calendar, but when Mother Nature deems herself ready.

I raise my beer in salute.

I'm also not oblivious to the similarities in the relationship between myself and Lily.

I'm finding myself relenting to her needs.

What I feel—*what I want*—it's delicate.

And impossible.

The lyrics from one of my favorite bands pulls me from my internal tirade.

"Nothing's impossible…"

I snort into my beer at the timing.

Yeah, life's some treat, alright. More like a tablespoon of arsenic.

The thought is a bit more sardonic than normal.

Whatever I saw in the song *Nothing's Impossible*, by Walking on Cars is obviously lost on me today. I don't even—

"… gazing at the stars."

And there it is.

That one line.

I snatch my phone from the table and replay it from the beginning, now desperate to give it another listen.

My heart pounds in my ears and my fingertips dig into the arms of my chair as the song plays.

Of course, I added it because of my connection with Lily.

And her love of the stars …

I wonder if she still loves looking up at the vastness of

the universe as much as she used to? Or is that a part of her that withered over the years of neglect?

A deep wave of sadness rolls through me and my mouth goes dry.

Somehow, I doubt that her insatiable curiosity ever went away.

At least, I hoped not.

That sort of passion never really goes away. It leaves its mark and bides its time, waiting for the best time to claw its way out.

The way she was always so excited to uncover something new—*something mysterious* ... God, I loved seeing that spark light up in her eyes when we were kids.

It was infectious.

I was always trying to surprise her with something new, just to see that light.

Like the time I told her about Atlantis.

She had been so enthralled, hanging on my every word, and never once caring whether or not an eight-year-old could ever be an expert on the subject.

Then, she'd spent weeks researching, reading, and talking with me about it.

If I'm honest, I think that's why I brought her to the Upper Tier yesterday. That innate, stupid desire to see the spark light in her eyes.

My thoughts once again drift to how the rest of the evening played out, like I hadn't already spent the past day and night parsing every moment apart.

The sexual tension. Her small inhalations when she

was surprised—or turned on. The way her body felt against mine.

That explosive kiss.

It was like all of our pent-up frustrations and feelings were unlocked and allowed to scream out of the box we'd locked them up in.

Briefly.

Fuck me.

I was supposed to get this out of my mind, not continue to play it on a continuous, torturous loop.

Groaning, I push off the chair and head to the kitchen to grab another beer. One is obviously not going to be enough today.

By the time I sit back down, Ed Sheeran's song, *Perfect,* haunts me softly from my phone. The weight of the song's lyrics mess with my already fucked up head and I question whether or not listening to this playlist is really all that helpful.

Yet, I can't seem to bring myself to hit pause, opting instead for more torture, just to drive home how careless I'd been.

My breath catches as I listen to the lyrics. The serendipity of it.

If stomachs could tie in knots, I'd swear, mine just did.

The song continues on and, yup, now my heart stopped beating.

Damn, I'm practically on the verge of tears here and it's all because of a stupid song.

When I first heard *Perfect*, I immediately added it to my favorites playlist on YouTube.

Funnily enough, I never questioned why. But deep down, I knew ...

I've always loved her.

I did. I knew it.

Hell, *Cal* knew it.

But I lied to myself to protect my stupid heart because I knew someone as amazing as Lily wouldn't be waiting around for me. She would have gone on to live her life—as she should have.

I lean forward and run my hands over my face.

What a mess.

Shaking my head, I reach out for my phone to shut it off. Instead, I fumble with the buttons and it shifts to a new playlist.

Instead of a song, the opening to the 1938 radio broadcast of *War of the Worlds* starts playing.

My heart stutters its beats and I stare at the screen, dumbfounded.

When I came across the broadcast twelve years ago, YouTube was still in its infancy. But still, I was desperate to save it. If I ever had the chance to see Lily again—if we ever became friends again—I wanted to show it to her.

I've listened to it myself at least a dozen times throughout the years because it always made me feel closer to her.

The night before my family moved us to Colorado, I had snuck out of my bedroom so I could spend one more night under the stars with her. I'd hid blankets and risked being grounded for life. But it was worth it.

I told her that night about the broadcast and her eyes had lit up, just like I knew they would. That night, I'd wished so hard that I had a magical way of being able to share it with her.

I snicker under my breath.

Funnily enough, the magic I hoped for wasn't far off. The internet came along and YouTube was invented. We only missed it by six years.

A zap of *knowing* courses through me, forcing me to my feet as a plan starts to form.

What if...

What if I shared it with her? I could recreate that night, laying out under the stars ... It could remind her of the connection we've always shared. How much we meant to each other before. I could explain how much she still means to me.

Quinn had said last night that I should win her over.

And while I wasn't convinced last night, I'd be crazy if I didn't admit a part of me wanted to. Even if it's wrong.

Even if I'm stepping on another man's toes. A man who *hasn't even tried* to show Lily how special she is.

Even if I desperately want her to end her marriage so I can call her mine.

Would this kind of a gesture be the way to show her what's been in me all this time?

I bite my lip, thinking it through, because, shit ... now I'm not so sure.

The last thing I want to do is come across like an insensitive ass—or move too fast for her. All I know is, everything inside me is screaming that we belong together.

We always have.

It's obvious now.

But will she see it that way?

I rake my hands through my hair as I wear a path on my deck.

What if she sees this kind of gesture as manipulative? Or worse, as an attempt to capitalize on a vulnerable moment in her marriage? Sharing something so intimate, so connected to our shared past might just push her further away.

She's married.

She has a life now that's separate from mine. Am I being fair to her by trying to rekindle something from our past?

But on the flip side, she deserves to know how I've always felt. If she's ever felt even a fraction of what I have, doesn't she deserve to explore that, to know what it might mean? We shared so many special moments, and this could be our chance to create new ones.

If she's happy in her marriage, she'll tell me. She can always say no and walk away.

But if there's even a glimmer of doubt in her mind, don't we owe it to each other to see what's there?

One wrong move could ruin any chance I might have with Lily, not just for romance, but even for friendship.

But doing nothing, staying passive ... that might be the worst decision of all.

"Gah," I ground out, slamming my hands down on the deck railing.

There's so much at stake.

Her feelings.

Her marriage.

Our friendship.

But if I never take the risk, I'll go to my death wondering, *what if?*

Being torn between my own desires, what I think is right for Lily, and the potential fallout of making a move is enough to drive me crazy.

Is sharing this broadcast a grand romantic gesture or a colossal mistake?

Can I live with the consequences of either choice? I know I have to do something ... I can't sit here and let her go through this alone.

She needs to know she means something to me.

She's so damn special.

The sound of an incoming text has me leaping for my phone, in the hopes it's Lily. That somehow, the universe has bound us together enough that she can feel my excitement wherever she is.

Instead, Quinn's name is in the notification.

Heaving a sigh, I flick open my phone and read the text.

> Heard some news you might find
> interesting. Give me a call, asap.

CHAPTER 26

Lily

My heart races as I pace back and forth in our living room. This is where we've had the majority of our more heartfelt conversations over the past few years, so the setting just felt right.

I glance at the clock and a lump gets stuck in my throat.

Seth texted fifteen minutes ago to let me know he was on his way home. Based on his estimate, he'll be here any minute.

Under my skin is a live wire of energy that's causing me to shake from its intensity.

I don't know how this conversation is going to go—but one thing's for sure, things won't be the same when it's over.

For better or worse.

I laugh humorlessly at the irony in the thought.

Despite myself, as I wait, I can't help but notice the lack of anything overly personal from our decade together. There are no pictures of us as a couple on the walls—or anywhere else, for that matter. No displays of the love we once shared.

If anything, it looks like a staged home, ready for sale.

I don't know why I never realized ...

Maybe I was just too busy. Or maybe I was trying to shield myself.

Either way, it should have been a sign.

Internally, I jump at the sound of Seth's key at the backdoor, and my hands immediately start to sweat.

Swallowing hard, I will my breathing to slow. It doesn't listen.

Instead, it staccatos in type with my heartbeats.

Shaking off the extra energy, I take a seat on the couch and press my hands between my knees to keep them from shaking.

After the longest few minutes of my life, Seth walks into the living room.

A shadow of a smile flits to his face and he takes a deep breath. "Hey."

I mimic his inhalation and return the greeting.

"So," he whispers, shoving his hands in his pockets. He doesn't venture beyond the doorway and it makes me more nervous than if he sat beside me.

There's a palpable tension in the air as his gaze drops to the carpet and his lashes flutter against his cheeks.

An unwanted thought springs to mind, making my own anxiety worse.

Does he know about London?

I blow out a breath and stand up. I'll be the first to speak. It's the least I can do.

"Seth, we need to talk," I begin, my voice quivering. I pat the spot beside me in the hopes he'll sit down.

His blue eyes flit to mine and he nods slowly.

"I know," his reply is barely above a whisper.

On another deep breath, he accepts my invitation to sit on the couch beside me. For a moment, silence fills the space between us until it's its own force.

When he doesn't say anything, I gather my courage. If I don't speak now, it will tear me apart.

"Seth, I ... Things aren't working." I raise my gaze to his and tears threaten to emerge. "Between us, I mean."

His mouth twists to the side and his nod is almost imperceptible. "You remember our fifth anniversary?" Seth's voice wavers slightly but he holds my gaze.

I can't help but notice the distance that's still between us on the couch—he's on one end, I'm on the other.

Rather than speak, I tip my chin in acknowledgment.

"We went to that fancy restaurant on the lakewalk— the one with the view of Lake Superior that everyone was raving about."

"Va Bene," I whisper.

"Yeah, that one," he confirms, pointing at me. A small inhalation later, he continues, "I saved up for months to afford that dinner. I squirreled away a few bucks here and there so you never noticed it. I wanted everything to be perfect ..." His eyes close and he makes a face.

"It was a beautiful night," I respond, remembering what a surprise it was and how beautiful the sunset had been that night.

"That's just it—it was perfect on the outside. All through that night, there was this ... *nagging feeling*." He looks to the ceiling, as if asking the Heavens for some assistance.

My breath hitches and I wait for whatever truth he has coming.

"On the inside, though, I felt ... *hollow*. And I've been feeling that way for a really long time. I've been trying, Lily. Trying so hard to be the husband you deserve, but every time I look in the mirror, I can't help but see a man who wants ..." His voice almost cracks and he places his hands on his knees.

My eyes prickle with tears. "Seth ..."

"Please, let me finish," he whispers, holding my gaze. When I nod, he takes another deep breath and continues, "I've watched you, you know. I've seen the light in your eyes dim. I've felt the distance growing between us and I blame myself for it. Maybe if I was more, or different, or better—I don't know. Maybe things would be different."

The tears now spill over, hot and stinging their way across the spans of my cheeks.

"I thought I could do it. Be the man you needed me to be," Seth says, shaking his head. "I just ... *can't*."

"What do you mean?" I ask, my voice squeaking out.

"I want you to be happy, Lil. I want that happiness for myself, too, but I'm lost. I kept thinking that if I traveled enough, maybe I'd find myself out there somewhere.

But there's always been this tether—" He exhales and looks pointedly at me. "—to you."

I open my mouth to speak, but he holds up a hand.

"Look, I've been lost for a while. It's not you or your fault. But the guilt—the guilt of not being enough for you, or being here when I've been gone—" He laughs humorlessly. "No matter what I do, I can't find a way to win here. I thought I could prove to myself I could be what you needed by getting a job here. It's what you always begged me to do. But ..."

"You can't stay," I whisper, realizing what he's saying.

His blue eyes darken and his lips press tight. The slight tilt of his head tells me I'm right.

This isn't about me and London.

It's about his own inner turmoil. Turmoil I never realized he was going through.

My heart breaks for him. It breaks for me, too. For the life we shared and the life we tried to build.

"Lily, I'm sorry. I really am. I wish I was more—" his lip quivers and his emotion shines in his eyes. "But I can't stay here. Locked in one place like this. I knew before I took that job I was making a mistake. I could feel it, I guess. Still, I had to try."

I take a deep breath and scoot across the couch to him. I press the palm of my hand to his cheek.

"Seth, for what it's worth, I've been feeling the same way for a while, too. Things between us—they're differ-ent. *We're* different. I'm sorry I didn't see how much you were hurting ..." I whisper, dropping my hand to my lap.

"It's not your fault. I tried hard to keep that from you. I didn't want you to know—it was too much."

Silence expands between us again as that statement settles in.

"You could have talked to me, you know," I finally offer, wishing he would have. Maybe things *would* have been different had we communicated to each other sooner. Maybe we would have been able to strengthen our marriage. Maybe not.

Even if things had ended sooner—perhaps I wouldn't be in this tug of war with my heart.

Seth shakes his head. "That's just it, Lily. I couldn't."

I blow out a slow breath.

His confession is so vulnerable, so heartfelt, that guilt rises up and threatens to consume me whole.

I don't want to make him feel worse by speaking my own truth. Will it serve a purpose anymore? Or will it just cut him deeper?

I swallow hard, wishing I could see into the future to know what to say.

If I don't tell him about the kiss, I feel like I'm keeping secrets. But if I do, will it only make things worse?

"I just ... I want us to be happy," Seth admits softly. "But I think it means finding happiness on our own."

My phone buzzes from the coffee table, lighting up with London's name as he tries to call me.

Seth's gaze lands on my phone as I reach for it and silence the call. "London? Is that—?"

I flip the phone over on the coffee table and turn to

face him. My heart hammers in my chest, but I know I need to come clean. At least a little.

I guess we're doing this.

"Yeah, that's London," I admit, nodding. "He, um ... He moved back a while ago, I guess."

Something akin to relief flashes in Seth's eyes and it takes me aback. He doesn't say anything, though. Simply waits for me to continue.

"I should have told you sooner. I just didn't know how to bring it up."

His eyebrows flicker upward. "I guess communication was never our strong suit."

"It really wasn't." As soon as the words come out of my mouth, I realize the way they sound. The finality in them.

Seth's lips press tight, twisting to the side with the same absent nod I've seen for years.

How did I not know by keeping him tied to me, I was holding him back, too?

"He's my new boss—" I blurt out.

Seth's eyes shift to mine and confusion crosses his features.

"I mean, the event I've been planning ... He's the one who gave me the job," I clarify.

"Oh," he murmurs, his features relaxing.

Do I tell him?

Should I tell him?

"Well, that's good. You should have someone—" Seth says, his voice breaking. "Someone who you trust. To talk to now."

The meaning behind his words hit heavy.

I meet his gaze and the tears are back—in both of our eyes. "So, we're ..."

I can't bring myself to say the rest.

"Yeah, I think so," he whispers back.

The dam breaks and the tears fall. No matter what I do, I can't stop them.

I'm sad. Sad for all that's ending.

But there's a little glimmer of hope—that tiny bead of light that's guiding me into the future.

Even though I know it will be okay, I can't help but grieve.

"Sweetie," Seth says, reaching for me.

"No, don't call me that. Not—*not anymore.*" I shake my head and shrink back from him.

I can't. Not when we've decided this is over. It'll break me in two.

His face blanches, but he drops his head and nods. After a beat, he jabs a thumb behind him. "I'm gonna ... pack."

My chin quivers as I watch him stand up and walk away.

There's suddenly not enough oxygen in this room.

Not enough space to allow me to breathe.

I stand up, snatching my phone, and shoving it in my pocket. Then, I stride to the front door.

I need a walk to clear my head.

I need to think about everything that just happened.

I need to ... *get out of this house.*

CHAPTER 27

London

Sitting in my truck, I debate for the hundredth time whether or not to just drive to Lily's house to warn her.

Instead, I clutch my phone like a lifeline and dial again.

No answer.

I drop it to my lap and run my hands through my hair.

"Fuck," I ground out.

Then, a notification comes through.

It's a text ... *from Lily.*

> London, I need you. Things are falling apart. Please, can you come?

My fingers fly across the keypad.

> Where are you?

A second later, her response comes through.

Home.

She texts me the address, but I have it memorized from her employment records.

On my way.

The escalade is on the road before I have time to question it but it's still the longest drive of my life.

When I pull up, I find her sitting on her front porch steps, her face in her hands.

Slowly, I make my way over, not wanting to startle her. "Lily ..."

She glances up and her face contorts into one of so much heartache, that I can't help but wrap my arms around her and tug her into me.

Her body wracks against mine and the tears flow effortlessly.

My eyelids slam shut and my heart sinks as I hold her close.

Too late.

I'm too late to warn her.

For the longest moment, we stand there on her steps.

Her body trembles from her tears and I'm acutely aware of the fact that her husband must be inside somewhere. Every so often, the sounds of movement on the other side of the door draw my attention, but I can't find it in me to guide her away.

If he tries to make a spectacle, then so be it.

I'm here for Lily. No one else.

She's what matters.

And I'm willing to go to bat over it.

So, I hold her, listening to her breathing surrounded by the ambient sounds of leaf blowers and lawnmowers in the neighborhood. The lingering scent of clipped grass hangs heavy in the air.

I don't know what she's thinking. What she's feeling. *What was said ...*

"Lily," I finally whisper, drawing away enough to see her face.

The rims of her eyes are red and the tears cling to her long lashes as she pulls back slightly.

"Are you okay?" I murmur, tucking a stray strand of hair behind her ear.

Stupid question. But it has to be asked.

Her lips press into a thin line and she shakes her head.

I glance over my shoulder. There's still an hour or so of daylight.

"Wanna get out of here? Go for a walk?" I suggest, tipping my head toward the street.

She inhales sharply like she's shocked at my words. Again, instead of speaking, her lips twist slightly and she nods.

"Okay, let's go," I offer, taking a step back, and allowing her to take the lead.

Her silence is unnerving. I wish I knew what happened—what's going on.

Did Seth tell her he quit his job? Did they fight over it?

I wish Quinn had been given that little tidbit from his cousin sooner. Or that he'd come to *me* sooner, rather than spending the afternoon trying to get in touch with Lily. She'd clearly been ignoring her phone all afternoon.

Maybe I could have driven over here and warned her before …

When we hit the sidewalk, I take her hand and steer us to the left, walking slowly toward Lester Park. I'm not as familiar with these streets as I used to be. But as kids, Lily and I would ride bikes all over town. Lester Park was one of the places we loved to go because there's so much to do there.

There's a perfect spot to lie on the ground and stare at the stars—a favorite pastime of ours in the fall, when nighttime came earlier.

The peaceful sounds of water rushing over stones, thanks to the Amity Creek and Lester River cradling the park, are just what Lily needs to relax.

I've even found myself there once or twice since I moved back, not even realizing how close I was to Lily's home. Had she visited the park, we could have bumped into each other.

It's almost as if I knew on a subconscious level where to find her. As corny as that sounds.

It doesn't take us long to enter the park. She still hasn't said a word and that's weighing on me more than anything else.

I need to know what happened. How can I help her if I don't?

We walk over the Lester River bridge and I guide her to a bench on the edge of the park for now. There are a couple of kids playing on the playground, but we're far enough away that it doesn't matter. If anything, their laughter and giggles might help lighten the mood a bit.

We sit, facing the playground and I'm taken back to the days when it was the two of us running around the park, *our* laughter in the air. She always loved the swings most. She'd lean back, pumping her legs hard until she was practically flying. Then, she'd stare up at the sky and talk about all the things that are out there ... beyond the blue canopy.

Her face was always so radiant as she swung back and forth, her brown hair swaying in the motion.

Things were so much simpler back then. I miss that light she'd shine most—especially in times like these. I'd do anything to get her spark back.

She shudders slightly beside me and I reach out, drawing her nearer. I wrap my arm around her and she rests her head against my shoulder, letting go of a strangled breath.

Frogs and crickets have begun singing their nighttime songs as twilight descends. For a while, we sit there, listening to their serenade and the relaxing sounds of water flowing.

Somewhere in the distance, a horn honks, bringing me back to the moment at hand.

"Quinn's been trying to get ahold of you," I say, finally breaking the silence.

She doesn't lift her head or even really acknowledge my words. I almost think she didn't hear me, until she whispers, "Why?"

I hesitate for a moment, wondering how much to share and when. "He heard something ... about Seth."

Her body tenses beside me, and she raises her face to mine, her eyes searching for answers. "What did he hear?"

I tug my bottom lip through my teeth, gauging her emotional state. "It's about his job, Lil."

She pulls back slightly, confusion evident. "What about his job?"

Taking a deep breath, I finally offer, "He works—well, *worked*—with Quinn's cousin. Apparently he made a decision."

Her brown eyes widen. "What decision?"

Shit, she didn't know.

My heart thuds unevenly as I contemplate my next sentence. Instead of telling her what she wants to know, I ask a question in its place. "Lily, what happened back there?"

She raises her face to the sky and sits up straighter. Her teeth worry her lip, drawing my attention to them, so I shift my gaze to the kids to keep myself grounded.

One of the kids on the playground squeals, ducking into the slide. When she hits the bottom, she races to the other end of the equipment as her friend dashes after her.

A smile creeps onto my face.

Such innocence.

Finally, Lily whispers, "Seth and I ..." She lets a whoosh of air blow past those lips. "We're getting divorced. He doesn't want—" Her voice cracks.

I turn to face her. "Seth *broke up* with you?" My stupid heart damn near prances in my chest but I have to shake it off. However, I can't eradicate a tiny glimmer of hope that blooms like a goddamn golden sparkler. "Are—are you okay?"

She shudders again and shakes her head *'no.'*

Sighing, I pull her close again.

"Seth quit his job, apparently," I admit after a beat of silence, watching the kids play. "That's what Quinn wanted to warn you about. He thought maybe it would be important."

"Oh."

My mind whirls through the ramifications of what Lily's just gone through. This has been one helluva few days. I can only imagine the pressure she's under. The devastation.

"I'm sorry, Lily," I mutter softly. And I mean it. I *really* do.

As much as I wish she were mine, the last thing in the world I want for her is to be hurt. It's obvious how much she still cares for Seth. Even if things weren't ...

She laughs softly, humorlessly. "You don't have to do that, you know."

I stiffen. "Do what?"

"Lie to me," she responds.

"I'm not lying, Lil. I—" I begin.

Again she sits up, then places a hand on my thigh. The contact of her warm hand so close to other sensitive areas does strange things to my body—which I promptly work to tamp down.

I place my hand over hers, then stand up, pulling her along with me. I need to put a little space between us—and give my body a second to settle. It's not something she needs to concern herself with, that's for sure.

"Where are we going?" she asks, surprised by our sudden movements.

I turn back to her, grinning. "Come on."

We walk into the open field beyond the picnic pavilion. When I'm sure we'll have a good view, I sit down on the grass.

She lets out that soft squeal I love so much as I gently tug her hand so she'll join me.

"Lie back," I command, as I do the same, propping my head in my left hand.

She hesitates slightly, shooting me a sidelong glance, but she lies down to my right. The sun has set and the sky is darkening. Still, the first star hasn't made its appearance yet.

Good.

This was always her favorite time of the day.

We lay there for a few minutes, as a comfortable silence passes between us. The energy has shifted slightly, perhaps because of this location—perhaps because of the impending night.

I weigh my options for how to proceed, not wanting to mess anything up.

Do I take her to her sister's house? Tasia's? I could drive her somewhere that won't remind her of what she's lost.

Then again, Angie and Tasia will want to ask questions and if I know Lily, she won't be ready for that. At least, not yet.

Do I take her to my place? We could watch a movie or she could just sleep somewhere that doesn't remind her of her marriage ...

"I forgot how beautiful this is ..." she breathes, pulling me from my internal questioning.

The shadows of night creep closer to us when I turn to look at her. There's a slight smile gracing her lips as her eyes are fixed to the sky. I follow her gaze and realize not only did I miss the approach of the first star, but five of them.

"It's been years since I did this," she admits quietly.

My eyebrows tug in. "Why?"

I feel her shrug beside me. "I just ... *couldn't.*"

Pieces of my heart clench as if it had been slowly pulling itself back together. But that confession—I'm not sure what to make of it.

"I don't mean to sound like a toddler repeating myself, Lily, but ... *Why?*" I press. Part of me is hopeful—wanting the reason to be me. But that would be presumptuous.

She raises an arm and points. "Shooting star."

I follow her finger and watch the star fade behind the treeline. A smile floats to my lips. "Make a wish."

"I already have," she whispers. She tilts her head,

glancing in my direction. While the tears still cling to her lashes, there's a tiny fleck of something else in her eyes … Something real, and raw, and maybe just a little bit hopeful, too.

I know better than to ask her what she wished for. But that doesn't stop me from wanting to know.

She returns her gaze to the growing starlight and for a few moments, she simply watches them while I watch her. A simple serenity has taken hold of her features and I wish like hell I could reach out and run my fingertips across her lips.

Instead, I study her.

The way her eyes crinkle when she spots a new star. How her cheeks mound with the slightest smile.

"It was because of you," she says, keeping her gaze fixed on the stars.

"Hmmm?" I ask, confused.

"I didn't want your memory tainted by watching the stars with anyone else," she confesses. Then, she rolls over onto her side so she's facing me. "Maybe that's silly, but it was one thing that was just ours. You know? It felt like— without you, it didn't hold the same meaning."

I roll onto my side, mirroring her position. "I get that."

"Have you? With anyone else, I mean," she asks tentatively.

The question stems from her insecurity and hurt, so I reach out and run my fingertips over her cheek.

"No one else," I whisper.

She exhales a jagged breath.

"Though," I continue, "I have done it on more than one occasion on my own."

A smile floats to her beautiful lips. "Really? Why?"

I roll my eyes and boop her chin. "You already know why."

Her smile broadens slightly and she nods. Then, she rolls onto her back and looks up again. "Yeah, I think maybe I do."

A comfortable silence settles between us and I return to my own stargazing, my mind whirling through the past few day's events.

Beside me, Lily takes a deep breath, and her voice is barely above a whisper. "London, what happens now? Between us?"

I turn to her, searching for an answer in her eyes. But all I see are the reflections of the stars above, and the question that lingers in the air, unanswered.

CHAPTER 28

Lily

One by one, the stars twinkle to life like tiny diamonds as they scatter across the vast canvas of the night sky. To me, each one holds a story of its own—a tale of timelessness and wonder. Much like the memories of my childhood with London, if I'm honest.

The night is beautiful, but the fragile connection we've been rekindling in its embrace feels even more precious.

A wave of guilt sweeps over me when I realize I'm equating timelessness with London—and not the man who held my hand for the past decade.

The realization of this evening's events crash over me again and I inhale a deep breath, trying to center myself and move through it.

There's a strange sense of relief in the undercurrent, but I can't seem to fully grasp it.

Yet ... laying beside London like this—with the soft

glow of the stars illuminating his face—the bond of our shared history presses against my heart.

The silence and comfort he brought with him tonight speaks volumes to me. I don't know what I would have done if I had to endure this evening alone.

The city has started to settle down and the distant sound of rushing water provides a serene background music to our quiet contemplation. This was the perfect place to go.

He's always known what to do. How to make me feel better.

My fingers unconsciously play with the grass beneath me, seeking some tactile connection to the earth to ground my scattered thoughts.

London's breathing is steady, but every so often I can hear him swallowing hard or exhaling a little sharper than before. He's trying to be strong for both of us, but I know he's also navigating through his own storm of emotions.

"Remember that summer when we tried to count all the stars?" London's voice, although soft, breaks the stillness.

It draws a chuckle from me, so I turn to face him. "We gave up around three hundred something," I recall, unable to hide a slight grin.

He chuckles. "Simpler times, weren't they?"

"Simpler, but not necessarily better," I muse, recalling both the good and bad times of our past.

We continue to reminisce, reliving some of our favorite memories and laughing over our childish antics.

This trip down memory lane feels like a salve to my wounded heart, reminding me that even amidst the pain, there's light waiting to embrace you in its warmth.

However, as the night wears on, the weight of my reality starts to settle back in, and I can't help but wonder about the future.

What will my life look like now?

Where will I live?

How do you start a divorce? Will Seth start it? Or should I?

There's so much to consider.

"We should probably head back," London murmurs, probably sensing my internal shift.

"I don't want to go home," I admit, my voice nothing more than a strangled whisper. His gaze searches mine, silently asking for clarification. "Not to that empty house ... not tonight."

His eyes soften with understanding. "You can stay at my place," he offers. "It's not much, but it's a change of scenery. Or, if you'd rather go to your sister's—"

"Your place would be nice," I say, cutting off his uncertainty. Even though Angie offered, I can't deal with her questions right now. So, instead, I just whisper, "Thank you."

The idea of being somewhere new, even just for the night, feels inviting.

London stands up, brushing grass from his backside. Then, he reaches a hand out for me. I slide my hand in his, so grateful for his support. It means more to me than he'll ever know.

As we begin our walk back, the city's nocturnal sounds surround us. The distant hum of traffic, the muted conversations from late-night trail walkers, and the rhythmic cadence of our footsteps on the pavement create a comforting ambiance.

I didn't know what to expect from tonight—from that conversation with Seth—but if this is how it ends, I'm at least glad it didn't end in a heated argument, or overly hurt feelings.

Instead, it just sort of fizzled.

Like my marriage.

The sidewalks are lit by the gentle glow of streetlights, casting long shadows in our path. Each step feels like I'm straddling two worlds—the melancholy of the past and the uncertainty of the future.

"So, how far do you live from here?" I ask, trying to distract myself from the looming thoughts about the dissolution of my marriage.

"Actually, I bought my parent's old place," London replies.

I turn to him, unable to hide my surprise. "Really?"

He grins sheepishly.

My eyebrows tug in, wishing I could read his mind. Instead, I murmur, "It's strange ... How some places just embed themselves in your heart."

He smiles, that familiar lopsided grin that used to make my heart so happy as a kid. "Some places ... *and some people.*"

My heart skips a beat and a soft smile tugs at my lips as we continue walking.

A comfortable silence settles between us, but it's punctuated by the occasional sounds of the city—the laughter of a group of friends heading home or the distant rumble of a train.

As we approach the park's boundary, the houses become more frequent, giving way to rows of old houses and apartment buildings. The sound of our footsteps is accompanied by the distant hum of traffic from Superior Street.

"You've been quiet," he observes, casting a sideways glance at me.

"Just … *processing*," I admit. "I never imagined my life turning out this way."

He nods. "Life rarely goes the way we envision. But sometimes, the unexpected turns lead us to where we need to be. At least, I hope."

His optimism is touching, but the reality of my situation is hard to escape.

Before I know it, we've passed my house and we're standing beside his Escalade.

"This is me," he says, pointing to his vehicle. "Do you want to grab anything from inside before we leave?"

I glance toward the house. The soft glow of light filters to the street from a lamp in the window.

I don't know if Seth is still inside. If he is, I don't want to go back in.

"No," I reply, shaking my head.

A mixture of anxiety and gratitude churns inside me as I realize I'm leaving with London.

Every little sound is amplified—the chirping of the

late-night crickets, the rustling of the leaves in the trees, and even our own steady breathing.

With a nod, he unlocks the doors to his truck with a soft beep. Then, he guides me to the passenger side and opens the door for me—a chivalrous gesture that makes my heart beam.

Settling into the plush seats, I take a moment to watch London as he circles the vehicle and gets in. The dim interior light casts a soft glow on his face, high-lighting his features—like the little grooves between his eyebrows as he thinks.

For a brief moment, everything else fades away, and it's just the two of us—two old friends, or maybe some-thing more ... seeking comfort and understanding in a world that feels so overwhelming.

London starts the vehicle, the engine purring to life, and gently maneuvers us away from my neighborhood and out onto the street.

I stare out the window, barely taking in the familiar streets of East Duluth as they pass by. Instead, I focus on the street lamps, as they cast their fleeting beams of light. Each block we pass holds memories—fragments of a past life that seems so distant now—while others become more vivid.

London occasionally steals glances in my direction, and I can feel his concern rolling off of him.

"You okay?" he finally asks as he makes a left turn, steering us toward West Duluth.

I give a small nod. "Just ... a lot to take in."

He exhales softly. "Understandable."

The drive is almost meditative. While I've lived in East Duluth for a while now, it's the other side—the west side—that holds my most cherished memories.

Before I know it, London pulls into our old neighborhood. I haven't been back here in ages. Not since I went to college and my parents moved to Two Harbors.

He pulls up to the quaint two-story Victorian home I know like the back of my hand. Or at least, I used to. When I stare at the two homes side-by-side, despite small changes, like the fact that our treehouse is missing, I can almost envision that no time has passed.

"Here we are," he says, turning off the engine.

His house stands proudly, its wooden facade bathed in the glow of his porch lights. Even in the dim lighting, I can make out a well-maintained garden and the silhouette of a swing hanging from a tree in the back.

We exit the vehicle in relative silence, London once again guiding me.

As we approach his front door, he pauses and turns to face me. "Lily, before we go in, just ..." He chews on his bottom lip for a moment before continuing, "just know that you're safe here. No judgments—*no expectations.*"

While I hadn't really processed enough to think that far, I give him a thankful smile, and the weight on my shoulders feels a tad lighter.

Inside, the house is a blend of old-world charm and modern comfort. It's clear someone—maybe London— has remodeled the home in recent years. The living room is cozy, with a plush, dark leather sofa and walls adorned with various paintings depicting the stars.

I can't even fight back the smile that brings.

He gestures for me to sit, so I do, drawing my knees up.

"Would you like something to drink?" he asks, already heading toward the kitchen.

"Just some water, please," I reply.

While he's gone, I take the opportunity to study the room. It feels lived in, warm. I spot a telescope propped up against one wall, a stack of vinyl records on a shelf, and numerous books scattered about.

Returning with two glasses of water, London sits down beside me, handing one over. Our fingers brush in the brief exchange, and an electric current of familiarity and something more courses through my hand.

"Thank you," I whisper, glancing down.

For a moment, we simply sit in silence, sipping our water. The night's events, the emotional rollercoaster, seem to catch up with me all at once.

I stifle a yawn with the back of my hand.

"Hey," London says softly, nudging my shoulder. "If you want, the guest room is all set. You can rest."

I nod, appreciating his understanding. "Yeah, that sounds good."

He guides me to a bedroom upstairs. It's not his old bedroom, which makes me wonder what if he's sleeping in there now. The room is softly lit with a comforting amber hue. The bed looks inviting with its fluffy pillows and blankets.

"Get some sleep," London says, pausing at the door. "We can talk more in the morning."

I nod, already feeling the pull of sleep. "Goodnight, London."

A ghost of a smile curves his lips. "Goodnight, Lily."

As the door softly clicks shut, I'm left with my thoughts, the comfort of his house, and the overwhelming realization that, amidst the chaos, I've somehow managed to find a safe haven.

I undress down to my t-shirt, folding the rest of my clothing on a chair in the corner, and slide into the soft bed.

Despite the allure of sleep, the events of the evening replay.

Over, and over, and over.

Amidst my emotional storm, a single question keeps pressing on my mind—one that I hadn't dared to ask myself yet ...

What would it be like to be loved by London?

CHAPTER 29

Lily

Muffled raindrops patter against the window pane, lulling me from a comfortable sleep. As I open my eyes, soft morning light filters through light gray curtains, casting a gentle glow over an unfamiliar room.

For a moment, my insides clench and my heart skips a beat. Then, the events of the previous night rush back in fragmented memories. I close my eyes and let the waves of guilt and hurt and hope wash over me.

After a few moments, when the brunt of it has subsided, I sit up, rub my eyes, and glance around. The guest room in London's house is a blend of nostalgia and unfamiliarity. As much as we explored this house, I don't think we ever went into this room when we were kids.

The walls are adorned with pictures of London's family and even some photos of shared memories from our childhood together.

I pick a framed photo up off the nightstand beside

me and smile. We're dressed up for Halloween. Me dressed as Hermione and London as Ron. How he even has this photo is beyond me.

Back then, I thought it was strange that he'd pick Ron over Harry. We had so many mock fights about it, but all he'd tell me was that he liked Ron better.

My heart constricts again—but this time, in a way that stirs up my suspicions.

The scent of coffee wafts up the staircase, followed by the soft clang of pans. With a deep breath, I swing my legs over the side of the bed, still feeling the weight of the previous day's revelations pressing on me.

Divorce.

I'm getting a *divorce.*

The idea still feels surreal. And a little bit hollow.

And yet ...

I hesitate for a moment, debating whether to head straight downstairs or freshen up first. Deciding on the latter, I grab my clothes from the chair, and tug them back on.

Then I make my way to the small bathroom across the hall. After doing my business, I catch my reflection in the mirror and pause. With mascara and makeup smeared beneath my lids, haunted, dark eyes stare back at me.

Inhaling softly, I turn on the water, letting it flow through my fingertips as it heats up. When it reaches temperature, I wash my hands, then cup them together and bring the water to my face.

I let the warm water wash away the tears still clinging

to my cheeks from the night before. When my makeup is gone, I pat my face dry and try to tame my unruly hair.

When that last task seems impossible, I take another deep breath, throw my shoulders back, and venture downstairs. The comforting aroma of breakfast grows stronger, guiding me towards the kitchen.

So much about the house has changed, yet the layout, the one I could have run with my eyes closed as a kid, is still the same.

When I enter the kitchen, I find London, standing beside a large island—something that wasn't there before—wearing a casual tee and sweatpants, his focus on flipping pancakes.

The sight of him like this does strange things to my stomach.

He glances up, his eyes meeting mine, and a soft smile plays on his lips. "Morning, sleepyhead."

I chuckle, feeling a blush creep into my cheeks. "Morning."

"I hope you're hungry," London says, adding bacon to one of the pans.

My eyes open wide as I take a seat at the kitchen island. "You cook?"

He glances up, holding my gaze for a beat. Then, he winks. "Only when I have special guests."

"Special guests, huh?" I ask, raising an eyebrow. "Have lots of those, do you?"

He narrows his eyes and scrunches his face, then turns back to the stovetop, letting that go unanswered.

The sizzle of bacon fills the room, coupled with the

sweet aroma of his pancakes. I watch as London's hands move, deftly flipping a pancake here, stirring something there.

"I didn't know you were such a culinary expert," I tease.

He chuckles softly, but glances up at me from under his eyebrows, "There's a lot you don't know about me these days."

The comment hangs in the air, and the familiar tension between us rises again. There's so much we haven't said, so many emotions tangled between us.

In an attempt to diffuse the atmosphere, I ask, "Need any help?"

Without missing a beat, London reaches across the island and hands me a bowl filled with mixed berries. "You can toss these with some honey and lemon zest. Should be over there, on the counter." He jabs a thumb to the space behind him.

I nod, getting up from my seat and making my way to the ingredients. As I mix, I can't help but sneak glances at London, who seems lost in thought, his eyebrows knitted slightly.

"So, just a week until the big event," I begin, not entirely sure if it's the right thing to bring up but I need to bridge the silence. "I sent the invitations out a few days ago."

He glances over to me and grins. "Yeah, coming up fast."

I drop my gaze. "Yeah."

"Are you—" He clears his throat and shifts to his

other foot. "Will you be attending the night of the event? Or—?"

I shrug. "Honestly, I don't know. But I hope so."

London raises an eyebrow, a hint of mischief playing in the flecks of gold light sparkling in his blue eyes.

I inhale sharply, returning my eyes to the bowl of fruit.

London shuts off the stove and begins laying out the breakfast. He grabs the bowl from me, spooning fruit onto each plate.

I stand there, my fingers drumming lightly on the counter, as I watch him move. The way the muscles of his shoulders press against his t-shirt. The way his sweatpants hang from his hips.

For a split second, I let myself imagine ...

What if this were my life?

Waking up to this every morning—this warm, comforting, and safe place?

To him?

I catch myself before my thoughts spiral any deeper and shake my head, trying to rid the vision from my mind. But the seeds of those thoughts have already been sown, causing a rush of guilt.

I'm not even divorced yet, and here I am, having breakfast with London, and wondering about a life together.

London tilts his head slightly, his lips curving into a playful smirk. "Penny for your thoughts?"

"Just ... thinking about the pancakes," I reply with a small laugh, attempting to deflect. However, I'm pretty sure my cheeks betray me. I pick up my cup of coffee, trying to hide behind it.

He raises an eyebrow, an all-knowing glint in his eyes. "Just pancakes, huh? Not imagining me as your personal chef, serving breakfast in bed every morning?"

I choke on my coffee, trying to suppress my surprised laughter. "Oh, definitely not. I mean, who would want a handsome man cooking breakfast for them every day? Psh. Definitely not me."

He chuckles, sliding a plate filled with pancakes, fruit, and bacon in front of me. "Eat up, before you get more *imaginative* ideas."

We share a smile, but beneath it, I feel a tug—a blend of temptation, guilt, and excitement.

I take the first few bites and have to hold myself back from moaning. The breakfast is *perfect*. And so delicious.

The whole time, I sneak glances at him and I swear I feel him doing the same.

After taking a bite of his pancake, he says, "Remember when you used to steal bites from my plate when we were kids?"

I laugh, feigning innocence, as I press my fingertips to my chest. "Who, me? Never. I was just taste-testing. Making sure they were safe for consumption. I was obviously trying to protect you."

He leans in playfully, his fork pointing at a piece of his bacon. "Don't you dare try it now."

The thrill of a challenge rushes over me and I reach out, snatching the bacon with my fork just as London tries to pull his plate away.

I don't even wait. I pop it in my mouth and moan loudly like it's the best tasting thing I've ever had.

His eyes widen and his throat bobs. "You, uh—you always were a step ahead," he says, admiration—and maybe something else—reflecting back at me.

I bite my lip, dropping my gaze back to my plate.

The air between us feels charged again, so I focus on eating—quietly this time.

"Do you remember that summer we built the treehouse in your backyard?" London asks, humor painting his tone. "We thought we were brilliant architects."

I shake my head and giggle. "You mean the one that nearly fell when we tried climbing into it? Then, my dad had to get involved and fortify it so we didn't tumble to our deaths? That one?"

"Yep, that's the one. At least it was a great place to store the blankets the night before I—" London stops, then clears his throat. "Uh, anyway ... In our defense, we were just kids. But hey, no broken bones, so ... *success?*"

I smile, trying to push past the haunting whisper of a memory. "We were quite the pair, weren't we?"

"Yeah," he murmurs, his eyes darkening. "We were." A smile begins to creep onto my face, but then he continues, letting out a deep sigh, "We had something special, Lily. Something that I'm not sure ever truly went away."

The weight of his words hangs in the air, leaving us both lost in the silence.

Because I couldn't agree more.

CHAPTER 30

London

A week ago, if you would have told me that I'd have kissed Lily ... Or that she'd spend the last four nights at my house due to her crumbling marriage—something which had nothing to do with said kiss, *thank fuck*—I'd have said you were out of your mind.

Yet, here she is.

Sitting at my dining room table with her sleepy eyes and disheveled hair, looking more gorgeous than I've ever seen her, simply because this is a new side of her that she's allowing me to see.

How anyone could walk away from this—*from her*—it's beyond me.

To be honest, though, it takes me back to when we were kids. When I'd wake her up early and she'd still be in her pajamas and unicorn slippers.

A smile floats to my face before I can stop it.

"What are you grinning about?" she asks, narrowing her eyes.

My eyebrows flick upward in surprise.

Sleepy, but evidently still observant.

I let loose a sigh. "I was just thinking back to when we were kids and I'd drag you out of bed early. You look the same."

Her face crumples and she fusses over her hair, only making my heart ache more.

I chuckle, reaching out across the table to stop her hand. "You look lovely. Leave it."

"Oh yes, an absolute angel, I'm sure." She laughs dryly as she rolls her eyes.

I lock eyes with her, holding our gaze for a full beat before saying, "You look like one to me."

Color rushes into her cheeks and she drops my gaze to stare into her coffee cup.

"Well, thank you." Her voice is so soft, I barely make it out.

I grin, knowing full well, that saying thank you was hard for her to say when a million rebuttals were probably ready to spring off her tongue.

"So, what's on the agenda today?" I ask, changing the subject so things don't turn awkward.

This has become our routine now. Breakfast together, find out what the other has planned for the day … Then we'd work from my kitchen table until I needed to check in at Nocté or she had something she needed to attend to.

Most of the time, though, we've traveled together to the club so we could hammer out the last-minute details for the Upper Tier event.

Once or twice she'd had to leave to take care of personal things on her to-do list.

She even went back to her house to retrieve some of her clothing—but only when she knew for a fact that Seth wasn't around. At least, that's what I gathered from our talks. How she knew that, I had no clue and I hadn't pried.

Lily never outright said it, but I could see in those big brown eyes that relief was starting to replace the more intense feelings she'd been dealing with the past few days.

With a heavy sigh, she splays her hands on the table in front of her and I can't help but notice her wedding ring is no longer adorning her finger.

"Today, I have to meet with my lawyer," she says softly. "Seth's lawyer got in touch yesterday, and I want to make sure things run smoothly. And *quickly*. You know?"

She scrunches her nose at the end of the sentence and it's the cutest thing but I make an attempt to pretend it doesn't affect me.

Instead, I reach out, placing a hand over hers. "Are you okay? With everything?"

Her eyes meet mine and early morning sunshine cascades across her features as she nods. "I'm getting there."

"Good." I grin, rubbing lazy circles with the tip of my middle finger on the back of her hand. Her eyes flit to the place where we touch and I ask, "Do you want me to stop?"

She swallows hard and shakes her head.

So, I keep doing it, allowing that tiny point of contact to be a reminder that I'm here. Whenever she's ready—if she's *ever* ready. And if she's not, I was her friend first. I can find a way for that to be enough.

"London—"

She says my name like a big talk is coming, so I pause my motion to watch her. "Lily?"

Her eyelashes flutter on her cheeks and she takes a moment before saying, "Thank you. For letting me stay here. For not—" She bites on her lip, drawing my eyes in the motion. "For not expecting anything from me. I know this must be weird ..."

"It's not," I say, cutting her off.

She tilts her head and shoots me a *get-real* expression.

I shake my head. "Seriously. I like having you here. I wish—" I clamp my mouth shut, knowing damn well the confession that nearly slipped out is too much.

Too soon. Too fast.

"You wish?" Lily prods.

I clear my throat. "I wish things were easier for you."

A hint of a smile plays at her lips. It's almost as if she knew what I wanted to say even though I hadn't said it. "You've definitely made things easier."

That brings a smile to my face. "Good."

"London, I know ..." she begins, her eyebrows knitting together. "I know there's more—*between us.*" Her eyes flash to mine and she holds my stare for a beat. "More than friendship. More than a crush. I've been thinking a lot. About what's right. What's wrong. About *timing.*"

I inhale sharply, trying to ignore the pounding in my chest because it feels like it's going to crack open any minute.

"You've made things, this weird transition, feel like it was meant to be," she whispers.

I smooth my hand over hers, hoping like hell it's the right move. "What do you mean?"

Her lips shift to the side before that faint blush creeps across her cheeks. "I didn't realize it—*not at first*—but I think I've been wishing for you. For a long, long time."

My heartbeat kicks up another notch and I reach out, letting my palm graze her cheek.

She leans into my touch for a moment, letting her eyes drift closed.

Her words do something strange to me. Warmth spreads through my body and I let go of the breath I didn't even realize I was holding.

"I never needed to wish for you," I say, standing up and walking around the table when I meet her confused eyes. I reach out, and she takes my hand so I can pull her to a stand. "Lily, I never needed to wish for you because I *knew*. I knew from the time we were kids that you were something special. I knew I loved you then. So if anything, I was *waiting*."

Her eyes go wide. "You did?"

I nod. "Always."

She glances away from me, letting her gaze drift out my kitchen window and into the backyard. "I don't know what to say."

"You don't have to say anything. Or do anything. Just

know I'm here. When you're ready. *If* you're ready," I whisper, my gaze drifting to her lips. Without thinking, I reach out, brushing my thumb across her bottom lip.

She sucks in a sharp breath and again her eyes drift closed. "That's just it ... I feel like"—She swallows hard—"I feel like moving on should be harder than this. *Take* longer." She shakes her head, then opens her eyes. "But all I can think about is how much I want you to kiss me again when you look at me like that. Isn't that terrible?"

I grin, trying desperately not to full-on beam from that statement. So, instead, I tease, "Wow, you know how to make a guy feel special."

She pins me with a glare. "You know what I meant."

I chuckle softly. "I do."

She sighs.

"But for what it's worth, our situation is a little unusual," I offer, continuing to rub my thumb across her bottom lip.

"How?" she asks, her voice turning breathy.

I finally pull my hand away from her face and instead, slide it into hers. "We've known each other a long time, Lily. We were so close. And your marriage—" I glance at her, hoping I'm not stepping into things. "It sounds as though your marriage ended a while ago. You just hadn't made it official."

"I hadn't thought of that." Again, she licks her bottom lip, and it drives me crazy before she continues, "No, that's a lie. It's all I can think about." She snickers under her breath, then reaches out to scratch her forehead. "God, why is this so hard?"

"Expectations?" I suggest.

"What do you mean?" Her eyebrows tug in and I reach out to press my index finger at the place where they scrunch. Instantly, she relaxes them.

"Societal expectations, mostly." I shrug. "People assume you have to behave a certain way when a marriage breaks up and so you shoulder that expectation."

She narrows her gaze. "I suppose."

"Lily, you've never wanted to hurt people. Never wanted to have someone tell you that you did a terrible job. Or hell, be *mad* at you. So, you're trying to weigh the consequences. I get it," I say, squeezing her hand.

"It's like you're in my head." She huffs a humorless laugh.

A slow grin spreads across my face. "Maybe I am." When she rolls her eyes again, I say, "Or maybe ... I just *know* you."

She takes another deep breath and her eyes glisten with emotion.

With my free hand, I place my index finger under her chin and tip it up. "I see you, Lily. I see *you*. And I'll follow your lead. I don't care what others think of us. I couldn't give two fucks—but I know *you do*. So, I don't care how long it takes. If you need to keep me at a distance for a decade before you feel comfortable, I'll—"

Before I can process her sudden movement, Lily's lips are on mine—a soft, tentative touch, like the whisper of a dream. Her fingers tighten on the nape of my neck, drawing me deeper into her embrace and the scent that is all Lily—a combination of cherry and vanilla—floods my senses.

As our lips move together, they're in a delicate exploration. It's not just the merging of mouths, but a blending of past memories, unspoken desires, and buried feelings. Every nuance of her kiss tells a story, one I've been longing to read for what feels like an eternity.

The world narrows down to just the two of us as she deepens the kiss. The slight taste of her morning coffee, the warmth of her breath, the soft hum of satisfaction she lets out—all of it sends electricity zinging through me.

Her hands travel from my neck, over my shoulders, and down my chest, as if she's trying to memorize every inch of me.

I respond by sliding one hand into the silken strands of her hair and tilting her head to gain better access. The other hand rests on the small of her back, pulling her closer, wanting to bridge any remaining gap between us.

The feel of her pressed up against me is intoxicating, grounding, and terrifying all at once. Because while this kiss feels like coming home, it also holds the weight of every unsaid word, every missed opportunity, every year spent apart when we should have been together.

When we finally pull apart, it's not a break—but a pause. Our foreheads rest together, our heavy breaths mingling in the space between us. I can feel the rapid pulse of her heart, and I'm sure she can feel mine, racing just as fast.

There's a moment of silence, a wordless exchange, as

if we're both trying to find our bearings in this new reality we've just created.

The reality we're intentionally *creating*.

Lily is the first to speak, her voice a breathless whisper, "That was ..."

I chuckle softly, finishing her sentence, "Overdue."

She laughs, a soft, tinkling sound that makes my heart soar. "*Very* overdue."

And in that shared moment, with the early morning light filtering through the windows and the lingering taste of her on my lips, everything feels possible.

"Will I see you tonight?" I ask a bit dreamily, pulling back enough to see her face.

Her smile is all the answer I need.

However, she replies, "It's Thursday."

I narrow my gaze, confused. "And?"

"And," she draws out the word with a mischievous glint in her eyes, "It's book club night. I think it's time to have a conversation with the Dirty B's."

CHAPTER 31

Lily

"Holy shit," Vivian says, absolutely vibrating with excitement. "*Holy shit.* She finally did it."

"Pay up," Anna mutters, flicking her fingertips at Vivian without even looking up from her phone.

"I can't believe it," Vivian chirps, shaking her head as she pulls out a twenty-dollar bill from her purse and hands it over to Anna.

I narrow my gaze and point at their exchange. "What's all this?"

Anna levels me with a borderline bored stare. "No one thought you'd finally pull the trigger and divorce Seth."

"And not for lack of scheming," Tasia adds with a chuckle. She leans back in her chair and shakes her head. "Believe me."

My mouth gapes open. "What?"

"Oh, honey. You have no idea the Machiavellian lengths we've all gone through," Quinn grins, taking a seat on the arm of the loveseat. "All I can say is, thank the Heavens above for London."

A catlike grin spreads across Vivian's face as she twists to face me. "Yes, how is *sexy* London?"

"Sorry, I'm late guys," Carlie says, entering the little nook in the back of Dirty Books. In her arms is a large brown bag, presumably full of wine, since it's her week. "I've got a big event coming up next weekend," she continues, unloading a variety of bottles onto the small coffee table, "and I've been trying to figure out what to wear. Nothing fits the way I want it to and I'm mortified that I can't get my weight under control."

"What are you talking about? You're hot," Vivian counters, shooting Carlie a look of admonishment.

Color floods Carlie's cheeks and she almost misses the table with the last bottle. Luckily, she scrambles, catching it before it can become one hell of a mess on the carpet.

"Whoa," she breathes, setting the bottle gingerly on the table. "That was close."

Tasia shoos her from the table, then picks up the bottle opener to start passing out the wine.

"What did I miss?" Carlie asks, taking a seat on the empty folding chair meant for her.

"I'm thrilled to finally be indoctrinated as a Dirty B," Quinn announces with a sly grin. "At least, every once in a while."

Carlie tips her head and smiles. "Yay."

Vivian swipes a hand in the air. "Yes, yes. That's all very exciting. However, the big bomb drop goes to Lily."

All eyes once again turn on me and I sigh, mustering up the courage to say it once again. "I'm getting a divorce."

Carlie gasps, planting her hands over her mouth. "Oh my gosh."

Anna drops her phone a couple inches to quirk an eyebrow at Carlie.

"And now that we're all caught up, I'm dying here," Vivian cuts in. "Please, please tell me London has made his move."

I shake my head in disbelief, even though I should have expected nothing less from Vivian.

"I second that query," Quinn interjects, narrowing his gaze. "What *is* going on with London?"

I bite my lip, weighing how much I want to tell them. While they're my closest friends in the world, everything with London is so new. So ... *tentative*.

"Well," I begin, letting my gaze float around the room. "I've been staying with London."

"What?" Quinn fires off, gawking at me. "Why is this the first I've heard of this? Tell us *everything*. I'll flog him later, that minx."

"How long?" Tasia questions, a hint of scandal in her tone.

I swallow hard, scooting forward to grab one of the glasses of wine. After taking a sip, I lean back and offer, "Since the night Seth and I called things off."

Anna's eyes dart around the group, gauging reactions, and then they land back on me. "You've been with him every night since the split? Like, every single night?"

I nod, my face warming under the intensity of their stares. "Not ... not like *that*. He's ..."

Vivian leans forward, her wine nearly spilling in her excitement. "So have you two ... ?" She wiggles her eyebrows.

I take a deep breath, laughing a bit nervously. "We've had moments. Tender, confusing moments. But we haven't, you know ... At least, not yet."

"But you want to?" Vivian presses, practically biting down on her knuckles.

I chew on my lip and try desperately not to show my true desires. I don't think it works, though.

Carlie interjects with a thoughtful expression, "You're both in a vulnerable place right now, especially you. He knows that. London wouldn't take advantage. If I were writing your love story, I'd have him wait for you to come to him."

Quinn sets his wine glass down and grins. "Well, I for one, can't wait to hear when the fireworks over that event go off."

Anna snickers. "What are you going to do, Quinn? Camp outside their bedroom door until you hear them moaning in ecstasy?"

I bury my face in my hands, trying desperately to hide the intense blush.

"Maybe," Quinn fires back.

Tasia laughs, her attention unwavering. "Oh, come on, guys. We all saw this coming, didn't we? Their chemistry has been off the charts from the moment they found each other again."

I lower my hands and blink hard at her.

Anna grins knowingly, flipping her fingertips toward Vivian again—who in turn, pulls another twenty from her purse and cusses.

"And that bet was on whether or not you'd end up with London immediately after," Anna says.

How that woman notices anything beyond her phone screen is beyond me. But dang, she's good.

I shake my head, chuckling. "I shouldn't be surprised. But look, it's not like we're jumping into a full-blown relationship. I need time to figure things out, and he's been very respectful of that. We're taking things slow."

Quinn leans forward, his voice softening. "Just promise us you'll be careful, okay? His heart is fragile, too."

I press my lips tight and nod, touched by the genuine concern in his eyes. I kinda love that my friends care so much for London already.

"I promise. But guys, I can't deny there's something there. Maybe it's been there for a while, buried underneath everything else."

Carlie reaches across to squeeze my hand. "We just want the best for you. Always."

"Thank you," I whisper, trying hard to hold back my emotions.

Vivian, ever the one to break a somber moment, lifts her glass in a toast. "To new beginnings, unexplored feelings, and the hope that Lily breaks her celibacy streak soon."

Again, my face heats, but laughter fills the room as we clink glasses in cheers.

The tension in the room dissipates with our shared laughter and lightness. Being with the Dirty B's feels like a sanctuary from the heavy, complex world outside.

I catch Quinn's eye, and there's a mischievous sparkle in his gaze I've come to recognize over the years—a sure sign that Quinn has a story to spill.

Inwardly, I cringe just a bit knowing full well, it's going to be about me somehow.

He clears his throat dramatically, drawing attention as he often does with his natural flair for the theatric. "Speaking of unexplored feelings," he begins, waggling his eyebrows in my direction. "I believe I had a front-row seat to the rekindling of Lily's epic romance. Would everyone care for a trip down memory lane as I describe how this meet-cute went down?"

The group leans in with interest, their gazes flicking between Quinn and me. I narrow my eyes at him, a nervous thrill running through me.

"Well, don't keep us in suspense," Tasia urges, her eyes wide with anticipation.

Quinn's grin widens, the dramatic pause only heightening the intrigue. "Picture it—a fine Thursday afternoon, and our dear Lily in Dirty Deeds—on the hunt for Tasia's bookmarks. Anyone remember?" There's a group consensus and he continues, "Well, as I'm describing the absolute many uses of our new vibrator line, who does she bump into but London—the prodigal son returned."

My cheeks are burning—even the tips of my ears feel

hot. The memory of that awkward yet electric encounter floods back.

"Quinn, they know all of this," I protest, though there's laughter in my voice. The embarrassment is real, but so is the fondness for that memory.

I can't believe I practically dong-slapped London's box of stir sticks out of his hands.

"Oh, let him speak," Vivian interjects with a delighted cackle. "This is the quality content I live for."

Ignoring my feigned outrage, Quinn continues, narrating the encounter with an added flair that only he can muster. He describes the charged air, the unspoken tension, and the undeniable chemistry that even a casual observer like him evidently couldn't ignore.

As the tale unfolds, the room is filled with laughter, teasing, and the kind of camaraderie that has seen us through the best and worst of times.

Despite my initial hesitation, I find myself drawn into the reminiscing and the memories that paint London in a light that's both nostalgic and new.

When the laughter dies down, there's a moment of silence, the kind filled with unsaid words and unexplored territories. We're on the brink of something, something terrifying yet thrilling—at least I am.

"See," Quinn concludes with a wink, "destiny has been knocking on this door for a while, my dear. It's about time you answered. I, for one, bow down to the Fate's matchmaking skills."

I clear my throat, trying to shift the spotlight a bit. "Speaking of destiny, what's this event you're going to next weekend? And why does it have you questioning your worth?"

Carlie shrugs. "I've had a hard time maintaining my weight and since I spend so much time sitting down at a computer, it's only gotten worse the past few years. I guess, I just want to feel sexy and desirable. You know?"

Vivian opens her mouth like she's going to interject, but Anna cuts her off. "Desirability is all in your head. If you feel it, so will your partner."

We all turn to give Anna a surprised once-over with that little nugget.

She simply shrugs.

"Well, I've got an appointment with a nutritionist next week, and then I'm starting with a personal trainer on Monday after the event. My hope is just to get to a point where I feel strong and healthy again," Carlie says with a shy smile.

Tasia, ever curious, asks, "Oh? Who's the trainer?"

"Just a sec," Carlie says, reaching down to rummage through her purse. As she pulls out a card, the edge of a lavish-looking invitation gets snagged. In classic Carlie fashion, it slips from her purse, gliding to the floor, the familiar golden embossment shimmering in the dim light.

My heart skips a beat as I stare at it.

Everyone pauses, their gazes shifting between the invite and Carlie.

Vivian's eyes glint with her brand of mischief as she makes an attempt to reach for the envelope. "Oooh, what's this? The invite to your fancy event, Carlie?"

Carlie's cheeks turn a deep shade of crimson as swiftly reaches out and snatches it up before Vivian can. The way she holds it to her chest, it's obvious she's trying to conceal the details.

"Yeah," she breathes, her voice slightly shaky, "it is."

As her eyes briefly meet mine, a chill zings straight down my spine.

Carlie is planning on heading into the very heart of Nocté—the Upper Tier event I've been meticulously planning.

CHAPTER 32

London

"I can't believe it's already down to this," Lily muses, setting out the remaining floral arrangement on the extended dining room table. She fusses with the tablecloth and turns to me with a smile that lights up the room.

"I can't either. It feels like we've been planning this event for ages." I take a deep breath and glance around.

The Upper Tier has been completely reimagined, thanks to Lily's attention to detail.

As part of our rehearsal before the big night, the lights have been dimmed low and candles lit, flickering gently. Music filters into the space—the haunting sound of violins creates the perfect ambiance in the background.

Everywhere I look there are large plants and more flowers than I've ever seen in one place. The main flower, of course, is *lilies*. All varieties, all sorts of colors.

It's an oasis of colors, textures, and smells.

No matter where you go, the lingering scents follow, hanging heavy and sweet in the air. And it's intoxicating.

Maybe I'm biased. Or maybe it's because I've been working so closely with Lily for the past few days and things have been *so good* between us.

She moves from the flowers, fiddling for the hundredth time with the masks that are laid out with meticulous care for the guests to use tomorrow night.

I lean against the wall, watching her, and loving every minute of it.

Her attention, her focus, her drive.

How much she loves what she does—it shows in the way her eyes light up and that adorable smile creeps across her face.

Just like it is now.

Evidently satisfied, she turns to me.

"What are you grinning at?" she laughs, crinkling her nose at me.

My eyebrows flick upward and I shake my head. "I, uh—I was just thinking about what an incredible job you've done."

She beams back at me, her eyes sparkling in the candlelight as she folds her hands in front of her. "You think they'll all like it?"

I move toward her, reaching out a hand so I can take hers in mine. "If they don't, it will have nothing to do with what you've created here."

She narrows her eyes, then glances around again. "So, if you were participating in this event, would this put you in the mood?"

As if she realized what she said—or perhaps who she said it to—she bites down on her lip. Her brown eyes are wide but there's something in them that stirs my body to awaken more than anything she's decorated.

I huff a laugh, brushing my knuckles across her cheek. Slowly, I bend forward and whisper next to her ear, "I don't think you want me to answer that."

Lily inhales sharply, her chest heaving in the motion. "You know, I think maybe I do."

I grin, taking a small step back, unable to stray too far, but needing to put a little space between us.

She seems momentarily taken aback by her own words, as the candor of the moment hangs between us. Then, with a small, challenging smile, she steps closer.

"Prove it," she whispers.

I blink in surprise, totally caught off guard. "Prove what?"

"That this," she gestures around the dimly lit Upper Tier, "doesn't affect you as much as it affects me."

I swallow hard, our close proximity causing my heart to race. "You're playing a dangerous game, Lily."

She tilts her head, her gaze locked onto mine. "Am I?"

Then, she reaches out, plucking a black and deep purple velvet mask from the table. The design is intricate, with feathers that brush her fingers as she holds it. "Would you wear this?"

"If I were a guest?" I press, watching her every move closely.

Her lips twitch and she bats her eyelashes. "Sure."

I nod slowly, knowing damn well this *really is* a dangerous game. Because if she starts something, I'm not sure if I'll be able to stop her. Hell, *stop myself.*

She steps closer, raising the mask to my face and securing it. The world goes slightly dark, the eye holes only allowing a limited view of her through the fabric. I can vaguely make out her form, and that's about it.

Everything suddenly becomes more focused, more intimate. And my body goes on high alert.

"Better?" she murmurs, her fingers brushing against my jawline, and sending shivers straight through me.

"Depends on your definition of *'better,'*" I reply, my voice huskier than intended.

She chuckles softly. "Do you trust me?"

"With my life," I answer without hesitation.

She takes that as an affirmation as she grabs my hand, leading me somewhere beyond the dining room. When we arrive at her destination, she pushes me gently so I take a seat.

My senses heighten further, thanks to the limited vision the mask provides and this line we seem to be treading.

Lily moves behind me, her fingertips ghosting over my shoulders as she leans down. "Close your eyes," she whispers.

"You know I can't really see you." I chuckle.

She places a fingertip to my mouth, cutting off any further teasing from me.

"Do it," she commands.

Obliging her, I close my eyes and wait, trying desperately to settle my heart and what my body wants from her. I shift in my seat and think calming thoughts. Not that they help one little bit.

Then I hear the soft rustle of fabric, and the clink of glass. A moment later, I feel something cool and soft against my lips. She drags it slowly from one side to the other, teasing against my lower lip. I open my mouth slightly, tasting a rich, decadent chocolate, followed by the sweet tang of a berry.

Fuck. Me.

I moan softly at the taste and the unexpected intimacy of the moment. I had no idea how sexy something like this could be.

She leans down, her breath warm against my ear. "Tell me this doesn't affect you."

I swallow hard. "I can't."

She lets out a soft laugh, the sound vibrating through the charged space between us. "Good."

I reach out, searching for her, and when my hands find the soft curve of her waist, I pull her gently in front of me.

"Now what?" I ask, the challenge implicit.

Lily's fingers dance over my mask, tracing the intricate designs before she slowly lifts it.

As it comes off, our eyes meet. No longer shielded by the fabric, the raw intensity of the moment makes everything else fade into the background.

The fact that we're at Nocté.

That anyone could walk in at a moment's notice ...

None of that matters.

She leans in, her lips so close, but not quite touching mine. "What if I told you this affects me just as much—*maybe more*? And it has everything to do with you."

My heart thunders in my chest like a storm demanding to be unleashed. "Then I'd say, why are we still talking?"

Lily hesitates for just a moment, the weight of the decision clear in her eyes.

If we cross this line, if we do anything more than kiss ...

I'm not sure she's ready for that.

But then, with a certainty that sends another shiver down my spine, she closes the gap between us. The world narrows down to a single point of contact—our one shared breath as she takes my face in her hands and kisses me like it will bring us both to life.

God, it will never get old having her do this—take the initiative.

Kiss *me*.

Like she means it. Like it's all she wants.

No fears.

Just *us*.

My hands grope her hips, pulling her on top of me. She wraps her legs around mine, sitting directly where I want her—where I need her. If only with less clothing.

I tip my hips slightly, groaning from the friction it causes between us—because *damn*.

It doesn't just affect me, either. Lily's moan is swallowed by my mouth as my kiss turns frantic.

For a moment, I swear, I've lost my damn mind.

All I can think about is this kiss, this beautiful woman sitting on top of me, and how I've wanted this for so long.

I can't take much more of it—this tension and desire.

But I know I have to... I *might* have to.

Should I have to?

God, what are we doing?

Coming up for air, I practically pant, "Lily, we should stop."

Her eyes are hooded as she leans back slightly, breathing as heavily as I am.

"There's so much more I want to discover about you, Lil. Beyond the masks, beyond the pretense. Just us," I whisper.

She smiles, a touch of mischief in her eyes that instantly has me suspicious. "Then let's start tonight."

I narrow my gaze, uncertain if she means what I think she means. "I don't want to push you to before you're—"

Again, she presses her fingertips to my lips, cutting off my words. "London, I've been thinking about this a lot since"—Her eyes hold mine for a beat—"well, you know."

I tip my head.

Because I do. I know all too well.

She runs her hands down the plane of my chest, causing me to shiver. "There's no one up here but us. The doors are locked until tomorrow, to keep the Upper Tier in suspense. The club is open downstairs, so Myles and Cal are preoccupied." She shoots me a sly grin and my heartbeat ratchets up further. "We might not be participating in the event as guests tomorrow, but for once—*just once*—I want to know what it feels like."

My eyebrows tug inward and I splay my hands over her lower back, trying desperately to keep them from roaming. "Lily, I want more from you than one night."

One side of her lips curls upward. "But that's just it ... *It's perfect.*"

I shake my head. "I don't understand."

"*One night* in the club," she whispers, bending in close to my ear. "Then, the rest of the nights are ours."

Realization dawns and I lean back in my chair.

The rules.

She's talking about the rules of Club Nocté ...

"What if..." I swallow hard, trying to calm my emotions. Am I really considering this? "What if we do this and you decide I'm not—"

She levels me with a pointed stare.

"Lily, I don't want to be a rebound," I admit, raising my hand to trace her jaw.

She meets my gaze squarely, her eyebrows drawing together. "You think I see you as a rebound?" There's a challenging tone in her voice, mixed with a hint of vulnerability.

"It's not that—not entirely," I whisper, carefully choosing my words, "It's just ... After everything that's happened, I don't want us rushing into something. No matter how much I want to."

Lily's expression softens, but there's still a fire in her eyes. "London, I get it, I do. But I don't want to be perpetually defined by my past. And when I look at you, I don't see a rebound. I see *home—my future.* I see someone who has known me, *all of me,* for so long. I just want to share one more piece of myself with you."

I swallow hard, taken aback by the raw intensity of her words. "Lily ..."

She slides her hands to the nape of my neck, halting me. "I need you to trust my feelings. To trust that I know my own heart. Can you do that?"

I nod, not trusting myself enough to speak because I think my mouth has just gone dry and my heart has stopped beating all together.

"Good." A playful twinkle lights up her eyes and she begins slowly unbuttoning my shirt. "Then let's not waste another moment questioning what we already know to be true. Tonight, is the beginning of ... *us.* That is, if you'll have me."

CHAPTER 33

Lily

As I wait for London's response, a tense silence envelops us, but I continue to work his buttons.

Slowly, I lift my eyes from his chest, finding myself lost in his silent, searching gaze. In the muted glow of the distant candlelight, his eyes shimmer like they're the epitome of living starlight.

His warm hands settle over mine, stilling my work. "Lily, are you sure? Because I can—"

I inhale deeply, wishing he could see into my mind and heart. "I've never been more sure of anything in all my life. I only wish …" I bite my lip before continuing, "I wish it hadn't taken us so long to get here. Now, shut up and kiss me."

Thankfully, he doesn't make me wait this time. Instead, his kiss is powerful as he drops my hands to pull me in closer.

My fingertips return to his shirt, unbuttoning it as quickly as I can, so I don't lose my nerve. I've been thinking about today for a while now. About how I was going to ask him and how I would initiate this evening.

Carlie was right. I'm the one who had to go to him. I'm the one who had to make this first night happen.

Now that it's here ...

My heart is about to explode with excitement and nerves.

A part of me still feels like I'm cheating on my marriage. It's such a strange feeling.

Or perhaps it feels like this is too good to be happening. That I shouldn't feel *this good* right now.

I shove that part of me aside, willing myself to move through it. Trusting that this is all part of the process. A part of moving on.

Especially now that I know what I want. What *I've always wanted.*

London suddenly stands up, taking me along with him. I let out a small squeak of surprise, only to have it drowned out by his smiling kiss.

"God, I love that sound," he murmurs against my lips.

My chest feels like it's about to burst open and I weave my hands through his dark hair, wishing this feeling would never end. Wishing this new chapter we're both creating would last for eternity.

Before I realize it, we're moving. I don't break our kiss long enough to orient myself until London kicks a door shut behind us and I slide down to the floor, standing directly in front of him.

Suddenly enveloped in a room we've staged for the Upper Tier, the gravity of this moment settles over me.

I'm here. In the *One Night Stand Club*, ready to explore the *one man* I should have always been with. The *one man* who has always had my heart.

I hear the lock click into place and I smile to myself.

Even if, *God forbid*, one of the others came upstairs, it won't matter. We're fully, and totally alone, and now, privacy envelops us.

Elation swims through my veins as I untuck his shirt from beneath his pants. I slide my hands over his broad shoulders, so I can remove it fully. As I do so, my eyes snag on the tattoo—the one right above his heart. With a smile on my lips, I trace the petals.

London watches me, not moving a muscle as I take it in.

"It's—" he says breathlessly, wrapping my hand in his as he presses it to his chest. "Lily, for me, it's always been you."

My breath hitches as our eyes meet again. There's so much there in the depths of his—love, longing, a fierce determination to make sure I understand where this is heading.

I kiss him again, harder this time—needing to show him how much he means to me, too. How much I need him. Want *him*...

Slowly, London presses forward, never breaking our kiss as he walks us to the edge of the bed. When the backs of my knees hit the fabric of the bedspread, he prowls forward, helping to settle me against the mattress so gently, that I can hardly stand it.

"I hope you're ready for a long night, Lily," he whispers, fire burning in those lust-filled eyes of his. "Because I intend to take my time."

My breath catches in my throat and a thrill of excitement races through me at the promise of those words. Everything tightens—my heart, my core, my breasts ...

Holy *hell.*

Quivering with anticipation, I don't think I've ever been this turned on.

He moves with a deliberate sensuality as he crawls backward to removes my shoes. I never would have thought something as simple as that could be hot, but dear lord above, I'm practically a puddle on this bed.

When both of have been removed and thrown to the floor, he kneels at the edge of the bed, watching me with a seductive grin for a moment. Then, with a slight shake of his head, he crawls forward, hovering slightly as his lips crush mine.

I groan as he settles on top of me, his hips tipping just enough that I can feel exactly how much he's affected. His hard length presses against my pelvis, but it's not enough—*not nearly enough.*

I open my legs wide, inviting him to settle between them. When he does, a guttural sound escapes his lips and he drops his head to my clavicle.

"Christ," he mutters between labored breaths.

"We need less clothing," I whisper at his ear, nipping gently.

He shudders, then raises ever so slightly so he can slide his hands beneath my shirt. His warm palms graze against my abdomen, traveling upward. When he reaches the bottom of my bra, his breathing goes shallow and his hips tip again, pressing his length against my center.

Heat pulses and I swear, I'm about to combust.

"Off—take it off," I command, trying to reach down to my shirt's hem and do it myself.

He swats my hands away. "I say when."

I gasp, unable to believe that such a small sentence could turn me on more than I already am.

"You wanted a one-night stand, Lily," London says, his voice gruff and intense. "I'm going to ensure this is the last one you'll ever have."

I'm full-on panting now, every part of me a live wire and ready—so ready for whatever he has in mind.

"When we're done here, I want my name to be the only one on your mind. My body to be the only one you think about. Do you understand?" he continues, kneeling up enough to unbutton my dress pants.

I swear, I nearly come from those words alone.

Outwardly, though, I nod, trying to calm myself enough to reach for him.

Again, he swats my hands away.

Toying with me.

A mischievous grin crosses his features as he unzips me and drags my pants off like he's part-sloth. So torturously *slow*.

"Oh, my god," I breathe, my head falling back to the

bed. Partly in total frustration and partly in complete, desperate desire.

I swear I can hear the smile in his words when he says, "Patience was never your strong suit."

Then, with my shirt still annoyingly in place, he settles himself over the top of me again. Only, this time, with one less piece of fabric separating us, I can feel him even better as he works his hips, grinding against me. He peppers kisses along my collarbone, my neck, and then the edge of my jaw.

My fingertips press into his skin, silently demanding he move faster.

Suddenly, his hands are beneath my shirt again as he traces the edge of my bra with his fingertips, never going under it, never palming over it.

I wiggle my hips, trying to build the friction in the hopes it might unhinge the iron-clad grip he seems to have on his control.

It only takes a few thrusts for him to press back slightly, his eyelids slamming shut. "Fuck," he mutters, breathing slowly through his nose. "You're evil, woman."

With his eyes still closed, he makes a valiant effort at breathing deep. I take the temporary distraction as a way to slip my shirt off. When he opens his eyes his lips press tight.

"What?" I ask, demurely.

"You're—" He shakes his head but takes in my body sprawled out before him. His eyes glass over and he bends forward, licking his way up my torso.

I groan. "God, no. No more teasing ... *Please.* I need you, London. Inside me. *Now.*"

London's eyes narrow, but the same frantic energy lurks in their depths. "I'll give you round one. But then ... you're mine to do with as I please."

My breath hitches and I nod, willing to accept anything at this point.

Then, he winks and reaches over to the nightstand, which by the look of it, is supplied with enough condoms to sheath a hundred guys.

My eyes widen, but I reach for his hand and whisper, "I'm on the pill."

He stills his motion as he turns to me still breathing heavily.

"And I'm clean," I admit in a rush, frowning slightly, pushing away any thoughts about how long it's been since I last has sex. "I mean, *obviously.*"

London's expression softens with understanding and he kisses my right eyebrow.

Then, my eyelid.

My cheek.

My nose.

Then, his tongue skirts the place where my lips meet and I fall back into the pillow with a moan.

"I'm clean, as well. I was checked a while ago. But I haven't—" London begins, speaking between kisses.

I run my hands over his muscled back, dragging my fingernails in an upward motion. "I trust you."

"You will be my undoing. I hope you know that," he

mutters, pulling himself off me long enough to kick off his shoes and shuck his jeans to the floor.

I can't bring myself to tear my eyes from him. He's so fucking beautiful—I could stare at him for days and never get bored.

But right now, I need more. I slide to the edge of the bed, and unhook my bra, letting it fall to the floor.

Now, we're even.

He sucks in a deep breath, his gaze straying over my chest. "Fuck, Lily, you are so incredibly sexy."

Until now, I never felt it.

Never had those words uttered to me in the way he says them. Like I was somehow molded by the gods solely for the purpose of being perfect for him.

Yet, despite all of that, I know the feeling.

Because he's the sexiest thing I've ever laid eyes on.

He's standing right in front of me and I look up at his handsome face, my heart pounding in my ears—and just about everywhere else.

"You were made for me," I whisper.

A ghost of a smile crosses his features and I reach out, slowly removing his black boxer briefs before he can stop me. His erection springs free and my breath catches.

Sexy doesn't even begin to cover all this man is.

Only one word comes close.

Soulmate.

When his briefs hit the floor, he steps out of them and I wrap my hands around his length, needing to feel him.

He groans, his head falling back. "I wouldn't do too much of that."

A grin floats to my lips and I quirk an eyebrow. "Why is that?"

London levels me with a desperate glare as I smile sweetly before I flick my tongue across the slick moisture pooling at his tip.

I moan, enjoying the feel and taste of him on my tongue.

He flat-out growls at me, planting his hands on my shoulders and pushing me back onto the bed. "For the same reason you don't want me to go slow."

Then, in a movement so swift, I barely register it, he slides the last remaining piece of fabric from my body. It flies over his shoulder as he prowls forward, nudging my legs wider as he settles between them.

My chest heaves with my breaths, every nerve alive and sparking with anticipation of what happens next.

Before he gets too close, he reaches out with one hand, finally sliding his palm over my breast. My eyes roll shut at the contact and my hips thrust forward.

With his other hand, he presses a fingertip to my clit and circles slowly. I just about jump out of my skin.

He chuckles softly. "That's a new sound."

It's an incredible amount of effort to open my eyes and flick him off, but I manage it.

Again, he laughs. "So vulgar." Then, he slides his finger inside me, causing me to buck against him. "And wet."

I writhe against his hand, desperate for him to remove it because if he doesn't …

"No, no …" I gasp, feeling the rush of my orgasm overcome any sense of control I thought I had. Light explodes behind my eyelids and throughout my body. Everything combusting with so little warning.

He doesn't remove his hand even after that, instead, he continues to thrust it in and out, building me back up with an incredible amount of precision. With my nipple between his thumb and forefinger, he pinches softly and bends in close. "Fuck, that was hot."

I cover my eyes in the crook of my arm, fighting off embarrassment. It's been so long—so long since I had sex and it's never felt like *this*.

London removes his hand from my breast to push my arm aside. When I open my eyes and connect my gaze to his, he says, "I love that I can make you do that."

Warmth spreads to my cheeks.

Then, without another word, his lips connect with mine and his other hand pulls away from my core as he inches closer. He nudges against me slowly, applying pressure as he slides his tip along my entrance.

"So fucking wet," he murmurs against my skin.

I bite down on my lip, trying desperately to keep myself still when all I really want is for him to thrust inside.

"London, I want you. *Please*," I plead, gripping his ass.

He smiles, a devastatingly gorgeous thing, as he

finally obliges. Slowly—*still so slowly*—he pushes into me.

And life as I know it will never, *ever* be the same.

He fits me in a way I never knew could be accomplished as he presses his enormous cock to the hilt. So full *... so blissfully full.*

A guttural sound escapes my lips and he's there with me, groaning and cursing to any gods who are brave enough to listen.

"Harder," I cry out, clinging onto him as if my life depended on it. "Fuck me harder."

That smile is in his words again when he repeats, "So vulgar."

But I plant a foot on the bed and rotate my hips, flipping us over.

His startled gaze meets mine as I slide down on top of him.

"Holy," he breaths a jagged breath, "*fuck.* You feel ..."

My heart beams, knowing he's as affected as I am—that this means as much to him as it does to me. Because God, I love this man.

The realization hits me hard.

I almost stop my movement, but his hands slide up my hips, helping to set a rhythm between us. Then, they slide up to my breasts, squeezing and pinching in a way that sends lightning threatening to unleash.

I press his roaming hands into the bed above his head and lick his lower lip, still riding him in a way that makes him squirm beneath me. Two hard thrusts, then pull up until he's almost out. Almost … but not quite. Then, I slam back down to the hilt.

Bending down, I kiss his jaw, his neck, and the lily over his heart.

His breath goes shallow and I flick his nipple with my tongue before nipping gently.

"Lily …" There's a warning in his tone and I smile against his chest, continuing my work. Having my way with him.

He sneaks a hand from my grasp—or perhaps I let him—and it finds my breast. In the same teasing way, he pinches my nipple, rolling it between his fingers in rhythm with our thrusts.

"Oh, fuck," he mutters, his voice tightens as he pulls both hands from me and plants them firmly on my hips. "Shit, you're going to—"

I feel him pulse inside me as he bucks his hips and I shatter around his climax. My body quakes from the energy, the torrent of emotions, the physical exertion—this incredible connection.

Never in a million years …

Never in all my life.

No dirty book could ever do this justice.

Every piece of me is in ecstasy and I know right here and now, this is everything I've been dreaming of.

He's everything I've been dreaming of.

And now, there's no turning back.

CHAPTER 34

London

I wake up with a jolt, totally disoriented.

Then, when I take in the dark hair in my field of vision, it all rushes back.

Lily is sprawled across my naked torso—and other naked places. Some of them haven't gotten the memo that exhaustion should have set in by now.

I don't know how many *rounds* we went through. Too many to count.

But damn, I've never felt this good.

I don't think this high will ever get old.

Smiling to myself, I reach up, feeling the tips of her hair as they glide through my fingertips. I don't even know what time it is, but I know one thing's for sure— it's gotta be late. Or *early*, depending on how you look at it.

I glance down again, brushing a stray hair from Lily's face.

She's so fucking beautiful, it hurts.

And after last night ...

She sighs softly, her eyes fluttering open. When she takes in our setting, she relaxes into me and smiles against my chest. "Hey."

My heart beams at her easy-going greeting.

"Hey, beautiful," I whisper, rubbing my hand across the bare skin of her back.

I feel her smile against my skin as her hand smooths across my chest. Then, she fiddles with my chest hair, running her fingertips through it. "I feel so ..." A grunt of satisfaction escapes her lips and she glances up at me. "Peaceful."

A smile floats to my face and I continue to rub my hand across her back.

"Though, I have a feeling, I'll be sore later." She chuckles softly.

I shake my head as I inventory my body. Warmth and heat still pool throughout all of my sensitive areas. "I think that goes for both of us."

A comfortable silence fills the space between us as she continues to stroke my chest.

I wish we could stay like this forever, but ...

"We need to get going," I whisper.

Lily presses up onto her forearm, her eyebrows tugged in. "What?"

"We can't stay here. I need to call housekeeping to have the bedding changed, so it's ready for tonight," I reply, meeting her questioning gaze.

Her forehead wrinkles. "What time is it?"

I shake my head. "I'm not sure. My phone's ..." I

glance around the space, spotting it on the floor near my jeans. I nudge my chin in its direction. "Way over there."

A lopsided grin lights up her features. "We certainly know how to take over a room."

"That we do." I grin.

Lily's eyes search mine for a moment and she inhales softly. "I wish we could stay here, but I suppose ..."

I kiss her temple, sliding my arm out from around her so I can exit the bed.

I hear another soft sigh as I walk over to my phone and pick it up.

"You have a sexy ass," she murmurs, her voice husky.

Shaking my head, I throw her a smirk over my shoulder. If she's not careful, I might have to take her again before we leave. Hell, my cock is already ready to go.

With effort, I tap on my screen to check the time. "Shit, it's almost five in the morning."

"Well, *wow*." Her eyes widen and she moves to the edge of the bed, letting the bedding drop to her waist. My body jolts from the visual but any thoughts of going again will have to wait.

I smile, searching the floor for her clothing. Bundling them all together, I hand them to her and start hunting for my own. Walking around naked in front of her—it's strange and yet, so natural at the same time. Like it's always been this way with us.

However, the gravity of last night hasn't fully impressed itself upon my brain yet, but I can feel it yawning like a chasm, ready to swallow me whole.

The panic flutters in my chest, but I shake out of its grasp, hoping it fucks off.

This is good. Things are *good*.

And yet ...

I tug on my briefs, then bend down and do the same with my jeans.

Lily busies herself, dressing in last night's outfit. As she does so, flashbacks of removing those articles of clothing stir up the visceral memory of everything we did.

God, I hope she doesn't think I only wanted sex ...

I slam my eyelids shut and reach for my shirt. Each button locking into place is a staccato, reminding me that I intended to take things slow with her. I promised myself I would go slow and it had gone out of the fucking window the moment she initiated things.

But I never wanted to rush this ...

"Are you okay?" Lily asks, pulling me from my inner tirade.

I spin to face her and shrug, trying to go for nonchalance, but not certain I pulled it off. "Sure. Of course."

She narrows her eyes as she slips into her shoes.

Yep, definitely failed at nonchalance.

"London," Lily begins, her voice wrapped in a warning.

I itch the side of my temple, unsure what to say. Instead, I bend down and slide my feet into my shoes.

When I stand back up, I smile at her and press my palms to her shoulders. "I'm fine. Really."

She steps into my space, wrapping her arms around

my waist and placing her cheek on my chest. Together, we sigh in utter contentment.

It's not that last night wasn't the best fucking night of my life.

It's just ...

"Your heart is beating so fast," she whispers, leaning back.

I swallow hard. "That's what you do to me."

She smiles at my words, but I can sense the energy in the room has shifted and it's all my fault.

Dammit, I'm messing this up.

"Come on. We should get going," I say, kissing the top of her head before I reach for the door handle.

She nods, straightening her shirt, then glancing around the room. My heart flutters when a nostalgic smile is hanging on her lips as she returns her gaze to me. I can see it in her eyes.

And yet for as happy as she appears, I know that if I'm not careful, she's going to freak.

This was a big step.

Big. Huge.

Monu-fucking-mental.

I don't want her to bolt. Not again.

I don't think my heart could take it.

So, I suck in a deep breath, hoping to steady myself.

Her eyebrows crinkle in the middle, but I turn away, so she can't see the storm brewing in my eyes or on my face.

Twisting back the lock, I open the door to find a folded piece of paper with my name written on it taped to the wood. I shoot Lily a questioning glance and unfold the paper.

> *The next time you decide to stage this whole place, then lock yourself in one of the rooms, at least have the courtesy to blow out the rest of the damn candles, you prick.*
>
> *PS - Tell Lily I said hi.*
>
> *Cal*

I crumple the paper in my palm and shove it into my pocket.

"Everything okay?" Lily asks, placing a hand on my arm.

I nod. "Yeah, just Cal."

Her eyes widen. "Did he—?"

I sigh, glancing toward the ceiling. "Possibly ... *probably.*"

Color stains her cheeks. "Oh, god."

"Exactly what he was hearing, I'm sure," I tease, trying to lighten the mood.

She slaps my bicep. "First of all, I'm pretty sure it was *your name* I was screaming. Not God's."

It's my turn to feel the rush of warmth that creeps from my neck and into my face.

She grins like a cat who caught a canary and walks past me.

I glance around the room one last time. With the exception of the bed being a total disaster, it's virtually untouched. At least housekeeping shouldn't be too pissed.

With Cal's words still in my mind, I blow out the remaining two candles and follow after Lily.

She's standing in the dining area, her eyes floating around the space. "We forgot about—"

"Cal," I say, cutting her off. "He blew them out."

"Oh," she whispers with a nod.

I can see the wheels turning in her eyes and my stomach starts flipping.

Please don't be second-guessing this.

I brush my hand across her lower back, urging her to follow me to the stairwell that leads to the parking lot.

We walk in silence, taking in the way she's decorated the stairs with beautiful sheer curtains and flowers. It's an entirely different space since she got her hands on it.

When I open the door, the inklings of the morning are just starting to paint the sky.

"Do you want something to eat? Or should we head back home?" I ask, the words feeling strange on my tongue.

Even though she's been staying with me for the past week and a half, and I've said the same sentence since then, the word *home* has a different context now.

I flinch, hoping it doesn't scare her away.

"Home, definitely," she says, patting me on the chest and walking over to my Escalade.

The parking lot is devoid of any other vehicles and I

glance around, wondering what kind of hell I'm going to get from Myles later. She would have noticed my car was still here, even if Cal hadn't told her what we were up to …

I shake my head, raising my gaze to the brightening sky as I throw up a quick prayer for it to be quick and painless—whatever torture she has in mind.

The drive home is a quiet affair. Both Lily and I are lost in thought and I can feel her withdrawing the closer we get to the house.

The panic that started settling into my chest earlier has now got me on full alert.

"Are you hungry?" I ask, turning to her.

She blinks back in surprise. "Hmmm?"

"I can make omelets—or pancakes again," I offer. Anything to keep me busy and take my mind off of this dread welling inside me.

"Sure. Whatever you want," she replies with a fleeting smile.

I turn back to the road, my eyebrows tugging in.

This is wrong, it's all wrong …

After my feeble attempt at raising a conversation, the rest of the drive is just as silent. I don't know what to say or do to make things feel right again.

When we pull into the driveway, I park with a sigh, trying to loosen this tightening in my chest. I get out of the vehicle but before I can make it to Lily's side to open her door, she's already out and walking over to me.

She reaches out, grazing her fingertips through mine as she makes her way past me and into the house.

I watch her, my heart pounding like some kind of a war drum.

She always lets me open the door for her.

Thump, thump, thump.

Why didn't she wait for me?

Thump, thump, thump.

Then, the insight comes rushing in. A reminder of what I wanted to do like some sort of inspired guidance from the Heavens.

I know how to fix this.

CHAPTER 35

Lily

The soft thrumming of Nocté's neon sign is louder than usual as I approach the lower entrance to the Upper Tier. Each luminous pulse sends a wave of unease down my spine.

Its ethereal glow should have been comforting, a blissful reminder of what London and I share, but instead, it echoes against the flickering doubts that are beginning to spring to my mind.

What happened this morning?

My gaze flits to the staff entrance and the sinking feeling plummets a bit further.

I blow out a puff of air, trying to shake it off.

I just need to get through this night ... Then, I can sit London down and we can talk this all out. Whatever it is, I'm sure it's no big deal.

My heartbeat stumbles a tiny bit.

Right?

The rest of the parking lot is filling with patrons

eagerly waiting to get inside Nocté, completely unaware of the sexy new offering being presented to the Upper Tier tonight. I half-wonder what they'd think if they knew.

Would they wish they could go? Or would they be appalled?

A sharp gust of wind tugs at my hair, and I pull my spring coat tighter, trying to block out the chill and my growing sense of dread.

There's still lots to do before the guests arrive.

I want everything to be *perfect*.

However, this looming event isn't the only thing weighing on me. Instead, it's the echoing silence between London and me that stretched onward throughout the day.

Every attempt at conversation was like trying to ignite a wet matchstick—futile and frustrating.

And I didn't understand what had happened.

Things were good. *So good.*

Did I do something wrong?

The moment we arrived back at the club, he had sauntered off, claiming he needed to finalize some things before we opened the doors. Evidently, he thought I could handle the rest of the arrangements upstairs alone.

But deep down, I think I know why he's avoiding me.

Why did I have to push things with us?

In his workplace, no less. He *was working.*

And his co-worker—*his employee*—Cal knew.

He knew what we'd done and ... I slam my eyelids shut.

Cal was already upset with London for that kiss on the rooftop. I could see it on his face when he realized our situation.

"Don't do anything else stupid ..."

That's what he had said to London when he left that day.

And then, there's the other aspect. I'm certain London wanted to wait, to take things slow, and I ...

I'd been so impatient.

Things just clicked and I knew—or I thought I did—what I wanted. What *he* wanted.

I sigh, sneaking into the club and walking up the back stairs to the Upper Tier. From here, enticing aromas already waft around me, inviting me to go deeper into this Eden.

The flowers, lights, and fabrics in the stairwell are the perfect touch—something I'm certain will surprise and delight the guests. Especially the ones who have been already using this place.

And for those who haven't ... hopefully, it will be just the beginning of a beautiful experience.

I take a deep breath when I reach the top landing, then push open the heavy doors of Nocté's Upper Tier. Candles are already lit, the coat racks ready, and the table with the masks is highlighted in the soft glow of a spotlight.

The comforting hum of preparations fill the air—the

soft whispers of staff in the kitchen, the delicate clinking of glasses as the wait staff prep for the night.

But London's absence is a gaping hole in the middle of it all—and absolutely impossible to miss.

We were doing this together.

Walking in, I'm immediately inundated with last-minute details. Staff approach me to confirm everything: the lights, music, and the special drinks for the night.

Each decision makes my head spin a little more—each choice a stark reminder that I'm doing this alone.

Where the hell is London?

Stepping away from the main entrance to review the seating chart one last time, I'm momentarily distracted as I look over the names.

Carlie isn't on this list.

And yet ... she had an invite for this event.

I'd personally written out every single envelope, using calligraphy to make it more beautiful.

"What name are you hiding under, Carlie?" I muse, looking through them all.

My eyes snag on a name I hadn't thought anything of at first: *Zoey Cummings.*

Carlie is an steamy romance author ...

I pull out my phone, consulting Google to see if my hunch is correct.

Bingo.

After a few clicks, I'm on a sexy romance author website. My eyebrows flick upward when I peruse the titles. There are nearly a hundred books written by this author.

I tap on the 'About Page' and sure enough, Carlie's smiling face beams back at me. She's wearing more makeup and looks more seductive than I've ever seen her in real life.

But it's her.

I glance back at the sheet with details of her as an Upper Tier member.

She was invited nearly a year ago but has never used the club.

Not once.

"Hmmm," I muse, now curious about what happened to her to warrant an invite. She's never talked about her past relationships, but clearly, she must have been cheated on.

I'm startled by the scent of fresh cologne. Before I can turn around, a hand gently lands on my elbow.

"Everything okay, Lily?" Cal whispers. His usually playful eyes now radiate concern, which doesn't help ease the anxieties I had been able to forget momentarily.

My cheeks flush and the memory of London's words haunt my mind.

"Possibly ... probably."

He'd been up here last night. He'd checked to make sure things were secure and heard us ...

"Have you seen London?" I ask, trying to keep my voice steady and the embarrassment from my tone.

Cal's eyes hold mine for a moment longer than is comfortable. "He's around, probably busy with last-minute preparations. You know how he gets."

I nod, though his words do little to assure me.

London hasn't been up here at all. What last-minute preparations would take him this long?

"I've already done my rounds," Cal continues. "So, Myles sent me up to see if you needed any help."

His words surprise me. "London didn't send you?"

Cal shakes his head, a flicker of something I can't quite decipher crossing his features. "No, it was Myles. She figured you could use an extra pair of hands with Saint ... *occupied*."

His choice of words feels pointed, like there's something he's not saying. My worry intensifies and my stomach clenches in its wake. "Is he okay?"

Cal hesitates, then offers a comforting smile. "He's London. Always trying to be a saint, you know." He winks at me and I get his double-meaning. "He's always in his head a bit more than necessary. But, it's probably best if you two talk when you get a chance."

"Talk about what?" The raw edge in my voice surprises even me.

Cal holds up his hands defensively. "Hey, I'm just here to help."

"Lily, do you want the strawberries cut in half and placed on the edge of the glass for the signature drink? Or inside the cocktail," Stefanie, one of the servers, asks, walking over to us and holding up a mock drink.

I blink hard. "Ummm."

"Try slicing it three or four times, then fan them out across the edge of the glass. Like this," Cal offers, taking over and showing her what he means.

I stand back, watching the two of them. It's a helpful

distraction, but the weight of London's absence remains, pressing down on me, and Cal's words echo in my mind.

We need to talk.

God, I've messed things up.

He kept talking about not wanting to rush *me*. And here, I was the one rushing *him*.

Despite the internal turmoil, the professional in me pushes through. Directing the staff, ensuring the setup is immaculate. Each time a staff member calls for my attention, a part of me wishes the event would be over with already so I can hunt London down.

Cal's words are a haunting refrain, and unsettlingly vague.

What did he know? What had London told him?

Every whispered conversation and subtle glance seems suspect. Every smile, tainted with undisclosed meanings.

A text message lights up my phone.

It's from Myles.

Everything on track? Need anything?

I stare at the message, tempted to divulge the cyclone of confusion, doubts, and fears swirling inside me. But I refrain. This isn't her burden to bear. Even if she and London are close.

So, instead, I type back, the lie heavy on my fingertips.

All good.

Over the next hour, the final aspects of our setup are completed, and every detail is in place ...

Yet the masterpiece feels incomplete.

It's a symphony missing its lead violinist. A painting lacking its final stroke of brush. London's absence is a void, echoing in the silent corners of the room.

The clock on the wall chimes 8:00 p.m.

It's time.

"Are you ready for this?" Stefanie asks, a hint of a smile floating to her dainty features.

I nod. "I think so."

"Are you alright?" she questions, her expression shifting to concern.

"Yeah, just ... pre-event jitters, I guess," I reply, trying to give a convincing smile.

She doesn't seem entirely convinced but nods nonetheless. "You've done a wonderful job here, Lily. Just breathe. Everything will go off without a hitch. Just you watch."

I nod, appreciative of her kind words, though they do little to quell the storm of uncertainty inside me. The weight of today, the unspoken words between London and me, the physical distance that feels like miles at this point—it's all a heavy burden.

With a final tip of her chin, Stefanie heads downstairs to open the doors.

I find myself ready to survey the incoming crowd, but hoping to catch a glimpse of London.

But first, the reveal.

The unveiling of a reimagined Upper Tier, an experience that promises an odyssey of sensual discovery is about to unfold. I've poured my soul into this, yet the pride is dulled by the shadow of the morning, and the silence that looms large between London and me.

Just down the hallway, where guest will be having their own adventures, I had mine with London.

That moment feels so far away.

Was it really just last night?

The staff, all prepped and polished, look to me for the signal.

I nod, the cue to usher in a night of decadence. The doors swing open, and the first of the patrons step inside.

The reaction is immediate—a collective gasp, eyes widening as Stefanie announces what's to come and asks each of the guests to find a mask.

Compliments and awe filter through the air, yet each word of praise feels hollow without London by my side to share in this moment of triumph.

I stand back, somewhat in the shadows, as the room fills. There's a dazzling dance of lights and shadows, mystery and revelation, but the absence of one person tinges every success with an undertone of melancholy. Every accolade, every exclamation of wonder, is a reminder of the silent space between us, widening with each passing moment.

Minutes seem to expand into hours. The influx of the Upper Tier guests transforms Nocté from a quiet hum to a symphony of laughter, chatter, and music.

More guests trickle in—no sign of Carlie yet.

Though, a part of me is excited to know what she thinks ... If she likes what we've done.

Or if this will be taking things too far.

Just when the crescendo of my anxiety is about to overwhelm me, a familiar touch on my shoulder pulls me back.

I turn slowly, meeting London's intense gaze.

A small sob threatens to unleash from my throat but I swallow it down.

"Lily," he begins, his voice lower than the ambient lighting, "will you come with me?"

CHAPTER 36

Lily

My heart hammers in my chest as London takes my hand and leads me to the staff elevator.

I glance back just in time to witness Stefanie giving me two thumbs up and a quick wave before we slide behind the curtain.

The commotion of the Upper Tier event fades into the background and the only thing keeping me from falling apart is the single point of contact I have with London.

His fingers are intertwined with mine and pray it's not for the last time.

The elevator ride is painfully silent, doing nothing to quell the thrumming of my pulse in my ears.

"London, I'm sorry," I blurt out, turning to him. "I didn't mean to—"

Just then, the doors ding open, but I refused to move a muscle.

Confusion floats across his face as he reaches for the

doors to hold them open for us. My gaze drifts to his hand, then beyond the elevator.

I double-take.

Once again, he's taken me to the roof—not his office, as I anticipated. Throughout the rooftop, it's a wonderland of flowers, lilies mostly, just like downstairs, and the romantic flicker of candles all across the space.

The Adirondack chairs that had once circled the fire pit are gone. Instead, a single air mattress rests on the floor. It's covered in blankets and pillows.

"What is ..." I begin, narrowing my eyes and shaking my head, *"this?"*

We step out of the elevator and London turns to face me, taking my hands in his.

His handsome face is filled with complexity and he hesitates slightly before saying, "Lily, last night ..."

"Please," I shake my head and squeeze his hands. "Please don't say it was a mistake."

He chuckles darkly and his eyebrows tug in. "Lily, it was *mind-blowing.*"

A rush of breath escapes me. "Really?"

Again, he laughs softly and places a kiss to my forehead. "Yes, really." Raising a hand to my cheek, he brushes it with the back of his hand. "But I need you to know, it wasn't just about how it felt physically. Last night ... it was a culmination of everything we've been dancing around. Every look, every touch, every unspoken word between us. It wasn't a mistake, Lily. It was *inevitable.*"

I swallow hard, fighting the tears threatening to spill over.

"What I regret is how we didn't communicate much afterward. It was totally my fault. I let my own worries and insecurities make things complicated between us today. I'm sorry for that," he replies, his words full of gravel.

I shake my head, confused. "What are you insecure about?"

He takes a moment, the slight breeze tousling his hair, making the ambient light catch the strands. "Lily, when I first got involved in Nocté and the Upper Tier, it was purely business. I never expected to get involved emotionally with anyone who walked through its doors. I never expected to—" He exhales a jagged breath. "But then, you happened. Your presence, your enthusiasm, the way you're so fiercely dedicated to everything you do. It's magnetic. It always has been. Participating the way we did, it's given me a new perspective on what it is we do here, oddly enough. But for us, I just don't want you to think ..." His eyebrows tug in and a slight frown forms on his lips.

I reach out, placing my hand along his jaw, silently urging him to continue.

His gaze is fierce when he locks it with my own. "Don't—I don't *ever* want you to think sex is all I want. Because," he pauses, his eyelashes fluttering against his cheeks.

A surprised laugh bubbles past my lips, startling him. I cover my mouth with my fingertips.

"London," I whisper, trying to convey with my eyes how silly that thought is. "I have never, for a single moment, thought that. If anything, I should have been worried you thought that of *me*. I was the one who started everything." I lift my eyes to the starlit sky. "We're ridiculous."

A grin graces his lips and he glances around the space. He still hasn't explained it, but I'm beginning to understand.

His thumb brushes my cheek gently. "I want you to know, I'm not insecure about *us*, about what we have. I'm *cautious* because I don't want to lose you by moving too quickly and not cherishing every moment. But I also realize that by hesitating, I risk pushing you away. So, *this*"—He raises his hands to suggest the space around us—"is my way of showing you how much you mean to me. How much you've *always* meant to me."

Once again, I glance around, smiling at the amount of effort it must have taken to get this place set up. There are drinks and food on a small table to the side. The ambiance is so ...

"Oh," I breathe, realization slapping me across the face. "This is what you've been doing."

A boyish grin flits across his face and it reminds me of all those little surprises he'd pull when we were kids. He was always up to something. Always trying to make me smile.

"This, Lily, is to help erase all the years we spent apart," he says, guiding me to the air mattress.

As I slip off my shoes and take a seat, I turn to face him. "What do you mean?"

He mimics my movement, taking off his shoes and settling in beside me. "You'll see."

I narrow my gaze, but a sideways grin floats to my face.

However, rather than answer beyond his cryptic response, he simply reaches for a couple of glasses on a table beside the mattress.

"Your drink, milady," London says, passing one of the signature drinks from tonight's event over to me. "So, you can celebrate your accomplishment of an incredible event and feel like you're still a part of what's going on downstairs."

I take the drink and swivel my wrist to get a better look. It's garnished with the strawberry, just like Cal had recommended downstairs. I can't help but wonder who inspired whom.

Then, instead of the tiny umbrella, there's a ...

"Is this ...?" I say, plucking the stir stick from the glass and spinning it in the low light. "It is. It's a dick stick." I turn to him with a smirk on my face.

His eyes twinkle and he shrugs. "Well, Myles won't use them."

I throw my head back and laugh. Like, full-on laugh. And it feels *so* good.

London laughs along with me and as it gradually subsides, I find myself wiping tears from the corners of my eyes, the emotional intensity of the evening making every reaction feel exaggerated.

The light-hearted moment lingers between us, a shared melody in the now silent night, and a stark contrast to the earlier tension.

London's gaze softens, the twinkle in his eyes illuminated by the moonlight and candles surrounding us. We share a quiet moment, and in his eyes, I see the reflection of years passed, of a connection that neither time nor distance could sever.

"This"—I wave the quirky stir stick in my hand, the laughter still tingling on my lips—"is so *you*. Even in a moment like this, you find a way to make me laugh."

"And that," he replies, reaching out to tuck a loose strand of hair behind my ear, his touch lingering on my skin, "is one of the million things I've missed about you, Lily. Your laughter is the best fucking sound in the world. It always has been."

Silence envelops us again, but this time, it's comforting.

The city's distant sounds create a soft symphony, and above us, the stars sparkle, each one telling tales of timeless existence.

London clears his throat, drawing my attention back to him. His fingers intertwine with mine again and he tightens their grip.

Inhaling sharply, I sense something profound is about to unfold.

"I want to show you something," he proclaims, his voice tinged with an emotion I can't quite decipher.

Dropping my hands after a final squeeze, he retrieves his phone and navigates to YouTube. The bright screen casts a gentle glow on his face, highlighting the seriousness etched in his features.

He selects a video, and the familiar opening to "The War of the Worlds" radio broadcast fills the air.

I can't count how many times I've listened to it at this point. Finding it on Youtube years ago helped me feel connected to London.

Our eyes lock, and in that moment, memories of a past life, of youthful innocence, and an unbreakable bond flood back. The broadcast, the night he left, our unspoken words—they all come rushing back with a breathtaking intensity.

"I've carried this moment with me, Lily," London's voice is a soft whisper, his words weaving through the haunting opening of the show. "Every day, every night— it's been with me, a constant reminder of what I left behind."

Emotion glistens in his eyes, mirroring my own. The magnitude of his revelation, the vulnerability in his admission, binds us together in a shared moment of truth.

"And now?" I manage to utter, my voice choked with the sentiment.

"Now, I want to create new memories. Ones that don't revolve around goodbyes, but hellos. I don't want to dwell on what was left unsaid and what we had no control over, but instead, focus on what we can say now, and every day moving forward."

He pauses, his gaze unflinching, as if searching the

depths of my soul for an anchor. "Starting tonight, I want to rewrite our story, Lily. Are you with me?"

The intensity of his gaze, the sincerity in his voice—it's overwhelming, yet exhilarating. A wave of emotions, as tumultuous and profound as the ocean, crash over me.

I'm at the precipice of a new beginning, a moment where the past and present converge, offering a bridge to a future yet unwritten—and yet, somehow, *foretold*.

The broadcast continues to play as I grasp his hand tighter, a silent, yet unequivocal *yes*. The stars above bear witness to our silent pact, their twinkling lights illuminating the dawn of a new chapter in our entwined lives.

Above us, the universe unfolds its cosmic dance, and beneath the stars, amidst the echoes of a haunting tale, London and I embark upon a journey where time is not a barrier, but a canvas—waiting to be painted with new memories.

We lay back, our hands still intertwined, as the broadcast weaves through the silence of the night.

In this moment, we are not just two souls marked by time and distance—we are cosmic entities, star-crossed lovers destined to find our way back to each other.

The old memories, the unuttered goodbyes—they still linger, but now they share space with something new, something profound.

After the final notes of "The War of the Worlds" dwindle to an end, London speaks again, his voice soft yet determined, "I used to think that some things are too broken to be mended, some distances too vast to be bridged. But tonight, with you here by my side, under this vast expanse of stars, I realize that sometimes, the universe is willing to give you a second chance."

I turn to look at him, tracing the lines of his face, each one telling a story of the years gone by. The weight of our past, the depth of our connection, and the possibilities of our future hang in the balance of this one, singular moment.

He continues, "I don't want to waste that chance, Lily. Not anymore."

Tears, born out of years of longing, heartbreak, and newfound hope, form in the corners of my eyes. I blink them back, not wanting to break our gaze.

"I know we can't change the past," I whisper, my voice thick with emotion, "but we have the power to shape our future. And I want that future to be with you."

Our eyes lock, and in them, I see a reflection of our shared hopes, dreams, and the promise of many tomorrows. We lean into each other, our foreheads touching, our breaths mingling, the world around us fading away.

The significance of the moment isn't lost on either of us.

It's a beginning—*a fresh start.*

In this timeless moment, with the world at our feet and the universe as our witness, we embrace the promise of a love reborn, infinite and unbreakable, ready to face whatever the future holds, *together.*

I pace back and forth in my office at Nocté, rechecking the clues and little notes for what feels like the hundredth time.

Everything has to be perfect tonight.

Cal pops his head in, a wide smirk spreading across his face. "You look like you're about to toss your cookies."

Despite feeling very much like a man about to puke his guts up, I take the opportunity to flick him off.

Just like always, Cal laughs it off and takes a seat opposite my desk. "Are you ready for the games to begin, lover boy?"

I inhale sharply, patting my pocket. "Is she here?"

He chuckles. "Well, Quinn says she's already seen him for his clue. The rest of the Dirty B's are in position and Tasia just messaged that she and Lily left her establishments. So, it should be any minute now."

A wave of nervousness sweeps over me. It's not just

about the proposal, but reliving our journey with our friends playing such a significant role.

Let's be honest here, as much as I adore them, they're all wild cards.

"You okay?" Cal presses again, this time his expression more pointed.

I breathe in deeply and exhale, trying to calm my nerves.

"I've always imagined this day, but experiencing it is something else," I admit, running a hand through my hair.

Cal smirks at me and nods.

I shake my head and itch the side of my temple. "It's like standing at the edge of a precipice, knowing the leap is worth it, but the fear of falling is still *very* real."

Cal watches me for a moment before finally saying, "Saint, she loves you, man. Remember that. All of this, the heist, the rooftop, the meticulous planning and hoops you've had all of us jumping through"—a pointed look in my direction—"It's just the setting for tonight's magic. Your story, your *love*, that's the real deal."

A small chime sounds, indicating a message on my phone. Both of us turn to look as the screen lights up.

It's a text from Quinn with an update on the clue trail.

> She's seen Vivian. Third clue done.
> They're on the move.

Cal leans back, rubbing his hands together. "And so it begins."

I can't help but smile. "Here goes nothing."

"Do you think she'll figure out all the clues? Some of them are pretty cryptic." Cal raises an eyebrow, his smirk returning full force.

"Lily's a smart woman. But just in case, I've got backup plans. And backup plans for my backup plans."

"Always the strategist." He chuckles.

The room falls into a brief silence, the weight of the night settling in.

Suddenly, Cal's expression grows more serious. "You remember the first time you finally admitted to yourself you were in love with her?"

I nod, the memory vivid. It feels like it was yesterday.

"You were scared shitless," Cal continues. "Scared of ruining what you two had, scared of not being enough for her. But here's the thing, Saint—she's always seen you. Really *seen* you. Even when you tried to hide, even when you doubted yourself."

I swallow hard, all of the memories flooding back. "I just don't want to let her down. This has to be special."

Cal leans forward, placing his elbows on his knees. "You won't let her down. All these clues, the planning, it's impressive, yeah. But it's the heart behind them that counts. And if there's one thing I know about you, it's that your heart has always been in the right place when it comes to her."

Suddenly, my phone chimes again.

Another update.

I glance at the message and my heart skips a beat.

> She's on the last clue. Won't take her
> long. Get your ass in place.

Taking a deep breath, I stand, smoothing down my suit. "It's game time."

Cal nods, standing up to join me. "Let's make this a night to remember."

I send a lopsided grin in his direction and walk out of my office and into the main area of Nocté.

Rather than head to my final location, I pass by Myles, who simply nods my direction—the epitome of her game face—as she slings drinks like there's nothing out of the ordinary going on tonight.

Hiding in the shadows, I wait for Lily to arrive.

After a few minutes, she enters the club with an entourage of our friends. Quinn, Tasia, Carlie, Vivian, and Anna surround her. She's dressed in a simple, but elegant black dress—the one with sparkles all over it that reminded me of the night sky the moment I saw it.

It was a perfect first prize and looks stunning on her.

Her eyes scan the dance club, already in full swing. Even from here, I can see that familiar fire of curiosity burning in her eyes. She walks over to Myles, who hands her a drink ... *and the final note.*

Watching from the shadows for a few more moments, I see her face light up in realization when she thinks she's figured out the clue, or when she shares a laugh with one of the Dirty B's.

All the while, I notice her searching gaze. The way she scans the room ...

Despite my nerves, my heart is so full, knowing she's searching for me.

Of course, this is not just about fun and games.

Each clue, each moment, was designed to be a reminder of our shared journey.

Of our destiny.

I've deliberately created it to be a reflection of our past, present, and hopeful future.

Some of the clues were inside jokes, others were memories from our childhood and our tumultuous new beginning. Like the one that led her to Dirty Books and Dirty Deeds—the spot where we ran into each other after all the years apart, or the one hinting at our favorite song.

Each step was like turning a page in our shared history, each destination a bookmark of our significant moments.

All of it leading to the place where I knew I would never, ever be the same.

Vanishing into the shadows, I make my way to the elevator.

With my heart in my throat, I reach the rooftop and slide into position.

Music is playing from the hidden speakers and the scene is a beautifully lit landscape. Twinkle lights surround the entire space and a fire crackles in the middle.

The team of attendants waits on the fringes for the party to begin—all of us eyeing those elevator doors.

Finally, the ding of the elevator snaps my attention to

it and my back straightens as the doors open. Quinn, Vivian, and Anna pour out first, but then ...

Finally, she's on the rooftop.

I stand there, hidden for now, clutching the ring so hard it indents my palm. My heart races as she looks around the space. Awe and wonder and so much love flood her features.

I can't wait to see what happens next.

The final clue leads her to the small ornate box hidden on the other side of the fire pit.

Quinn grabs hold of Tasia's arm and practically squeals.

Anna rolls her eyes, but they also glint with a bit of happiness, too.

Lily approaches the box, finds it, and picks it up so delicately. Hesitating for just a moment, her gaze sweeping between her friends before she opens it.

Even from here, I almost laugh out loud at the slight confusion on her face—because the box is empty.

With an exasperated sigh, she drops it to her side and turns her back to where I'm hiding so she can look over the space again.

Showtime.

Stepping out of my hiding spot, I drop to one knee, holding up the ring, and wait.

Quinn clutches Tasia closer and bites his lip, trying desperately to be quiet.

When Lily spins around again, only to find me waiting there, she gasps.

God, I love that sound.

"This," I say, my voice shaking more than I'd like, "is the stolen treasure you seek. But it only becomes priceless when you say yes."

She drops the box, pressing her fingertips to her lips. Her eyes shimmer with tears, and for a moment, we're the only two people on this rooftop, hell, in this *entire universe.*

Her soft *"yes"* as she reaches out to pull me to my feet is the only thing I need to hear.

The entire rooftop bursts into applause and the background sounds of muffled cheers and laughter can be heard all around us. I pull Lily into my arms, pressing my forehead against hers.

"Got you," I whisper, a smirk playing on my lips.

She chuckles, tears spilling from her eyes, and replies, "Always."

From the corner of my eye, Cal and the others raise their glasses for a toast.

Quinn, ever the dramatic one, stands on a chair and clears his throat, drawing attention with a flourish. "To London and Lily, may your journey ahead be as adventurous, unpredictable, and full of love as the path that brought you here tonight. But if he ever leaves you unsatisfied, you know we have you covered at Dirty Deeds. The Enigma will be waiting to show you that glimpse of Heaven." He winks at us both.

I shake my head, snickering under my breath.

Leaning in close, I whisper beside her ear, "You'll never have to worry about that."

She inhales sharply and bites her lip.

Glasses clink, laughter fills the air, and our *engagement party* truly begins. Music pumps louder, and people begin to dance, but Lily and I stay wrapped up in each other, swaying to our own rhythm.

As the night goes on, the rooftop starts to empty out, leaving just a few stragglers, lost in deep conversation or asleep nestled amidst the cushions or chairs. The twinkle lights continue to shimmer, casting a soft glow over everything.

Lily and I sit by the fire, her head on my shoulder, and my arm around her. We watch the first light of dawn paint the sky in hues of pink and gold.

"This feels like a dream. I can't believe I get to spend the rest of my life with you," she murmurs, tracing patterns on my hand.

I nod, smiling down at her. "And a lifetime isn't nearly enough time for all the adventures I want to have with you."

She leans in, capturing my lips in a soft, lingering kiss. And as the sun rises over the city, marking the beginning of a brand new day, I know without a doubt, we're both looking forward to the countless tomorrows we'll share, side by side.

**The One Night Stand Club continues with Carlie!
Read Dirty Books Now!**

Dirty Books |
Book 2

SNEAK PEEK

Carlie Taylor doesn't exist—*not tonight.*

Instead, I shed her like a skin, leaving behind the woman fraught with self-doubt, obsessed over every curve, and prone to clumsy missteps.

No, *tonight,* I am Zoey Cummings, a radiant *sex goddess,* armed with unshakeable confidence and a voracious appetite for adventure.

Zoey takes what she wants—*from whoever she wants it.*

No burdens to bear. No repercussions.

Zoey embodies her desires, claiming them with a boldness that Carlie can only dream of.

At least, that's the plan.

Nestled in the sanctuary of my car, just a whisper away from the venue, I retrieve the invite from my purse.

A shaky breath escapes my lips, and for a fleeting moment, I'm lost in the tactile dance of my fingers over the sumptuous dark paper—a detail I would have lingered on in a novel, painting the scene with words. The gravity of the impending night makes my heart flutter as if I'm on the precipice of my own story's pivotal scene.

The beautifully handwritten letters spell out *'Zoey Cummings'*—a pseudonym that promises a night of liberation.

This invite is more than just paper and ink—it's a golden ticket to a realm shrouded in mystery. Hell, it's a spell to forget.

Heart pounding, I wonder if I'm truly ready to be untethered to the past.

The wounds from him are still raw, his memory a lingering shadow in my mind and on my heart.

No, I *need* this.

I need to obliterate the ghost of him, even if just for one ephemeral night.

With trembling hands, I turn the envelope over and gently pull out the card. Sparkly silver type glistens on the black silky paper, and I read over the words once more, confirming the details etched in my mind.

"Zoey, it is under the veil of night..." I whisper out loud, then fall into silence as I read on.

An exclusive evening, shrouded in mystery and desire within Club Nocté's Upper Tier, beckons. The promise of an unforgettable experience fills the air, as tempting as it is terrifying.

Elegance is your armor, a mask your shield. Indulge in fine cocktails and decadent treats, lose yourself to the experience, and let the night unveil who you truly are when the world isn't watching.

The stage is set.

The night awaits.

All that's left is to step into the shadows and allow the adventure to begin.

Yours in mystery,
Club Nocté

The magic and mystery of this invite have done its job well. Nocté has woven their spell, captivating the author in me in a way that hasn't been summoned out for a while.

When the original notification of my 'exclusive membership' arrived months ago, a mix of emotions swirled within me—more mortification than thrill, to be honest.

To be selected for this secretive club as a consolation for being cheated on was not how I envisioned diving back into the world of romance and passion.

If anything, it felt like a slap in the face.

How Nocté had learned of his indiscretion, I'll never know.

Yet, as I sit here, on the brink of an unknown adventure, the allure of escape and the promise of a night shrouded in mystery is incredibly enticing.

It's been long enough.

Zoey Cummings is ready, even if Carlie Taylor is not.

Tonight, I choose the adventure.

Tonight, I choose to be Zoey.

Taking a deep breath, I open the car door, feeling the cool night air gently caress my skin. It's a small, yet poignant, reminder that I'm about to step out of my comfort zone in a big way. The sounds of the city at night surround me, a symphony of life that's both daunting and exhilarating.

Superior has a reputation for being seedy—or at the very least, the darker of the Twin Ports cities. Something about that feels so good. *Right.*

I straighten my dress, a sleek emerald number that clings to my curves in all the right places—at least, I hope it does.

No, that's a Carlie thought.

I banish it and button my long coat against the breeze.

Throwing my shoulders back, I adjust my mask—a delicate piece of dark green lace that hides just enough to make me feel mysterious. Zoey would wear this with pride and a mischievous glint in her eye.

My heels click against the pavement as I make my way toward the hidden back entrance of Club Nocté, the thumping bass from inside growing louder with each step. My heart races, not just from the nerves but also from the sheer excitement of what might happen tonight. What does this event have in store for me?

As I approach the door, a blond, broad-shouldered bouncer checks my invite, his eyes lingering just a moment too long on the name written in elegant script. "Enjoy your night, Zoey," he says with a smirk, stepping aside to let me through.

I step through the dimly lit doorway and into a stairwell that leads to an upper level. The transition from the bright city lights to the seductive ambiance of Club Nocté is momentarily disorienting, but the soft music and lush foliage that is strategically placed along the path invite me to proceed. It's like being invited into Wonderland.

The air is thick with anticipation by the time I reach the top landing. The soft murmur of conversation is punctuated by occasional laughter in the space beyond.

"May I take your coat?" the hostess asks, halting my progress.

I turn to her and smile. "Thank you, that would be lovely."

Her bright blue eyes survey me and I shrug it off, feeling far more exposed.

"Your mask is beautiful," she offers as she accepts my coat.

My fingertips trace the fabric and a smile floats to my lips. "Thank you."

She tips her head before vanishing into the coat room behind her.

I take a moment to steel myself, letting my eyes

adjust, as I take in my surroundings. The club is even more lavish than I imagined, with rich, dark colors and plush velvet. The décor speaks of opulence and decadence, and a thrill runs down my spine.

I'm at a—

"May I offer you a drink?" a server asks, appearing at my side with a tray of champagne flutes.

I nod, accepting a glass. "Thank you," I say, my voice steady despite the fluttering in my stomach.

Zoey doesn't get nervous, after all.

With the glass in hand, I venture further into the club, paying far more attention than I should on walking straight and not spilling the champagne all over some unsuspecting guest.

A little bit of Carlie is still with me, it seems.

The alluring sound of violins playing through the speakers guides me to a large dining area and the crowd grows. The room is a tableau of intrigue, characters in a scene I might have written.

Laughter and chatter fill the air, every one a protagonist in their own story, hidden behind masks of mystery. Some share knowing glances, like old friends or old rivals—details I'd note as an author to hint at stories untold.

That thought makes my insides flutter again.

I take a sip of the champagne, the bubbles tickling my nose as I let the atmosphere wash over me. I'm here to forget, to let go, and to embrace the adventure that awaits.

And who knows? Maybe, just maybe, I'll find something—*or someone*—that will make the night even more unforgettable.

With that thought in mind, I lift my chin, square my shoulders, and walk into the room.

"Miss Cummings?" another hostess inside asks when I enter the space.

"How'd—?" I ask, turning to her with my eyebrows drawn.

She smiles sweetly. "We have been given specific orders to know each of our guests so we can tailor the experience for each of you. Now, if you'll follow me, I'll bring you to your assigned seat."

A hushed anticipation settles over the room as the lights dim, casting long, dancing shadows across the walls. The flicker of candles becomes the heartbeat of the space, their warm glow softening the edges of masked faces and creating an intimate cocoon of secrecy and allure.

The transformation is swift but profound, and I feel the persona of Zoey enveloping me more fully, as if the dim light is a curtain, drawing closed and leaving Carlie firmly behind in the shadows.

The hostess, a vision of poise, guides me with a gentle hand on my elbow. She points to the final open seat at the table and I slide into it.

"Ladies and gentlemen, if I may have your attention, please," she begins, her gaze sweeping across the room, ensuring she has captured the attention of every attendee. Her voice carries a weight of authority that commands attention, even as it remains soft and melodic."Tonight, you are embarking on a journey of connection and discovery. In the spirit of trust and intimacy, you will spend the evening with the person seated to your left. We have taken great care in choosing your companions for the evening, seeking to create connections that extend beyond the superficial."

A murmur of curiosity ripples through the room, and I feel a prickling of excitement—*or is it apprehension?*—at the base of my spine.

"As we serve the first course, we invite you to share in an experience of vulnerability and care with your partner. You are not to feed yourselves, but instead, nourish the person beside you. Speak of your desires, your fears, your dreams—let the masks you wear be the only barriers between you tonight."

The room falls into a hushed silence, the gravity of her words settling over us. I can feel the gravity in the gaze of the man to my left, and I turn, offering a small, tentative smile. I don't dare look too closely.

The hostess gives a nod as if to say 'begin,' and the servers move gracefully through the room, placing plates of exquisite food in front of us. There are chocolate-covered strawberries, watermelon, and other finger foods. The aroma is tantalizing, a symphony of flavors waiting to be explored.

The entire room breaks out into a hum of conversation as we turn to our prospective partners for the evening.

If I were writing this as a story, I'd make sure the man

beside me was the exact opposite of the real me. He'd be gorgeous, fit, and adventurous in every way.

But this is no story...

My gaze drifts to the man seated to my left, a stranger cloaked in the anonymity of the night.

Who is he?

What stories lie behind those gray eyes?

The mystery entices me, and Zoey's boldness surges within, eager to uncover the secrets hidden by his mask.

I pick up a large strawberry, its chocolate coating melting into my fingertips.

"Well," I start, my voice steady even though my heart has galloped away, "I suppose we should dive in."

His eyes, a stormy gray, meet mine, and I sense a flicker of curiosity in their depths. The corner of his lips tilts upward in a half-smirk as if he's both amused and intrigued by the situation. I extend my arm, the strawberry held between my fingers, and I can't help but notice the slight quiver in my hand, a betrayal of my inner turmoil.

I swallow hard, my heart fluttering with the vulnerability of this intimate act.

The strawberry hovers before his lips, and for a brief moment, time stands still. There's a silent question in his gaze, an invitation to share more than just the sweetness of the fruit. I take a deep breath, steadying myself, and gently press the strawberry to his lips.

He accepts the strawberry, his teeth grazing my fingers ever so lightly, sending a shiver down my spine.

His eyes never leave mine, and in them, I see a spark of something indefinable.

Is it curiosity?

Interest?

I can't be sure, but it draws me in, compelling me to know more.

"So," I begin, my voice barely above a whisper, "tell me something real about yourself. Something you've never told a stranger before."

His pause lingers, and the weight of the unspoken stretches between us, taut as the violin strings being strummed in the background music.

"I've mastered the art of guarding secrets," he begins, his voice a hushed murmur that sends shivers down my spine. "But for you, tonight, I might be willing to share one." He leans closer, so close that the edges of our masks nearly touch. The scent of his cologne—a tantalizing blend of cedar and citrus—fills my senses. "Only if," he continues, the challenge evident in his stormy eyes, "you reciprocate with a truth of your own."

A torrent of emotions whirls inside me—curiosity, apprehension, excitement. His words are a dare, a high-stakes game of trust and revelation. But the night's theme revolves around vulnerability, doesn't it?

If I were writing this scene, my protagonist would face an internal dilemma, torn between self-preservation and the lure of the unknown. Tonight, reality mirrors fiction. My pulse races and the weight of my decision bears down on me.

After a heartbeat that feels like an eternity, I muster a

sly smile, matching his challenge. "All right," I whisper, my voice shaking with a blend of excitement and nerves. "Shall we trade truths, then?"

His lips twitch in response, a hint of satisfaction flashing behind his mask. But before he can answer, the lights dim even further, and a captivating melody fills the room, momentarily distracting us.

The game of truth, now hanging precariously in the air, promises a night that will either expose or ensnare. It's a gamble, and the stakes have never felt higher.

**The One Night Stand Club continues!
Read Dirty Books Now!**

About the Author

Carissa Knight writes steamy, emotional romcoms where second chances get messy, feelings get avoided (until they don't), and unresolved tension simmers for pages. Her books are built on tropes she loves deeply—especially second chances, forced proximity, and the occasional enemies-to-lovers situation that gets *way too personal.*

Though her romcom debut is recent, Carissa's no newbie to storytelling. Writing since 2010 as **Carissa Andrews**, she's an **international bestselling** and **award-winning author** of paranormal and urban fantasy. Now, under her romcom pen name, she's leaning into the chaos of love, heartbreak, and hot dumbasses who absolutely *do not* have their lives together.

Based in Minnesota, she writes for the readers who crave big emotions, found family, and characters who take way too long to admit they're in love.

Learn more at: romcomcarissa.com

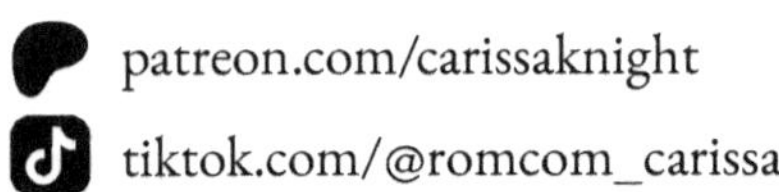

patreon.com/carissaknight

tiktok.com/@romcom_carissa